2.75

* HERE'S WHAT THE CRITICS SAID ABOUT
* THIS SPINE-CHILLING STORY OF ACTION
* AND SUSPENSE

"Brillian...

"Mr. Stanton gives the reader a countdown to destruction and leaves the reader biting his nails as he wonders what will happen."

—PITTSBURGH PRESS

"Moments of almost unbearable suspense!"

—LOS ANGELES TIMES

"A taut novel that deals in an adult and dramatic way with a situation that probably could happen, and just in the manner described here. We can hope—as with **On the Beach**—that it doesn't. But the possibility remains."

—OMAHA WORLD HERALD

* * * * * * * * * * * * * * *

VILLAGE OF STARS by Paul Stanton was originally published by the M. S. Mill Co., Inc., at $3.75.

Also by Paul Stanton

CALL ME CAPTAIN

Published in a PERMABOOK edition.

Are there paper-bound books you want
but cannot find at your retail stores? You can get any
title in print in these famous series, **POCKET BOOKS,
CARDINAL EDITIONS, POCKET LIBRARY** and
PERMABOOKS, by ordering from Mail Service Dept.,
Pocket Books, Inc., 1 West 39th St., New York 18, N.Y.
Enclose retail price plus 5c per book for mailing costs;
send check or money order—do not send cash.

FREE CATALOGUE SENT ON REQUEST

VILLAGE
OF
STARS

Paul Stanton

PERMABOOKS ⚓ NEW YORK
Published by Pocket Books, Inc.

Village of Stars

M. S. Mill edition published July, 1960

PERMABOOK edition published May, 1962
1st printing...March, 1962

This PERMABOOK Includes every word contained in the original, higher-priced edition. It is printed from brand-new plates made from completely reset, clear, easy-to-read type.

PERMABOOK editions are distributed in the U.S. by Affiliated Publishers, Inc., 630 Fifth Avenue, New York 20, N.Y.

PERMABOOK editions are published in the United States by Pocket Books, Inc., and in Canada by Pocket Books of Canada, Ltd.—the world's largest publishers of low-priced adult books.

L

Copyright, ©, 1960, by Paul Stanton. All rights reserved. This PERMABOOK edition is published by arrangement with the M. S. Mill Company and William Morrow & Company.

PRINTED IN THE U.S.A.

Only too well he knew them for a trap. A man sees a few stars at the issue of a pit and climbs toward them, and then—never can he get down again but stays up there eternally, chewing the stars . . .

But such was his lust for light that he began to climb.

Antoine de Saint-Exupéry: *Night Flight*

Contents

Solomon Grundy,
        Born on *Monday*,
Christened on *Tuesday*,
        Married on *Wednesday*,
Took ill on *Thursday*,
        Worse on *Friday*,
Died on *Saturday*,
        Buried on *Sunday*,
    And that was the end of Solomon Grundy.

*

Monday

FOR FIVE HOURS now, the man had waited.

Motionless all that time, he stood on the brow of a Caucasian hill, in the shadow of granite rocks around him.

The day was Monday. The date was October 12th. The time was three hours before midnight. The weather was clear.

Above him was Deneb. Cold as an ice-blue aquamarine, Vega sparkled high behind him. From halfway up the northern sky came the glimmer of the Pole Star; and on the horizon beyond flashed those big diamonds Dubhe and Capella. Alpheratz guarded the bracelet of Pegasus from the Lady in the Chair. Close by, the necklace of Perseus still gleamed; but in the west, the brooch of Bootes was already disappearing.

Arcturus vanished, followed by its attendants. But over on the eastern horizon, two others came up immediately to replace them.

Yet these lights did not twinkle. For stars, they seemed too bright, too yellow and they moved too fast. Now two more had appeared below them, and two more after those, and then very faintly another two, and still another two—till they formed an illuminated orderly pattern, far too symmetrical for any constellation.

This, after all, was what the watcher must have been expecting. From the folds of his cloak, he took out a horn and blew it twice, sending a thin high note echoing around the hills. Then he shielded his eyes against what was now a dazzling glare of lights.

A convoy of trucks was coming up the hill toward him.

Their headlamps reflected a hard going. This was no proper road, only what looked like a dried-up river bed, full of cracks and ruts, flanked on either side by rocks and boulders. The trucks bounced and rattled, their springs and brakes squeaking and squealing.

As the first truck approached him, the watcher jumped on the running board and peered through the open window. The slight light from the dashboard illuminated the flat round features of the Mongolian driver.

Smiling at each other, both of them shouted.

Cautiously guiding the others in a follow-my-leader, the first truck crested the brow of the hill, and then again moved downward into a wood, till around a bend at the bottom, suddenly the flare of oil lamps could be seen through the trees, and from a collection of mud huts, men in long robes came rushing forward.

This was the village of Tamarisk, on the Russo-Kanjistan border.

The vehicles slowed and stopped. The drivers climbed out, shook hands, made signs, never stopped smiling. Excited voices were raised. There was a concerted movement toward the rear of the trucks.

Obviously they were loaded with much-needed supplies—food perhaps, or medicine. Cords were untied. Tarpaulins were ripped off. Under the illumination of headlamps and flashlights, a lifeline was quickly formed.

One by one, rifles, machine guns, boxes of hand grenades and ammunition were passed from hand to hand into the waiting shadow of the huts.

At exactly the same time, a hundred and ninety miles south, a figure was climbing under the barbed wire encircling one of the biggest oil fields in the country.

And not five miles from there, at the Palace of the King there was the clatter of boots over marble steps. The guard was being changed, but this time the relieved men were not dismissed. The two commanders stood talking to each other, apparently making plans for the deployment of their troops. Behind them, silhouetted against the glow of the streetlamps, were the minarets and domes of the city of Karkarabad.

Two thousand miles to the west, inside the third room on the second landing at Number Ten, a meeting of the British Cabinet had just broken up. It was not quite dark when the Foreign Secretary walked down the steps into Downing Street. Though the sky was clear, fog was coming up from the river. He bought a paper from a seller on the corner of Whitehall, glanced at the headlines, saw OIL SHARES DIVE. "Wonder how the devil they find out?" he grunted to himself, and shivering a little in the autumn air, he began walking briskly over the frosty pavements in the direction of his Westminster flat.

Further north, England was being slowly extinguished in the fog end of this autumn day. The flats and fens of Essex and Cambridge had already become a uniform dun color. Along the B189 from Lincoln, a few cars already had their lights on. The countryside hovered between the gray of the sky and the gray of the darkening earth, between night and day. Mist was rising up from the dikes, rolling slowly over the neat fertile fields, so that the small farms and the haystacks seemed to float above ground. Distance was blurred to a pale whitish nothing. It might have been sea to the east; it might have been sky; or it might have been just more mist. The few figures that moved down the straight side lanes were smudged and huddled. The air was damp and cold and clinging, with the sharper smell of the sea in it.

But inside the Humber it was warm. The headlights cut easily through the smoky visibility; but to add to their power and effect, Corporal Kidd had switched on the twin yellow foglamps. The glow of the dashboard instruments accorded well with the fluttering gold and blue Air Officer Commanding's pennant on the hood. So did the sleek hiss of the fat tires on the road. So did the festive smell of the A.O.C.'s cigar.

Alone in the seat at the back, conscious of comfort through all her five senses, Helen Durrant closed her eyes and smiled.

With one small black-leather-shod foot, she felt for and found the suitcase on the floor. In her mind, she checked over again that she had forgotten nothing.

The dress, of course, she could hardly forget. But the new stole?

She had that. Her silver slippers? She remembered packing them, together with the silver hair ornament—which might or might not be used. She was undecided whether or not it showed off enough in the blonde of her hair.

Stockings? Her best and sheerest. And an extra pair in case of last-minute runs.

Bracelet? Dress ring? Perfume?

Yes, everything.

She opened her eyes, round and light blue, and satisfied now over the contents of her suitcase, began to contemplate instead the back of the A.O.C.'s neck. In the six months that she had been his Personal Assistant, she had never tired of studying it. It had three wrinkles going horizontally across, which were exactly like the character lines on anyone else's face. They reflected his mood as accurately as did his facial expression, his voice, his footfall. She prided herself on being a good P.A. She also prided herself on knowing her chief's character with a perception that would (she hoped) have appalled him.

The lines were satisfied and smiley now. The dance, of course. At twenty-four, she had learned never to be surprised at the eternal imagined youthfulness of man. It was at a much earlier age that she had learned about the eternal vanity of man. Not that she had any men in the family to study. Her father had been killed in the Air Battle before Alamein. She had no brothers. Her sister was much older, long married and very housewifely. Her mother still lived in the gray stone house east of Hexham, that had been *her* parents' and that had served as a place for Helen's father to hang his hat between R.A.F. postings and partings. Mrs. Durrant's life these days was placid and pleasant, and her few intimate friends were still spry, elderly ladies like herself, garnered from the surrounding countryside.

Perhaps it was rebellion from the confined feminine life that they drew her into, perhaps it was some vague yearning for the brief remembered pictures of her father; or perhaps the itching feet, the pull of the brass bands, the appetite for excitement, were handed down from father to daughter.

Whatever it was, after Oxford, she had rejected the suggested careers of teaching, the Civil Service—administrative class, of course—a really good secretarial job, and had announced that she was joining the W.R.A.F.

The Humber was passing through a village now. The houses were close together, gray and forbidding. A light was on here and there in a kitchen. She stared in momentarily, wondering who lived there, what they felt, what went on. Now came the suburbs of a small town, a jam factory, a sewage plant, a big grocery store.

Avondale, she supposed. Not far now. She wondered if she should lean forward and make some remark. The sweet hum of the engine had a soporific effect. And the two men in front sat so motionless, stolidly shoulder to shoulder, that they might almost have been asleep.

Briefly she wondered what qualities and opportunities in a man separated a driver from an Air Officer Commanding. For from behind, they looked alike. From the front not unalike, except that Corporal Kidd was a good ten years younger. She wondered what would happen if they changed places. Nothing, she supposed. Not a lot, anyway. It was the position that dictated the attitude, and the action would almost certainly be laid down in Air Ministry Orders.

Tiring of the two square blue backs, she wondered what

young men would be at the Officers' Mess dance that night.

"Oakwood approach lights."

As if conscious that her attention had wandered away from him, now the A.O.C. turned and pointed to the left at clustered lights, each on a tall stalk like giant Lords and Ladies. He began fiddling with the strap of a locked leather brief case. Looking businesslike, she thought indulgently. As if the whole Group (the whole Command, for that matter) didn't know that Air Vice Marshal Chatterton always managed to find the need to inspect a Station on the same date as a Station Dance.

She wondered how many dances he would have that night. One, perhaps. He would spend the rest of the time around the bar, tankard in hand, flanked by the Station Commander, the Squadron Commander, any other bright up-and-coming young pilots who knew a thing or two about the rungs on the ladder of promotion, talking first shop and then the War. Always the War! While the pretty girls would revolve around and around within eye's range and hand's reach, and he'd only want them that way. Like a rich woman in Bond Street, knowing she'd got the money but only really admiring the window dressing.

Suddenly a signpost broke the flat monotony of the Lincolnshire road. Arrow-shaped in the headlights, it stood out red and blue. And in big letters—R.A.F. STATION OAKWOOD.

Corporal Kidd slowed, waited for a passing truck which momentarily bathed them in a dazzle of light, then carefully turned.

R.A.F. Station Oakwood—up to now, those seventeen letters had been to Helen Durrant a flag on a map in Group Administration, four files marked *Secret*, a file marked *Confidential* in her own office, a line of tickets on the Group Strength Board, the home of 714 Squadron equipped with new long-rang V-bomber Vengers. It had a ration strength of twelve hundred and fifty, had eighty-one M/T vehicles, sixty-three R.A.F. Officers, eight W.R.A.F. Officers, six gasoline storage tanks, pens for twelve thermonuclear bombs. Also, in the Bomb Site, extensive alterations and excavations had recently been made—and a visit to these was the published reason for the Air Vice Marshal's inspection. They were the subject of files so *Top Secret* that Helen had not yet seen them, but she knew that they were to be the home of a newer and bigger type of atomic weapon, whose code name was K6. In addition, Oakwood last year had won the Group Award for the Best Kept Station, largely through the efforts of its commander, Group Captain K. N. Lucey, O.B.E., D.F.C.

Now, it began as barbed wire. Notices said AIR MINISTRY PROPERTY; KEEP OUT; POLICE DOGS PATROLLING. Six elms in a line stood by the first aircraft dispersal. The concrete of the maintenance huts was chipped. An old gun post left over from the war, gray-faced and baggy-eyed, glared over the top of a hawthorn hedge. Beyond were the runways—one long, one short, crossing each other near the center.

The mist was creeping over them now. Darkness was coming down quickly. The whole place had the sad emptiness of all these R.A.F. airfields. Why, Helen Durrant didn't know. But just the sight of them made even her, bright and self-possessed and rational though she was, feel the ache of something that has gone, of waiting for something that has not yet arrived.

Then they were around another corner, and lying slightly down, cupped by a small swell in the usually flat land, lay the upstart gaudy village of the Station proper.

Lights everywhere. Station Headquarters and the Barrack Blocks lit like illuminated crosswords. Main roadway lights on harebell stems. Blue lights from the hangars, long lines of lights from Nissen huts.

Helen Durrant leaned forward. "Do look at the Mess, sir! They've fairly spread themselves!"

A fountain was playing in the outside garden, that in the summer held standard roses. Multicolored searchlights continually changed its sprouting water-jet from red to blue to green to white. Fairy lights were strung out over the little fir trees that flanked the shallow steps. Two big yellow canvas pumpkins floated above the doorway, half disembodied in the darkness.

No music yet. She looked at her watch. It was earlier than she had thought—only half past six.

"You can drop Miss Durrant outside the W.R.A.F. wing. Then take me to the Station Commander's house."

"Yes, sir."

The Humber hushed to a halt. A small pathway led through the bare side garden to an imitation Georgian doorway of a red brick wing attached to the main Mess. A notice said w.r.a.f. officers only in white letters. All the windows were lighted. At two of them, dance dresses could be seen, hung on hangers. Water was running out of a bath. A woman was singing.

"You arranged your room, didn't you?"

"Yes, sir. I phoned yesterday. They're not full."

She had a ticker-tape memory. Two W.R.A.F. officers under strength.

"I'll be seeing you at the dance then." He smiled indulgently, briefly human. "Be good! Enjoy yourself!"

The corporal held the door open for her, saluted, closed it softly. A chauffeur nearly of her own, a luxury dance, plenty of partners, a clever confidential job. She stood for a moment watching the red rear lamps of the car lose themselves among the carnival of colored lights.

Life was good!

Carefully, in the dark, she picked her way. Beams of light stalked from the main Mess rooms. Figures moved. Distantly, someone tuned an instrument. There was a burst of men's laughter.

In through the white-painted door, the hall was warm. A girl in a crimson velvet bathrobe, her hair in pins, was saying, "For God's sake, hurry up with the bathroom—"

She broke off when she saw Helen, frowned, looked her over and said, "Section Officer Durrant, isn't it?"

"Yes. I came with the A.O.C. Sorry, should I have come in the other way?"

"Nothing to worry about. Visitors usually book in the Mess Office first. Still, who cares? I'm Everton. Signals. Hope you've had a bath. We're all queuing. Your room's at the far end. On the right. Switch off the hot water radiator if it's too hot—"

Breaking off abruptly, the girl began hammering on the bathroom door with her fists.

The room at the far end was like any other W.R.A.F. officer's bedroom on any other Station. Brown polished linoleum floor. Iron-framed bed painted black, spread with a white cotton cover. Brown painted dressing table, chairs, red and blue figured rug.

Helen opened her bag, laid out her dress carefully, then her underwear, then her slippers, her stockings, her bits of jewelry.

All these rooms, besides having furniture exactly the same, had a smell exactly the same. She didn't know what it was, but as the runways and the airfields had an aura of sadness and nostalgia, so the rooms had a smell of it, too. A kind of clean and polished wistfulness, haunted by past happenings, past memories.

She frowned, taking off her uniform jacket, unbuttoning her blouse, untying her tie, gazing around as if the odd mixture of odors was clearly visible, could be analyzed, broken down into their everyday elements, tabulated and then done away with.

Hurrying out of her uniform, now she took her make-up bag from her case and walked over to the severe rectangular mirror over the empty dressing-table.

Standing in front of it, for a long time she worked with absorbed care, so close that the mirror clouded over. Then impatiently she stood back, her head to one side. Her face remained obstinately the same as every day—perhaps a little fresher, a little prettier. Not the sort of face upon which one could paint the glamour of one's choice . . . pointed exotic eyes, penciled dangerous brows.

Through the half-open window, now she could hear the cars arriving, the extra high-pitched drawled-out voices of women coming to a dance, footsteps. . . .

The band had started a tentative foxtrot. More water gurgled down the drain outside. The bathroom door unlocked, then slammed shut again.

Leaving the mirror, still dissatisfied, she went back to the bed and the severe black dance frock. As she smoothed it out, she wondered if any of the Oakwood W.R.A.F. officers—existing now for her only in murmuring voices, snatches of giggles, slammed doors, and quick footsteps—would come in and offer to introduce her at the dance.

But no one came.

She slid the dress over her shoulders, sucking in her mouth to keep her lipstick smooth. The dress gripped her slender figure, accentuated her pale skin, dramatized her light hair, which now she fluffed over her ears. She dabbed on Chanel Number Five. She snapped in a pair of diamond earrings. She pinned on a brooch just over her high small breasts.

Then again she looked in the mirror—and this time took heart.

Just at eight thirty, when the A.O.C. should have arrived, when the dance should have warmed up, when the awkwardest, youngest officer should be feeling no pain, Helen Durrant opened the door of the room at the far end—and emerged.

As she passed down the corridor, the dark floor-length windows acted as mirrors. *Flattering* mirrors. It was odd how reassuring was the ring of one's own high heels, how intoxicating and confidence-giving was a good cloud of one's own expensive perfume.

The band was playing a rumba now. Soft pom-poms of

music bounced down the corridor. At the far end, under interminable Chinese lanterns, she could glimpse the party. A crowd of women, still in their fur capes, the lights glinting on their hair, waited to be escorted to the cloakroom. An arriving, a welcoming, a moving in the decorated Mess hall, laughter and voices funneled and muted by the corridor.

Just where she was, only her own high heels seemed to make any noise. Then just above her head, on the wall, the loudspeaker crackled. The Mess Corporal's voice—routine, languid, bored: "Squadron Leader Falkner . . . phone call, Number Two box. Squadron Leader Falkner, please!"

Now she was level with the row of telephone boxes used for officers' private calls. She could see herself reflected in their glass sides. The reflection was reassuring there, too. A lock of hair had come out of place, but somehow the effect given was casual, rather attractive.

A youngish man was coming down the corridor toward her. A girl called something after him. "Will do," he said over his shoulder, smiling down toward the floor, hurrying.

"Squadron Leader Falkner," she thought. "Bet he goes into Number Two box! Bet that's his wife! His girl friend, maybe." Waiting till he came almost level, eyeing him with the interest she always had in putting people to names, facts to faces.

Tallish and broad. In full Mess dress. Last-war medals. D.F.C., A.F.C. Why wasn't he more than a Squadron Leader? Too young for the big promotions before things tightened up? High-bridged nose, level brows, a serious face, the smile coming and going perhaps too quickly. Big hands and a forward-thrusting walk. Or maybe he was just eager for the call.

They passed. She turned, waiting to see if she was right. He stopped, turned too, caught her eye, smiled, winked. Then echoing down the corridor, puffing her into the party, he sent her off on a long shrill wolf whistle. Not till she reached the door of the bar did she hear the phone-box door slam.

She paused for a moment before turning the handle. Her cheeks had gone red. She was both irritated and flattered. Through the thick oak she could hear the noise of the party well under way . . . almost bursting out of the walls, so that she felt that when she opened the door, it would flood over her like a hot beery tide.

No one saw her for a moment. Even in her high heels, she did not reach over the shoulders of a group of Pilot Officers leaning on the counter, wetting someone's new ring. The place smelled of beer and whisky, perfume and powder, and the smoke of the big log fire in the stone fireplace opposite the bar.

But more than all that, despite the few senior officers, there was a smell of youth. She stood for a moment, neither lonely nor self-conscious, at the edge of the crowd, eyeing here a Flight Lieutenant's shoulders, there a white bare arm, ornamental with a silver bangle and a big vaccination mark, hearing unknown voices, loud, high, aimless . . . I thought I'd never *dare* tell him . . . on the ground-floor of Swan and Edgar's . . . ninety-five and still not flat out . . . touched down sweet as a kiss, and then the port oleo leg . . . *hell* of a good type . . . black velvet, with a heart-shaped neckline . . . posting to Aden . . . nine years as a Squadron Leader and no hope . . . oh, *definitely* . . . on a charge . . . no married quarters . . . whenever her husband's away on detachment . . . certainly . . . have another one . . . probably . . . my round . . . what'll it be?

Then Air Vice Marshal Chatterton saw her, and from his privileged position by the bar, took the few steps necessary to clear a way for her.

"Thought you'd decided to have an early night." He held her elbow in a loose cool grasp, leading her toward the splendid central group.

"Lucey . . . my Personal Assistant, Section Officer Helen Durrant. Helen . . . Group Captain Lucey. She knows all about you, Kenneth . . . so watch out! Mrs. Lucey, may I introduce Miss Durrant? Madge . . . Helen." All the way around the three Wing Commanders, four Squadron Leaders, one Flight Officer, down to a Pilot Officer, whose number could hardly be dry but who had already *learned*.

"What will you have?" The Group Captain waved at the bar, where a hundred different bottles glittered and glowed, and three white-clad Mess bar stewards hurried and sweated. "I think we have everything."

"Gin and lemon, sir, please. No ice." She folded her hands, refused a cigarette, smiled, waited to answer the usual questions . . . how long had she been a P.A., and by implication how had she wangled it? . . . did she like Group H/Q, and by implication old Chatterton? . . . when did she join, and by implication how old was she? . . . did she think she'd make the Service her career, and by implication had she got anyone lined up yet? . . . was she a long way from home?

"Quite a long way," she said to Mrs. Lucey. "My home's in Northumberland. I get up there fairly often . . . well, of course, I don't find it cold but I expect, being a native, I've got used to it."

Now that her drink was here, she could sip it decorously and let her eyes travel around. There was nothing quite like a Mess party. Nothing like one on a real Station. There was an odd-looking girl in the corner with her hair piled up in yellow curls, a girl drinking out of what looked like the Station Equipment Officer's glass. Someone started up a song in the corner, but Group Captain Lucey was tall enough to catch the culprit's eyes. The door kept opening and shutting, blowing in dance music and snatching it away again, like a gusting wind. The third time it opened, Squadron Leader Falkner came back in.

He came straight over to them, and the group made room for him, as if all the time they had been keeping his place warm.

"Well," said one of the Wing Commanders. "You've missed a round. I hope she was worth it."

"I don't think you've met my Personal Assistant. Miss Durrant, may I introduce Squadron Leader Falkner . . . 'B' Flight Commander of 714 Squadron."

"Oh, but we *have* met," Helen Durrant said sweetly. "Just a moment ago. In the corridor. Hello."

"Hello, *again.*" He smiled, but he looked neither surprised nor embarrassed. "I didn't catch your name that time."

He waved away a drink that the Wing Commander was making a great show of finding the loose change for. "I was wondering, Miss Durrant," he said, "while the floor isn't too crowded, if you'd like to dance?"

She put her glass on one of the wicker tables close by the bar, gathered up her skirt, and walked to the corridor door, keeping a little ahead of him till they were at the edge of the ballroom.

It was a waltz, and the lights were low. There was the usual crowd around the door, like swimmers afraid the water was too cold. But in the half-light, they were just a vague mass of heads and shoulders. High up at the far end, some-one was working a colored spotlight. Out of the darkness, filled only with the soft beat of the music and the soft scrape of rhythmic feet, would suddenly stand out a profile cruelly held and colored in bright blue or red or green.

He danced as she would have expected him to. Neatly and competently, but without all that much interest. Dancing to him was obviously a reflex movement that you made while you got to know a girl better.

"I suppose I should apologize?" The mixture of gloaming and the working of the colored spots highlighted his prominent cheekbones and long jaw. He had a consciously sweet and charming smile, which he turned on vaguely and without vanity . . . a necessary social easement.

"For whistling? No."

"Actually, I thought you were one of the girls from Oakwood."

"Those were some around the bar, weren't they?"

"Yes."

"Then you *should* apologize."

"I thought you were one of the better ones." He paused. "All right then . . . the best."

"Apologize."

"Sorry . . . sorry, ma'am. I didn't realize you were in such a powerful position."

"You should consider your future, you know."

The band stopped. They stood with the others. Momentarily the lights went up, and they blinked. Then Squadron Leader Falkner began clapping vigorously. Down went the light again, and up came the syrupy bubbles of drowsy waltz-time.

"Actually," he said, sliding his arm loosely around her, "I didn't even know old Chatterton could pick them quite so well."

"As what?"

"As you."

"Oh, I don't think he picks his P.A.'s . . . not for looks."

"Even he can't be that much of a fool. What d'you think I'm sweating on my Scrambled Egg for?"

She smiled up at him sweetly. "Can't you pick them without?"

"After all," he went on, ignoring the question, "what do you do at Group? Besides holding old Chatterton's hand all day?"

She held her head a little to one side. "What else *is* there to do?"

"Write bloody-minded letters to Stations? Lose files? Post the wrong people? Hang up spares? Refuse replacements?"

"We do all that, of course," she said. "But that's what we count as fun."

A sudden dizzy hilarity possessed her. She had never felt so young, never so silly, never so excited, so unknown and yet so known.

"How long have you been doing this job?"

Abruptly, the music stopped again. This time, it was she who clapped. But a W.R.A.F. waitress was bringing in a brimming tray of tankards—her hips wobbling, the beer slopping. Another came in with sausage rolls and sandwiches. The band pushed away their instruments. The lights remained irrevocably up.

"How long? Oh, about six months."

"How long have you been in?"

"Nearly two years."

"And he doesn't pick them for looks?"

Sharply she said, "He hasn't got a one-track mind."

"My heart belongs to Daddy, does it?"

"Are you always so rude?"

He paused halfway across the ballroom, and said quite seriously, "As a matter of fact, no. It's you. The way you affect me."

"I suppose," she said tartly, "I should apologize?"

"Not at the moment. Look, though. D'you want to go back? To the brass? Wouldn't you rather stop with me? You won't get the best of the eats. But I can promise you some stimulating conversation."

They were out in the corridor now. "I'll think about it," she said.

"Think fast! Ten more steps and we'll be back among them."

"Don't hurry me. I've got to weigh the pros and cons."

At the door of the bar, he stopped. "Well?"

"I'm not all that fond of eats," she said. "I'll try the conversation."

"Right!" He hurried her past the bar, opened the door of the supper room. "Hell!" he said. "Look at that!"

Already the long room swarmed with people. The display of stuffed pheasants, glazed ham and pigs' heads, the carefully arranged color scheme of savories and trifles and fruit and flowers was melting, losing shape, vanishing as the plates were filled, handed over, handed back and filled again.

"There's a corner over there. Don't move till I get back!"

When he returned, she looked at the meager plate. "The conversation," she said, "will really have to be something!"

He looked at his watch. "Beginning," he said, "*now!*"

"I'm listening," she said.

He made a queer deprecatory shrug of his shoulders. Close to, his eyes were hazel—candid, oddly confused. "I can't think of anything. Not at the moment."

He gave her a long slow look, as though he were memorizing her features.

"Tell me your first name," she said, confused herself now, feeling her party gaiety, her curious sense of being already known to this man, wavering into unforeseen, unwanted complications. "The A.O.C. didn't get as far as that."

He recovered his self-possession briefly. "He knew you might take advantage. You may just call me sir. I am, after all, a senior officer." He paused. "It's John."

"Nice to know you," she said, demurely lowering her eyes. "Anything else? Age?"

"Thirty-six."

"Married?"

"Of course not."

Someone bumped into them, spilled coffee down the sleeve of his uniform. He swore softly, good-naturedly.

"Let's get to hell out of here, shall we? You can't breathe without squashing someone." He held her hand to guide her through the room. Of all the delicacies, now only the pigs' heads remained untouched, side by side with a harvest-festival-like arrangement of fruit.

"The band's still stuffing itself," he said. "No music." And with sudden undeceiving inspiration: "Let's go and have a breath of fresh air."

"It's cold," she said, hesitating behind the main glass doors that reflected the lights on the artificial rockery behind them, and the shadows of couples moving up and down the corridor. She was not sure what he would expect of her. She was aware in herself of a cool, fastidious streak, that precluded necking sessions in the dark after a Mess party. She knew, too, that in some way she did not want this evening spoiled. Not so much the evening, but the picture that she now had in her mind of this man.

"Warm as toast," he said, and squeezed her hand. "Coming?"

The lights from the windows lapped in pools down the steps, spilled onto the gravel, just touching the stubby closeshorn autumn grass.

"You get a good view of the airfield past that hangar. Can you see it? How's your night vision?"

"Cat's eyes," she said.

They walked along in silence, listening to their feet crunching over the pathway, pausing on the grass verge as a truck came pounding down the main road.

"There!" he said. "Not a bad view, is it?" He pointed at the brightly-colored, ordered pattern of the airfield, the two rows of runway lights, inclined to each other by distance, leading like a ladder into the night sky. There was a curious boyishness in his voice—but underlying it, constraint.

"Wonderful!" she said. "I love an airfield at night."

"There's a Venger over there. Just outside the hangar."

She stood on tiptoe, peering past his pointing finger. The gray-white triangular shape, flat and dead-looking like a giant moth, lay on the hard standing, its pale anti-radiation paint catching a glow of indirect light from the hangar. Again the airfield lay flat and open in front of her, the spaces now filled with deep darkness, its lights puny, one by one disappearing . . . flat, austere, sad . . . and with the V-shaped Venger there, like some vast discarded Ku Klux Klan visor, now *something else.* . . .

She shivered.

"Are you cold?" His face peered down at her . . . warm, kindly, concerned.

"Not really."

"Would you like to go back?"

Oddly, now she felt only comfort in his presence. "Not unless you want to."

"*I* don't." He slipped her hand into his pocket for warmth. "Shall we just wander around? I'll show you the stars. You can tell me the story of your life."

"There's not much to tell," she said.

"Sure?"

"Quite sure."

Over beyond the hangars, the village church struck twelve. He glanced at his watch. "By the way," he said, "I'm doing an air test on that Venger tomorrow. Seventeen hundred. Like to come?"

It was neither the cold starry darkness of the night, nor the sight of the aircraft, nor the man in front of her, but a mixture of all three that suddenly made her have the desire to turn back to the warmth, the lights and the crowds of the Mess. The next second would be irrevocable—something gone, something gained.

Yet her own voice sounded bright, brisk and normal.

"Thank you," she said. "I'd love to."

When they turned back to the Mess, he held her hand lightly. Before they pushed open the glass doors, he touched her cheek, tilted her chin, smiled down at her and said, "See you tomorrow then."

The gesture was more formal, more possessive than a kiss. And her sense of having moved irrevocably to some unknown destination returned.

*

Tuesday

ON TUESDAY, October 13th, the sun rose above the horizon of Kanjistan at 0611 Local Time. It illuminated a countryside gray and empty, fretted to the north by the purple shadows of mountains. Nothing stirred, except a few sheep grazing on the lower brown-grassed slopes. A sudden and curiously timid police visit to the village of Tamarisk had disclosed only peasants and goatherds, sleeping peacefully in their huts. Further south, where the oil derricks stood like steel scaffolds, black against the slight drift of white morning clouds, the sun briefly struck a glint from the helmet of one of the drowsing guards. And in Karkarabad, the capital, everything was perfectly normal—except that the incoming train from the north was unusually crowded, and the Minister of the Interior had died, apparently from a stroke, quite quietly in the night.

In the neighboring country of Persia, stalls had already been set up in Teheran's main square. Most of the shops were open, and the usual weekday traffic, thick in the native quarter, had begun to hum gently into life near the flats and houses occupied by European residents. Inside the palace of the Shah, preparations for his forthcoming State Visit to Kanjistan were unaccountably and very abruptly shelved.

A thousand miles away in Athens, a shipping magnate diverted two of his oil tankers from Kanjistan to Bahrein. In a brilliant dawn, from Paris had gone instructions to selected French residents in Karkarabad, advising them to send their families home. In London, it was past seven o'clock before the sun, invisible behind the chokings of river mist and smog, allowed the city more than a pale lightening of night.

Inside the third room on the second landing of Number Ten Downing Street, the reading lamps were switched on all around the square mahogany table, giving an entirely spurious appearance of well-being.

Floating in through the fog, through the thick glass window hung with its dark blue velvet drapes, came the sounds of wakening London. It was quiet in the room, warm and ordered. Far too early in the morning for feelings to run high. Yet, leaning forward in his leather-armed chair, Air Chief Marshal Chester Duggane was conscious of a not unpleasant quickening of his heart.

It was not the Foreign Secretary's manner, his high-pitched, rather sanctimonious: "In the present crisis, provoked by the rebels under Ibrahim ben Sayid, the King of Kanjistan has asked police assistance from us in accordance with our treaty, and the Cabinet is entirely unanimous that this should be sent."

Duggane had expected that. The new government had come to power on the election cries of increased prosperity, increased power, increased discipline at home, increased protection of British interests abroad, and no more twisting of the lion's tail. Indeed Duggane had steered his vote (and those of his wife and two daughters) into the right ballot box for those very reasons.

Nor was it the monotonous, unimpassioned arguing about how this step should be presented to the United Nations in general and the United States in particular. Duggane had long ago arrived at an assessment of the swings and surges of American opinion which had proved up to now to be tolerably accurate.

No! The part that really concerned him was how, when, where, and by whom. The part, in fact, that they were coming to now. With some apprehension, he heard the creaking of the General's Sam Browne. He'd be getting his oar in, of course, trying to prove that the Army was the one indispensable Service.

"It seems to me, sir," the General said, capturing the initiative, "that a couple of battalions of the Parachute Regiment is the *first* essential. Get them in *quickly!* Land them *here . . .*" he pointed a stubby finger at the map in front of them. "Then you've got a police force capable of swinging north to the frontier, or west to the oil fields."

"Using 781 Transport Squadron?" Duggane interjected smoothly. If the General thought the R.A.F. would be content with running a bus service for the Army, he was sadly wrong. "That would be simple to arrange."

"We could leave simultaneously from Lyneham and Blackbushe."

"How soon?" asked the Prime Minister.

"We could have"—the General's light-blue eyes regarded the cornucopiaed ceiling—"the Second Battalion at Lyneham by noon. The rest say by twenty hundred hours."

Then the Chief of Naval Staff. Thin face, thin smile, thin voice cutting through the smoky atmosphere like the knife-edged bows of a frigate through the Channel.

"Communications, sir . . . they'll want watching. *Scipio, Scorpio* and *Centipede* could take up position in the Eastern Mediterranean."

"Unnecessary!" the General said. "Totally unnecessary!"

"They might be required," the Admiral went on, "to take off British subjects, should this develop into"—he hesitated, searching for an inoffensive recent campaign simile—"something like . . . like . . ."

"If we get in fast enough," the General said, "and stop shillyshallying, and asking every pipsqueak country's permission . . . the whole thing'll be nipped in the bud . . . finished before this *is* a civil war . . . or a crisis . . . or even a threat."

"That's exactly what I'm saying."

"We only need the paratroops."

Duggane bided his time. The Prime Minister needed a moment or two for strategic digestion. It was always the same in a Crisis. Jockeying for position like women around a bargain counter. As if the Army and the Navy didn't see that in this atomic age, they were finished. The trouble was, they were both rooted deep in the sentimentalities of the British people, and it would be a hell of a job to get them out. Time would, though. Time would!

"Now, gentlemen," he said at last, as the General and the Admiral continued to argue over warships, "we deviate. The keynote of our policy is surely . . . the *deterrent*." He looked around. "Is it not?"

Unerringly, he had struck the right note at the right time. He knew that the Prime Minister, torn between left of center and right of center factions in his party, between an aggressive mien and the electoral promise of peace, felt that at these meetings the Service Chiefs tended to stampede him into unripe action. Now he saw that the Prime Minister regarded him more kindlily.

"Of course, it's the deterrent," the General said sourly. "There's nothing aggressive about sending a paratroop regiment. It's a mobile fire-brigade!"

Ignoring him, Duggane went on, "And in the light of the deterrent policy it strikes me that these excellent and enthusiastic plans put forward by my colleagues"—he nodded politely at them in turn—"have certain lamentable disadvantages."

"Such as?" the General said.

"Specify!" said the Admiral.

"Gladly! First—" He held up one finger. "A landing in Kanjan soil, British warships in Kanjan waters . . . are likely to be misconstrued as armed intervention."

"Only," said the Foreign Secretary, "where any action of ours is *always* misconstrued."

Duggane looked respectfully doubtful. "World opinion," he

smiled, "has often been misinformed." He held up another finger. "Secondly, once in . . . difficult to withdraw."

He didn't mention Suez. But he hoped the Prime Minister would think of that himself.

"Thirdly, what if our plan *is* misconstrued . . . *what then?*" He leaned forward across the table. "What if other powers should similarly feel called upon to protect their interests? How do we follow up?"

No one said anything. The General knew, the Admiral knew, the Air Chief Marshal knew, that always to be reckoned with were those Russian intercontinental ballistic missiles that Mr. Khrushchev was always mentioning. And Britain, now the biggest storehouse of nuclear weapons, an American arms dump of goods not wanted elsewhere, not inadvisedly called America's off-shore island, would be a prize of a military target and would go up like a puff of smoke.

"Look here," the Admiral said. "You're not suggesting we just let the rebels get away with it?"

"Indeed no!"

"It wouldn't come to Russian interference." The General had that red-faced closed-minded look that Duggane knew so well among army types. "Complete nonsense!"

"I hope not. But it *might*. We must be prepared."

"What do you suggest, Air Marshal?" the Prime Minister asked thoughtfully.

And when Duggane paused, the General interjected, "A V-Bomber patrol, eh?"

These V-Bomber patrols had not been popular with the other Services—or with the public.

"*Not quite!*" He paused. "Not at *this* moment. Up to now, it isn't necessary. But there is something you should know." He smiled. "A week ago, sir, we took delivery of our first K6."

K6, he knew, was his trump card: Britain's biggest and most powerful secret. A new-type thermonuclear bomb—of infinitely greater destructive potential than anything possessed by either Russia or America. A neat, mobile, easily handled, deadly weapon, capable of no less than forty thousand square miles of complete devastation. He knew the Navy and the Army coveted it. But neither had the means of delivering it at that range.

The R.A.F. not only had the bomb—they could carry it vast distances. It made the tactics of the paratroops and the warships look as obvious as a wig and as useful as Dinky toys.

"Now, sir, *I'd* say that if it were well-positioned, K6 would provide a most cogent international argument."

"Where is it now?"

"Oakwood, sir. 714 Squadron."

"Where'd you suggest putting it?"

"Close to the troubled area, sir. If things quieten, back she comes. If they don't, the crew can take her . . ." he paused, "wherever required."

The Prime Minister stroked his chin. "Seems sound. No threat. But it's *there* . . . just in case—"

"Precisely!" Duggane was smiling broadly. "And I'm sure the General here will bear me out. The better half of tactics is . . . having the *right* weapon in the *right* place at the *right* time!"

There was still thick mist over the airdrome at Oakwood. Of the runways, nothing could be seen. Hangars loomed up out of nowhere like the prows of great ships. Figures of airmen moved uncertainly between blobs of yellow wool in shadowy buildings. Flanked on either side by Wing Commanders' residences, what was going on in the Group Captain's mansion was screened by the weather and velvet curtains. And beyond a scattering of lights in the Officers' Mess, the red-brick village of the Married Quarters was a mass of uncertain gray shapes, all armed with television aerials. The streets—all named after famous airmen—were wet. Nobody stirred along Tedder Avenue, where the married Flight Lieutenants lived inside nice detached four-bedroom houses—their garageless cars living outside in the damp. There was a little more activity along the terraces of N.C.O.'s and Airmen's houses.

And yet over to the east, what looked like the smothered beam of a lighthouse appeared to be trying to illuminate the Station.

Closer to, no lighthouse. Number Six Portal Street. A semi-detached house, laid down in A.M.O.'s as suitable for junior officers—with every window upstairs and downstairs blazing.

The dwelling of Pilot Officer Peter Pinkney, the recently commissioned Navigator/Bomb-aimer in Squadron Leader Falkner's crew.

The time was relentlessly approaching nine o'clock—the chaotic hour. The whole house reverberated with footsteps, calls, water running, food frying, clanks of cutlery, coal and crockery. Ever since his wife died two years ago, he had had to cope with five children on his own.

Now, sweating and puffing, he was scrabbling under hats and coats, trying to locate his youngest's mackintosh on the overcrowded pegs in the hall. He was a big red-faced man in his late thirties, with thick folds of flesh around his jowls, and rubbery boneless features that made him look like a plump Popeye.

"Elsie!" he called up the stairs. "Elsie . . . it's not here!"

From the bathroom in reply came the harassed voice of his eldest, who now worked—it was her only relaxation, she said —behind the counter in a Lincoln Ladies' Outfitters: "Stop still, Margaret . . . while I do your hair! Stop still, can't you . . . or you'll get a good smack!"

"Elsie . . . where is it?"

From the kitchen, a voice almost as deep as his own: "Bacon's burning, Dad!"

From the bedroom, the sound of a heavy bump, followed by squeals, followed by Elsie's voice, more threatening than ever: "If you two don't give over . . . I'll tell you this, I'll—"

"Elsie," Pinkney called up again, "Margaret's mac's missing."

"Then she can go without it."

"But the weather—"

"Serves her right for not hanging it up. She's been told enough. Now stop still! *Stop still!*"

Shrugging his shoulders, Pinkney gave up the search, and walked the four paces into the living room to lay the breakfast.

The family sat down to eat in dribs and drabs: twins of twelve, five-year-old Margaret, then Tom.

"Elsie," said her father, as brushing back a brown curl from a hot forehead, at last his eldest sat down. "You needn't come home to lunch. I'll collect Margaret from school."

"Thought you were flying," Tom said.

"Not till later this afternoon."

"Taking the bomb someplace?"

"Eat up your breakfast and stop asking questions." Pinkney reached for the mustard. "No . . . of course not. Just an air test. This bacon's fatty, Elsie."

The Pinkney family had been brought up in an atmosphere of aircraft, bombs and guns. Indoctrinated by long use and acceptance, they took such things completely for granted as part of their surroundings: life wouldn't have been the same without them. That under each big green mound in the Bomb Dump was something called an atom bomb, all of them knew. Though Pinkney did not himself speak about it, they also knew—intuitively, as children do—that occasionally their father flew with one of these things in the bomb bay of a Venger, where it became his special charge. "Don't think of it as anything else but another kind of bomb," he had told them. "That's all it is . . . and I should know. I've spent all my working life with 'em!" And that was how they thought about it—no less, and no more.

"Take your elbows off the table, Margaret! And eat up your egg! Go on! Eat it up!"

"Oh, she hasn't done too bad, Elsie!"

"Dad . . . you're far too easy with her. Lots of people in the world would be only too glad—"

But her father was not listening. The twins had started up again.

"St. John the Baptist had short hair."

"St. John the Baptist had long hair."

Pinkney banged his fat fist hard down on the table. "Stop it! *Stop it!* I've told you boys before . . . I won't have this scrapping! Not at breakfast!" And then, looking up at the clock on the mantelpiece: "Hurry up . . . hurry, everyone! Time's getting on!"

Cornflakes, bread, toast, and plates went zigzagging across the table. Tea and milk were spilt. A saucer fell off the table and broke on the floor.

Tom muttered something about missing the bus to the Tech, and disappeared through the back door with his mouth still full. Next off went Elsie on her bicycle. The twins were picked up by a fellow officer's car, to be taken to the village Secondary School along with his own children.

The two of them left together now, Pinkney fussed around his youngest. He managed at last to find her mackintosh—in the outside lavatory—produced her beret and satchel, and finally set off with her, hand in hand, to the R.A.F. Camp School at the end of the road.

Outside the iron railings, they stopped. Margaret was shy. Even though she only went in the mornings, she hated school. Pinkney knew it was an effort for her sometimes not to cry.

Now he could see the eyes blinking fast, as she went through the catechism of the questions she always asked him.

"I'll be all right, won't I?"

"Of course you will!"

"Miss Jones won't be cross with me, will she?"

"Of course she won't!"

"I won't feel sick, will I?"

"Of course you won't!"

"You'll be early, won't you?"

"Of course I will!"

She put up her face to be kissed. Reassured and smiling, into school she walked, and Pinkney, waving till she disappeared, began walking back up Portal Street.

Able at last to be more conscious of his surroundings, he was aware that the mist was lifting. There was a slit of yellow in the sky now; the airdrome buildings were slowly emerging from the uniform grayness into their individual natural colors.

He could see the Equipment Section quite clearly, and beyond it long orderly ranks on the parade ground. The A.O.C.'s inspection—he remembered it now, thanked his stars he wasn't on it. Before going into Number Six to do the washing-up and make the beds, he watched it for a while, located 714 Squadron turnout, managed to catch sight of the gold leaves—known as the Scrambled Egg—on Air Vice Marshal Chatterton's hat, moving just ahead of a number of variegated headgear among which was the softer crown of a W.R.A.F. officer's cap. . . .

At that moment, Helen Durrant was taking a surreptitious peep at her watch. Only ten past nine, and already the Inspection was well under way.

The slight wind that was helping to blow away the mist also kept the personal pennant of the Commanding Officer fluttering briskly at the top of the pole. At the yardarm below flew the R.A.F. ensign. Seven solid phalanxes of airmen —buttons burnished, boots blacked and dubbinged—and two smaller lines of airwomen cut a blue-gray, almost motionless rectangle out of the sunlit Barrack Square.

They were going down the second squad of airmen. The first squadron, backs as well as fronts now inspected, had been stood at ease. The A.O.C. paused momentarily to ask a pale-faced boy what Section he worked in. Walking behind ./im the requisite few paces, among the pheasant-like stalking of a covey of officers-in-attendance, to the tune of their clink-

ing medals, hiding all her thoughts behind a grave face, came
Helen Durrant.

During her six months as his P.A., she had attended some
eight or nine Station Inspections. Usually she had no strong
feelings either for or against them. They were part of her
two-year-old way of life. If the weather was crisp and fine
and clear she enjoyed them. If it was not, she loathed them.

Always fastidious, she liked her own extra-smart turnout.
She was amused at herself with her cap set dead straight on
her head instead of with its usual faintly rakish, very slightly
Beatty-angle. She liked the rhythmic clap of marching feet,
the hoarse voice of the Station Warrant Officer . . . they were
always hoarse and invariably red and fat. And the boom of
the band unashamedly excited her. She liked the drill, the
orders, the almost ritualistic pattern of the day's doings. She
liked her own secret smile most of all . . . at the huffing and
puffing, the strutting, the showing off, the bull and the
bother.

"Number Two Flight . . . atten*tion!*"

A hundred pairs of issue boots clanged hard on the concrete but caused not a flicker of interest in the A.O.C.'s eyes.
He was preoccupied; Helen Durrant had noticed it all the
morning. Not in the parade either—he moved in a mechanical kind of daze, saying things automatically as though he
wasn't thinking about what he was doing. No smiley lines
cut across the back of his neck today. No stern jaw-out
thrustings, either. The little convoy passed two airmen whose
hair-length would have been more appropriate for crooners,
but he made no comment.

"Number Two Flight . . . stand at *ease!*"

Again the clump of feet. An unbelieving, almost inaudi-
ble sigh of relief. Chatterton's reputation as a stickler for
discipline preceded him everywhere. His nickname among
the airmen was unmentionable in polite society.

Yet here he was hurrying everyone along almost at breakneck speed. Helen Durrant had difficulty keeping up with him.

"Number Three Flight . . . atten*tion!*"

The Officer in Charge of Three Flight advanced, struck sparks on the ground with the heels of his shoes. Another line of faces came up, the mixture as before: noses slightly pinched, indeterminate eyes staring ahead of them, glassy and reddened by the cold air.

And still no comment from the A.O.C. He had hardly opened his mouth the whole time, except to say a vague, "Thank you," or "Good turnout!" or "Keep it up!"

No one had been snagged. No one had been asked, "Haven't I seen you before?" Just as his P.A. prided herself on her factual memory, Air Vice Marshal Chatterton collected faces. Rarely was he wrong. Rarely was a parade unlightened by some almost time-expired men, some beribboned N.C.O. saying in reply, "Malta 'forty-one, sir" or, "Five Group 'forty-four" or "Thorney Island 'forty-five." A trick which he invariably pulled out of the hat, to the smiling admiration of the reigning Group Captain.

But today there was nothing.

"Number Three Flight . . . stand at *ease!*"

Helen began to wonder if there was anything the matter. Did he got to bed too late last night? Wasn't he best pleased with his accommodation with the Luceys? Was he ill? Had something upset him, knocked him off his perch, silenced both the jovial enthusiasm and the furious bark? Was he worried about something?

Concerned a little, she waited till he had turned ninety degrees to her, and momentarily she caught sight of his profile in the sunlight. An aircraft suddenly ran up its engines far away in dispersal, sent a wild whine across the parade ground, and as quickly died away. She saw his eyes narrow slightly, as though the noise had reminded him of something —that was all. No other expression whatever came over the glazed mask of his plump face.

But now he quickened his pace even more. Perhaps, like her, he felt the cold nipping his fingers within the leather gloves.

"Number Four Flight . . . atten*tion!*"

The Squadron. She had half-hoped to see John Falkner, magnificent in Best Blue, medals and brassed-up buttons. She had already decided overnight that she would enjoy a mild flirtation with him—no more. That way, she could allow her mind and imagination to wander through a glossy magazine of color and fiction—without getting herself involved.

But few aircrew, beyond a couple or so junior officers still almost on the bottle, were visible. It was a depleted turnout, all right. Trust the squadron to wangle out of parades! They always did. But again the A.O.C. made no audible comment.

Even the Women's Royal Air Force failed to kindle their usual paternal light in his eyes. He left aggressively thrust-out bosoms to be appreciated by the little band of officers that followed. During the march-past, standing at the salute alone on his dais, he seemed more preoccupied than ever. And afterward, almost blown off the parade ground by the rising wind, he led his party to their cars.

Then, at funeral pace, with the A.O.C. puffing with impatience, they moved down the Oakwood roadways, rounded a corner, stopped outside the first of the hutted camps.

Barrack inspection. Helen Durrant trod carefully. The floor was like glass and just as dangerous. Sometimes she wondered if all this paraphernalia of looking down lavatories, opening cupboard doors, admiring clean windows, was worth it. Around to the back now . . . a pretense of catching them out. Sure the coal bunker was clean enough to eat your dinner off—a good deal cleaner, she would bet, than the airmen's Mess kitchens on an ordinary day. But the A.O.C.'s *thing* about coal bunkers was well known.

Group Captain Lucey looked at the A.O.C. with expectant pride. But again, Chatterton said nothing.

Behind them, as they trooped down now toward the W.R.A.F. Mess and the gymnasium, the Wing Commander Administration tried to engage Helen in desultory conversation. "Section Officer Durrant . . . is there any particular aspect of W.R.A.F. welfare that you're *especially* interested in?"

A difficult one, that. She was about to shake her head, but thinking better of it, instead said loftily, "All aspects, sir . . . *equally.*"

The Wing Commander Admin looked suitably impressed.

Ten men in Persil-white shorts began a rhythmic exercise with batons as soon as the door of the gymnasium opened. In went the A.O.C. and party, and then out again. All that effort just for, "Carry on, don't let us disturb you!" And then the door closed and the party was off again—this time to the W.R.A.F. Mess.

The pace of the tour was quickening all the time.

Around the Equipment Section, the gardens still had a show of chrysanthemums. They had polished the brass knobs of the fire hydrants outside the M/T section. Freshly whitened stones edged the pathway invitingly up to the office. But Air Vice Marshal Chatterton did not go in. On he swept, past the hangars toward the Bomb Dump. As they rounded the main runway, the piles of excavated earth and two tractors clearly marked the pens for the hush-hush K6, the completion of which was the main cause of this Inspection.

Only two cars—the Group Captain's and their own—were going on to this part of the Inspection. All filled, Helen knew, with personnel who had been screened twice for Security. Idly, she watched the creamy-white of newly laid concrete glinting in the pale sunshine; saw the high barricade of steel fencing, the guards on the now open gate; wondered whether this time she would actually see the inside of the pens.

Probably not. Chatterton usually made the same excuse when it came to inspecting new atom-bomb pens. "Too dirty for you down here, Helen . . . you stay up there in the fresh air."

She was thinking, Perhaps he'll think of something new this time, or maybe in his present farawayness forget she was behind him—when suddenly there was a scream of a motorcycle overtaking the Humber. Abreast of them now, a dispatch rider signaled Corporal Kidd to stop.

"Sir—"

Under his crash helmet, Helen noticed, the airman had the large red earnest face of a butcher's errand boy. Two blue eyes bulged round and wide with the importance of this assignment.

"Wanted in Operations, sir. The telephone."

Normally, he would have exploded. He would have gone red with fury at being interrupted in this almost sacrosanct business. He would have wanted to know who and why and from where.

But to Helen's surprise, almost as though he had been expecting it, this time all he did was to nod and say, "Corporal—"

"Yes, sir?"

"Operations."

"Yes, sir."

"Drop me there. Then go on with Miss Durrant to the Mess. No need for you to come, Helen. You go and have some coffee."

The big Humber wheeled a hundred and eighty degrees around on its tracks, and without after all visiting the new Bomb Dump installations, began accelerating toward the squat flat-roofed building of Station Operations.

"Chatterton."

Sitting alone in the Controller's glass box, he spoke his name into the mouthpiece. But this was no ordinary telephone. This was the *scrambler*, direct to Bomber Command, the secret link that couldn't be tapped or listened to.

No answer yet. Only that curious burring background there always was to these damned things. They'd be looking for Thane now, telling him in hushed respectful tones that the A.O.C. of 93 Group was on the phone, anxious not to waste a second of the great man's precious time.

A frown on his forehead, Chatterton looked through what appeared to be a gigantic windscreen at the Operations Room below him. The Flight Lieutenant Controller—sandy-haired, freckle-faced—ousted from his eyrie, was talking to the Group Captain. And the two W.R.A.F. watch-keepers had put down their knitting and were trying to look busy.

Apart from the exit, seven doors led out of the Operations to the BRIEFING ROOM, CODE AND CIPHER, INTELLIGENCE, METEOROLOGICAL OFFICE, NAVIGATION, ARMAMENT OFFICER, SIGNALS. What was left of the wall was covered with notices and Squadron Orders.

And maps, of course. Maps of all colors: purple, red, green, white, spread everywhere in great dazzling daubs. The Air Vice Marshal's eyes, screwed up a little now, for they were not as good as they had been, studied the two opposite him: a map of the Middle East and a map of Oakwood, curiously juxtaposed.

His concentration was focused on two comparatively small areas of each: a ragged-edged country bordering on the Black Sea and Southern Russia called Kanjistan; and six rectangles newly drawn in the Bomb Dump area of the airdrome.

"Thane here. That you . . . Chatterton?"

Here he was now—that same honey-sweet voice that still managed to sound clipped and military, a sure-fire charm for politicians, foreigners and ladies.

"Yes . . . Chatterton."

"You've heard about the unrest in Kanjistan?"

"I've had some information . . . yes."

"Things are moving."

"Already?"

"Thought you'd be surprised. We're having no more of

this four-month fiasco." It was a curious thing, but Suez had already become a four-letter word with all the Services. "Second Battalion, Airborne Division is already on its way."

Which concerns the jet transports down at Lyneham only, Chatterton thought. Southern Group's pigeon.

"The Navy are sending to the Eastern Mediterranean *Scipio, Scorpio, Centipede . . .*"

For a moment, he closed his eyes, seeing them all at it, bickering around for something for their own particular boys, the politicians dealing out the cards: one to the Army, one to the Navy, one to the Air Force . . . *eenie-meenie-minie-mo-catch-a-nigger-by-the-toe-if-it-hollers . . .*

". . . as well as the Second Cruiser Squadron."

What's he telling me all this for? the A.O.C. thought. They've never been so generous with their information before. Unless—

"I expect you're wondering where you come in. I'll tell you. It's the K6."

For a moment, Chatterton said nothing. Then respectfully, evenly: "The K6 in what capacity, sir?"

"Chatterton . . . I know you're going to be pleased by this." The Chief of Bomber Command paused as though awaiting appreciative noises, and hearing none, went on: "The C.A.S. has at last persuaded the politicians to get it airborne."

"Premature, sir . . . in my opinion."

"Chatterton"—the smooth rich voice went very slightly sour—"we've got to get the aircrews used to flying with it!"

"But why *now* . . . sir? We've only got the one, after all. What's the hurry?"

The voice sounded nettled. "You know as well as I do the touchiness of the international situation. And Zweig has been angling to get us flying with it."

"It's flown at the Atlas Sinclair factory."

"Chatterton"—Air Marshal Thane's words were now coming thick and fast and hot—"that isn't the same at all! We've *got* to get our aircrews to accept it as they would any other weapon."

"But how does this tie in with the present situation?" He asked it, though he knew the answer: it was one of the cards the R.A.F. had been dealt, and the ace of trumps, at that.

"Just a flight down toward the troubled area."

"An *operational* flight?"

"Well . . . *semi*. Call it training. That's the idea."

Air Vice Marshal Chatterton paused. He pulled at the stiff white hairs of his stubby moustache. Loud-mouthed and blunt he most certainly was with his subordinates—but there was this very great compensation about him: he was exactly the same with his superiors. He said, "I'd call it stupid."

There was a very long silence at the end of the wire. Then, "You don't fully know the circumstances, Chatterton."

"I can have a good guess."

Again there was a silence. The Chief of Bomber Command was four years younger than the Air Vice Marshal, had been in the R.A.F. three years less. During the war, he had served more on the Staff than in operations against the enemy. Ambitious, flexible in his opinions, he had done extremely well in NATO, where Chatterton, unable to exchange enemies and friends with either the same speed or the same ease, had proved to be somewhat of an embarrassment. In spite of similar training and influences and indoctrinations, Chatterton had remained the man, while Thane had become the personification of the perfect Service officer. That was their essential difference.

"You don't guess in this business."

"I'm glad to hear it."

"Everything's planned . . . down to the last detail. You know that as well as I do."

"Well . . . if I'd had my say, sir . . . I would have suggested that familiarization with the K6 be done in a rather less explosive atmosphere."

"You're exaggerating both the need for training and the

degree of emergency. 714 Squadron crews are already ground-trained on it. The bomb-aimers and electronics officers have done an extensive course with Atlas Sinclair. You can get Zweig to come up to you straightaway—"

"This semi-training, sir . . . will details be sent to us?"

"We'll let you know them as soon as they're worked out."

"I see."

"Get a fully serviceable aircraft ready. And an operational crew available."

Chatterton was again about to say something. And then he stopped. In three years' time—if he wasn't made an Air Marshal, and it didn't look likely—he would be compulsorily retired at the age of fifty-five, on a pension that was hardly a just compensation, considering his services to the nation. However, three years was the maximum—not the minimum. Air Vice Marshals—he had known of several—were sometimes, by some curious mechanism working unseen above them, retired with an alarming suddenness.

Chatterton said, "Will do."

The voice at the other end of the line resumed its honeyed accent. "Haven't seen you for ages, Denis. Next time you're this way . . . come and have lunch."

Chatterton again said, "Will do."

They said good-by to each other in differing degrees of warmth. From the clock on the wall opposite, he saw it was 10:45. Lifting up the glass panel in front of him, he called the Group Captain over.

In a low voice, he said, "Things are moving rather fast. And they're so important that I must handle all the details myself direct. You understand, Kenneth?"

"Yes, sir. Of course."

"Then advance the airtest on 577 to twelve thirty, would you? Tell Squadron Leader Falkner and his crew. And if she's fully serviceable afterward, they're to bring her over to Number One Hangar."

"Yes . . . right, sir."

"And if the Armament Officer's asleep in his nest . . . smoke him out, will you? I want him."

"I'll do that."

With an energetic bang, the Air Vice Marshal closed the panel shut again. Then he picked up the receiver of the ordinary phone, and in reply to the W.R.A.F. telephone operator's husky query, "Can I help you?" growled, "Get me Atlas Sinclair at Stainthorpe . . . personal call to Professor Zweig. And no waiting, now! Immediately!"

At exactly that same time, not four hundred yards from where the Air Vice Marshal sat, Jean Halloran switched on the electric percolator in her kitchen at Number Nine Tedder Avenue. Then she unhooked two blue-glazed earthenware beakers from the dresser, and slotted a couple of slices of bread into the automatic toaster. From most of the other twelve Flight Lieutenants' houses, a similar smell had long ago emanated, and now as she glanced out of the window, here and there a small washing had appeared, a radio had started up, two children too young for school quarreled over first turns on a homemade swing in a bare strip of garden.

Those R.A.F. gardens! Practically all rough grass and thistles, except for last year's Christmas tree and the round of burnt ashes which marked the remains of the bonfire on Guy Fawkes' night. Aircrew were never long enough at one station to make it worth their while to plant anything.

The sight of those gardens would normally depress her. But not today. Today she felt fine. She crossed to the staircase and called up, "Are you nearly ready, darling?" And Mick's voice, muffled by the bathroom door, floated back to her, "I'll be with you in a tick."

"No hurry. Thought it about time we should eat . . . that's all." She smiled to herself and clip-clopping in her red velvet mules back to the kitchen, called out again, "Did Robin and Tony get the bus all right?"

"Yep. Watched them from the gate to make sure. Knew you'd ask."

Mick seemed to follow his voice down. He kissed the top of her head, and squeezed her shoulder. "You fuss too much, Mrs. Halloran! Lord, that coffee smells good! Just what the doctor ordered. Hey . . . you got a head?"

Sitting at the table now, she cupped her chin in her hands. "Do I look as though I have?"

"You never do. As a matter of fact, you look wonderful."

"I feel it."

It was only the obvious relief in his eyes that marred her mood. Not for a long time had she felt as good as this. The dance last night had been fun. She had slept like a top, and dear old Mick had been up with the lark to bring her morning tea in bed, and pack the boys off to school before she was out of her bath.

"My mouth's a bit like the bottom of a bird cage. But otherwise—" He grinned, helped himself to a piece of toast and buttered it. "I couldn't be better!"

"What were you drinking?" She loved these post-mortems on Station Dances. Mick was sweet and understanding, and would gossip if she felt like it as well as—and much more trustworthily than—another woman.

"Black and tan." He grimaced, rubbed his now slightly bulging diaphragm. "Mixture was too rich!"

"I stuck to gin."

"Wise girl! Most of the Oakwood floozies appeared to be feeling no pain."

"So I saw." She said it with satisfaction. "One was sick in the Ladies'."

"Please!" He held up a red square hand. "Not at breakfast." He began munching his toast, then described two curves in the air. "What did you think of John Falkner's . . . ?"

"All right. From what I could see. I didn't actually meet her, because I was caught by Mrs. Lucey."

"Bad luck!"

"You didn't rescue me, I remember."

"Someone else did. Don't worry, I saw!"

"Oh, *him!*" She tossed her head. "He was young enough to be Robin's elder brother!"

All the same, she was pleased. She smiled across at her husband, her mouth tremulous with love.

Flight Lieutenant Michael Halloran, navigator on Squadron Leader Falkner's crew, took a second piece of toast, and felt ten years slip away from his shoulders. When Jean was on top of the world, there was no one like her. Sitting opposite him now, her head cupped in her hands, she was a young girl again.

With a permanent commission in the R.A.F., with a good skipper and (with the exception of Beauchamp) a good crew, with a Married Quarter on a pleasant Station, two good kids, and only a few years to go for a full pension, there was nothing that Mick Halloran wanted out of life, except maybe that Jean would always be like this.

He knew it was partly the war, and partly never having a settled home, partly a bad time she'd had having Robin when they were stationed at Radlan, north of Singapore; but the last few years, Jean's nerves had been playing her up.

She had no other fault, if fault you could call that. She was sweet with the children, nice to the other wives, as unpushing and as worldly unambitious as he was. He knew of half a dozen other bods on the squadron who'd hesitate many a long day before they'd tell their wives that old So-and-so had got his other ring, or a Commendation, or sometimes even an invitation to shoot with the Group Captain and party. And thinking of what other men had to put up with, he just naturally arrived at Dickie Beauchamp. A vision of their second pilot—pale, thin, and nearly pretty—rose up in front of him now.

As if reading his thoughts, which sometimes she could, Jean said, "Did you notice Diana Beauchamp?"

"Did I not!"

"Revolting, wasn't she?"

"Not my cup of tea."

"I don't think she danced with Dickie *once*. Tight as a tick, and dressed just like a tart!"

Benignly, Mick Halloran said, "Miaouw!"

"So she was!" Jean wrinkled up her nose at him, blushing girlishly. A pale beam of milky sunlight was just touching the straggly branches of a solitary rose bush in their wilderness of garden. She thought she could see buds. Maybe she'd take some cuttings, plant a whole bed. Sitting here in the warm kitchen, with the boys safe at school, and only an air test laid on for Mick today and nothing for tomorrow, she could really know that there was nothing to be afraid of.

Not that fear was rational. At least she was intelligent enough to know that. It was some disease that each day scoured out just a little more from you, so that you were in the end a hollow shell. And the things that frightened you were only the little sticks that supported the monster growth of fear itself. Take one away, and it found another . . . and another . . . and another.

She never knew when she'd started with it. Perhaps it just grew naturally, out of being every day that little bit more afraid than yesterday. At the end of the war, when they'd been married just over a year, the thought of Mick staying in the peacetime Air Force had seemed like bliss. No flak, no bombing raids, no night fighters, no listening to the nightly grind of the bombers going out, awaiting their return, then trying to count them.

But it hadn't turned out like that. Where it had gone wrong she didn't know. Sometimes she told herself it was after Wing Commander Williams' Marlborough had blown up five years ago that she had begun to panic. It was all the fuss in the papers, all the theories, all the talk ending in . . . *nothing*. Because she knew and *they* knew and the aircrew knew that it was one of those things you expect in new aircraft. In new anything, for that matter. After that, she seemed to hear things she'd never even noticed before. She'd picked up over the last few years quite a bit about the sound barrier, the heat barrier, the effect of break-off, of metal fatigue, or pressurization failure. Six months ago, she had heard of radiation sickness and she had found out that one of the Security-screened airmen who worked in the bomb pens had had a bone graft, and that someone else had been badly burned. All these facts she kept to herself, added to them with careful listening and careful reading, stored them in a private Chamber of Horrors, into which occasionally some part of herself compelled her to retire.

But not today. No one could have looked solider, safer or more reliable sitting opposite her than Mick. Lovingly, her eyes traveled over his thick sleek black hair, now flecked with white, his square red face, the laughter-lines around his brown eyes. He rubbed his chin with a hand thick and stubby and capable-looking. "What's so funny about me?"

"Nothing. I was just looking at you, that's all."

"Happy?"

"Yes."

Generously, from his own wealth of well-being, Mick said, "You know, I wish you'd ask Diana Beauchamp around sometime."

Jean raised an eyebrow and laughed. "She wouldn't come."

"She might." He had a well-meaning, earnest look on his face. "You could try."

"I will . . . if you want me to."

"Might be an idea." He pushed away his plate, and throwing her a cigarette, lit them both. "After all . . . I fly with him."

"All boys and girls together, eh?"

"Something like that. In their own way, I think they're both lonely."

"Diana *lonely?*"

He ignored her derisively raised brows. "I think he's always putting up a front. . . . I think that's why he doesn't get on so well with the rest of us. . . ."

Suddenly, he knew he'd said too much.

Elaborately casual, Jean said, "Doesn't he? On the crew? Don't you like him? Doesn't John Falkner? Don't the rest of you? Isn't he much good?"

"Oh, he's *fine!* Just his ways . . . *you* know."

"Yes, of course." She smiled. "*I* know."

She wasn't really afraid. It was just that she remembered. Last year a Venger had disappeared on a training trip. There was something about dissension in the crew. . . .

The door of her private Horror Chamber started slowly to swing ajar.

Resolutely, she tried to close it. Brightly and casually, she said, "I'll give her a tinkle now, if you like."

"Good show!" He picked up the newspaper. "Can't do any harm." He yawned comfortably. "Worth a try."

She re-tied the cord of her housecoat and, pushing back her chair, walked into the hall and picked up the telephone.

A quarter of a mile away, in Number Two Trenchard Street, suddenly the phone rang out—and went on ringing.

"At least you could answer the damned thing." Diana Beauchamp's voice remained upward-pitched so that the unsaid words *if you can do nothing else* could clearly be heard by both of them.

In a low voice, Dick Beauchamp said, "You're nearer."

The shrill edgy trilling continued to echo around and around the disordered lounge, the standard-pattern sofa and chairs and lamps and curtains accorded by R.A.F. Stores to Flying Officers. For a moment, the pilot went on sitting, his long thin arms loosely between his knees, his head down, his eyes regarding the blue and red design of the standard-pattern carpet.

Diana said no more. She didn't have to. She simply opened her yellowish eyes wider and went on staring.

She was lying on the sofa, her well-shaped legs sheathed in skin-tight slacks, a pair of eastern jeweled slippers on her feet. Her cashmere sweater was black and low-cut. And her hair—specially done for last night's dance—glittered like spun glass.

She wasn't only staring to make him go, she was also trying to remember if she'd ever even imagined she was in love with him. Or had she just fallen for her own publicity? Jet bomber pilot, my dear, she'd told the other girls at the North Finchley Rep. Tall and handsome. Nephew of Sir Arnold Beauchamp. Heir to a mint of money. All very grand, all very wonderful.

All very true, of course. It was what you read into it that wasn't.

As if he could stand her stare no longer, he got up abruptly, just as she'd known he would, and loped the couple of yards across this box that they called home, and lifted the receiver.

The silence was deafening. Just as their silence had been when first it had rung, snapping off the rhythmic change of their insults to one another.

"Extension 304, Flying Officer Beauchamp," he said in that low cultured voice that used to *send* her at the start. She'd loved it when he phoned her up so often at the theater in the few weeks of their courtship. The voice didn't *send* her now. She got up and opened the silver cigarette box, a present from some rich maiden aunt of Dick's, and scrabbled around in it until she found a Turkish. She lit it and drew on it and felt slightly better.

"Oh, fine," he was saying. "Yes, thanks. She had a wonderful time."

"You didn't say that a moment ago!" Diana blew a ring of smoke up to the ceiling with malevolence, as though it were Dick's face up there.

"I thought the band was whizzo, too. Oh, *infinitely* better than last year." He sounded so affected. No wonder the others didn't really cotton on to him. Often she couldn't understand why she'd left a good career in the theater, for a nice enough boy, sure . . . but only twenty-five and a good three years younger than she was. And a jealous boy, at that. A jealous man might have been fun. But a jealous boy made her flesh go goose-pimply with distaste. They'd just had the most godalmighty row about last night's party. Who she'd danced with; to whom she'd given a peck or two in the artificial shrubbery; even the dress she wore, though the Lord knew, he'd chosen it, and his father's allowance had paid for it, which *should* have made it respectable enough.

If Dick had been nearer to her own fighting weight, she might have enjoyed the scrap. But he wasn't. And he left her dissatisfied and trembling with unquenched rage.

"Look . . ." he was saying now. "I'll get Diana . . . she'd love to have a word with you."

"She would *not!*" Diana swiveled her head swiftly around so that she was staring over the back of the sofa at him.

"Of course it's no trouble. I'll go and find her. We weren't doing anything, anyway."

"Much," said Diana.

"Just lazing around talking over the party."

"Oh, Christ!"

"Just hang on a sec." Dick put down the receiver on the small mahogany table, being careful not to disturb Diana's arrangement of the hothouse roses he had bought her yesterday.

Diana tossed her shoulder-length dark hair. "Who the hell is it, anyway?"

"Jean. Jean Halloran. She thought you might like to go and have coffee with her sometime."

"Then she thought wrong."

"I said I thought you'd like to."

"You must be mad! I saw her only last night, squinting down her long, long nose. At *me!*"

Briefly, his light-gray eyes glittered. "If she was, she wasn't the only one." And then suddenly he looked as though he wished he hadn't said it.

"Oh . . . ho . . . *ho?* Indeed?"

With an in-for-a-penny-in-for-a-pound voice, he said, "You behaved like a low-class whore."

"Christ! Don't start that again!" But she almost hoped that he would—only rather better this time.

"Everyone noticed Everyone! Even the G.C."

"No doubt he wouldn't have been averse himself." She crossed her legs and smiled.

"Diana!"

"Oh? And why not? He's a man, isn't he?" Again the amber-yellow eyes widened. Again words hanging unsaid in the air . . . *even if some others aren't.*

That got him. He took hold of her arm, his thin fingers digging satisfyingly deep. He jerked her off the sofa. Tripping over her legs, she would have fallen onto the floor, but he pulled her up. Her hair was flung over her face. He gave her a sudden push, so that her teeth jarred together.

"Go on!" he said, furiously shaking her shoulders. "Go and talk to Jean!"

"All right." She smoothed her hair. *"All right!* No need to get brutal. I didn't say I wouldn't."

She walked to the phone deliberately slowly, swinging her hips. She sniffed the roses before lifting the receiver.

The thing was making impatient ratcheting noises. Cradling it in her long crimson-tipped fingers, she said in her intimate stagey voice, smiling slightly, "Hello, Jean . . . this is Diana."

She glanced over at Dickie, to see if he was going to follow up the treatment. But he was standing with his back to her, his arms folded, looking out of the window.

For nearly a minute, nobody answered. Then a harassed, subservient woman's voice said, "Sorry to interrupt a personal call. This is Operations. Could I speak to Flying Officer Beauchamp, please?"

She shrugged her shoulders, called out, "Dick . . . Ops want you!"

And then back she went to the sofa and again lay down.

It was only a short call. When she heard him put down the receiver, she began rubbing her arms, wondering if she should lead him on to see if he *could* really get tough—aware of an odd mixture of anger and excitement stirring.

"God . . . you bruised me," she began . . . and then she became aware that he hadn't come back into the room, that now he was walking up the stairs.

"Did you get that shirt ironed?" he was calling out to her. "I'll have to get into uniform."

"That shirt?" Irritably she got up and stormed into the tiny hall. "No, of course it isn't ironed yet! Your air test's not till this afternoon. What's the flap, *anyway?* Why interrupt a call? What's happening?"

She watched him turn and look down at her from the landing. She expected to see exasperation, anger, or perhaps cool politeness.

But his face wore none of these expressions. It was puzzled and young.

And curiously apprehensive.

The next number the same Operations W.R.A.F. contacted was five miles outside the camp. Ilminster 22.

"No . . . I'm not going to get him," said a female voice in a Canadian accent. "Anything you want to tell Flight Lieutenant McQuade . . . you can tell to me."

Valerie McQuade listened for a few moments, then put down the receiver and said, "Well . . . whad'you know!"

She walked into the kitchen, and stood with her arms akimbo in front of her many-dialed brand-new electric oven. "For land's sakes! Putting the air test forward to twelve thirty. Just when my cheese soufflé was rising like a dream . . . and all set to go places!"

She kissed her fingers up to the ceiling in mingled hail and farewell, and aware of the figure now leaning against the open door, said, "Did you hear that, Terry McQuade?"

"Sure."

"And what have you got to say about it, Terry McQuade?"

"Nothing."

The figure pulled off a thick red sweater, and reached out an arm for a blue uniform jacket with a flying half wing above the left breast pocket. Shuffling his shoulders into it, Terry McQuade came toward his wife. He had a sideways, lopsided grin, a thin clever face, and the gangling loose-jointed walk of almost all Canadians.

"Wise guy!" Valerie smoothed her hair and untied her apron. She looked at her face in the mirror over the sink and said, "Wowie! After last night . . . my eyes look like two burnt holes in a blanket!"

As a matter of fact, she looked, smelled and was—sweet, immaculate, and dewy-fresh. Always, since the day he had met her at McGill University in '51, she had reminded him of a television soap advertisement, except that whatever she had went right through. Pretty, bright, warm-hearted, peppy . . . she made all the other wives at Oakwood look like a clinic for vitamin deficiency.

And this place they'd got—the top floor of an old house in a small town close to the airdrome—was exactly like her. The nearest thing they could fix up to the Montreal duplex of her dreams. Despite the drawbacks of two-hundred-year-old English architecture, it had the real true Canadian flavor. Their landlord—who was a real good head—had a job on the Bomb Dump up at the airdrome. Some secret thing, of which he was very proud. He helped them all he could; and she was quite glad there hadn't been a Married Quarter available on the camp.

This was much better.

Frilly drapes at the kitchen windows; a handsomely fitted bathroom with rugs and covers and chromium and a dandy little shower; fitted cupboards that Terry had knocked together in the evenings, while Val cooked or listened to the radio or watched TV; a red and white leather-upholstered breakfast nook; and the boxroom fitted up as a man's den. They had fixed sunblinds in every room—though in this goddamned climate they might be categorized as strictly sentimental only. Terry and Val were a couple of displaced persons, and they certainly liked to bring the best of Canadian civilization with them.

Not that they didn't like England. They just loved it. They were a couple of Anglophiles as ever was. Val's pop's great-uncle could trace his ancestry back to Robert the Bruce, and although with a name like he'd got, he couldn't miss a blind on St. Patrick's Day, Terry could still claim that on his mother's side he had a grandfather called Wellington, related—no doubt about it—to the family of the Duke.

When they'd got the news a year ago that he was to be seconded to the R.A.F. for development work on a V-Bomber Squadron, he and Val had been tickled pink. They both liked the English boys—in spite of their wives' cracks about Canadian rates of pay. And they'd got to know some real characters in the sixteenth-century pub down the bottom of their street.

In between pulling radios and televisions and anything else electrical apart, and putting them together again, Terry McQuade had written back peacetime dispatches of letters from England that would have filled volumes. In fact, a couple of his letters had appeared in the local paper at St. Lawrence, and the Daughters of the Commonwealth in Montreal had asked Val to be sure and find time to give them a little talk on her next vacation home.

But besides the fun and the history and the wonderful opportunity to see what went on in the rest of the world, Terry McQuade loved his job. He wasn't a born flyer in the sense that his skipper was. He got one helluva kick out of it, sure. But his real sensation was electronics. That was his baby. Electricity in all its forms—radio, radar, mechanical, vibrational—were to him the shot in the arm, the twist in the guts, the exhilaration that some other boys got just by being air-borne. Making something *work;* finding out just a little bit more in the field of electronics; interpreting formulae and wiring circuits. He'd told Val one hundred times that mathe-matics and electronics were the secret of the universe . . . the delicate manipulation . . . the fine meticulous breathless balance of it.

There was just *nothing* like electronics.

And somehow he'd gotten himself one helluva reputation. He told Val it was more than a bit because he was Canadian. If you were a Canadian, you could talk to the British about geology, oil, electronics, aluminum, asbestos, furs and atomic projects. And they'd take notice. Just as they'd take notice if a Frenchman talked about wine or literature or women or perfume or clothes, or an Italian talked about opera or eating, or the Swedes about films, or the Americans about mass pro-duction or high finance.

But Val knew that counted for only a part of it. He'd graduated well from McGill and got a research fellowship with the Maydecker Foundation. He'd joined the R.C.A.F. and he'd done three courses with them; he'd been seconded to the U.S.A.F. for another. And now here he was Elec-tronics Officer on Squadron Leader Falkner's crew on 714 Squadron, Oakwood, England. And here was an air test to provide a bit more flying time to write pridefully in his somewhat naked Log Book.

Padding into their peach-and-lime-green bedroom, he found his shoes cleaned by the bed. "Hi!" he called through the open door. "Who said Canadian girls were spoiled?"

"You did."

"Remind me to scrub it off the records."

She came and leaned against the door-jamb, watching him. "The Wives' Union'll drum me off the camp." She was lick-ing her fingers. "The soufflé's still rising. It's a dream!"

"I'll sniff out for it . . . while I'm up." He buttoned his

tunic, unhooked his cap, slung it on the back of his head. "Save me a bit."

"Soufflés are like good Canadian girls . . . they won't wait for anybody."

"Well, think of me when you eat it." He bent down and gave her a long kiss.

"Now I won't be able to eat it at all." She pushed him away. "Oughtn't you to be off?"

"I ought. What'll you do with yourself?"

"Sit down. Put my feet up. Turn on the radio . . . if it isn't in bits."

"It isn't."

"And if you get Ops to ring me when you're down . . . I've got a leg of chicken in the fridge I can fry for you."

She blew him a kiss at the top of the steps, and then opened the lounge window that gave a view of the garden gate. She watched him walk toward the little wooden garage where they kept the red roadster called *Angelique*. She knew he knew she was watching him. But then she always did. Before he slid the car out of the gate, he stopped for her to say, "Don't drive that thing too fast, honey! And remember . . . the wrong side of the road!"

When he'd gone, the morning seemed suddenly to go quiet. She tossed her head and waltzed around the kitchen as though to get a mood of the heebie jeebies out of her hair. Then, determinedly bright, she switched on the little white radio in the kitchen.

It was working all right. But it was bursting and crackling with some electrical interference, so that the sound was coming through distorted, half drowned in static.

She knew what it was, because Terry had told her. Switching it off, she said to herself, "Must be testing something up at the airdrome!"

Helen Durrant was sitting in the Mess ante-room, close to one of the radiators, when first she heard the whistling.

She looked up. None of the Squadron aircrew officers around her took the slightest notice of it. So she looked down again at the *Illustrated London News*, open on her lap.

The shrillness got louder. Still nobody took their eyes from their newspapers.

The noise reached a crescendo. A bright white triangle made a momentary appearance over the roof of the nearest hangar, streaming four long strings of gray smoke.

A bored anonymous voice behind the *Daily Mirror* asked, "Who's doing the dicing?"

Another anonymous voice, equally bored, answered from behind the *Daily Sketch*, "Falkner."

"In aid of what?"

"Just an air test."

"Which kite?"

"577."

"That bastard!"

"Flown it recently?"

"A week ago."

"Why?"

"Ask Chatterton. He laid it on."

"Doing what?"

"Nine-hour operational exercise. Three times around the island."

"Which island?"

"The British island, of course . . . clot!"

"Well . . . kept you occupied. Away from beer and women."

"Occupied is right . . . with 577."

"What's the matter with it?"

"Everything!"

Once more there was silence, broken only by the rustle of turning pages. But Helen had already reached the end of the *Illustrated London News*. She sat staring at the picture of a pretty girl in a railway carriage being self-consciously unconscious of a good-looking young man watching her from the platform: an advertisement for toilet soap.

So his Venger had gone off without her—and she had been particularly looking forward to the flight. She had not yet flown in any jet, let alone a jet bomber. A number of communication flights between airdromes in light aircraft, a trip in a Britannia to Gibraltar and back—that was all the flying experience she had.

She took the magazine back to its place on the table, and rather crossly looked at her watch.

One fifteen. Usually by this time, on Station Inspections, she would have been summoned to take her place beside the A.O.C. for a lunchtime session around the bar.

Well, today he was just too late. If he came in now, he'd had it.

Not feeling pleased with Royal Air Force Officers—Squadron Leaders and Air Vice Marshals in particular—she went in to lunch alone, and sat by herself at the oak table near the window.

It was here that John Falkner found her, half an hour later. He had caught sight of her the moment he pushed open the two big glass swing doors. She seemed slighter in uniform. Even like that, of all things finishing off bread-and-butter pudding, she had a curious grace, an aura of fastidiousness and freshness that he found both exciting and appealing.

He went up to the table, and took the empty chair next to her. "Hello."

She lifted her head. "Hello."

"Don't look at me as though I'm a spider that's sat down beside yer."

"*Aren't* you?"

"Sure I am . . . if you're little Miss Muffet."

"Sorry! Wrong girl."

She made a movement of being about to get up.

"Hey," he said, "no, you don't!"

"But I've finished!"

"Then you can sit still and bear my company." And then, when she sat back again, "Been busy?"

"Quite."

"How did the Inspection go?"

"Like the wind."

He smiled—a confident, superior sort of smile but warm, too. "Heard old Chatterton was at Full Boost. Maybe he's realized at last we're in the Jet Age." He leaned across the table for the menu. "What d'you recommend?"

"I had the beef."

"All right?"

"Well—"

"Not the sort of grub they give you at Group, eh?" And to the black-haired W.R.A.F. waitress standing beside him, "I'll have the steak pie, Eileen."

The waitress smiled and walked over to the serving-hatch.

"You shouldn't call the girls by their Christian names."

"All right . . . Durrant." He gave her a mock salute. "What's the matter with you today? Has Daddy Chatterton torn a strip off you?"

"He never does."

"Then he ought to. Don't see why his bile should be exclusively reserved for males." He began on the food the girl had put in front of him. "Come on . . . come on! Say something! Don't sit there dumb and glum and beautiful! I want to be entertained."

She said stonily, "And how did the air test go?"

"The air test?" He put his knife and fork down. "How d'you know it's been?"

"I heard . . . in the ante-room . . . a pilot talking."

"Well—" He began to eat again, talking slowly between mouthfuls. "I was going to get around to that air test . . . all in God's good time. But since you already know . . . wasn't my fault. They wanted it done very quickly, all of a sudden. Hadn't time to contact you."

"It was a quick one, wasn't it?"

"Yep. Nothing much we had to check. Bombing gear . . . that's all."

She said carefully, "Apparently 577 isn't exactly the squadron's favorite aircraft."

"Another bit of ante-room gossip you got from that character, eh?" He gave a short laugh. "Probably made a bad landing . . . last time he flew her . . . that's all. 577's fine. D'you think I'd have suggested you go up in a ropey aircraft?"

"And your crew . . . are they good?"

"Hey . . . what's got into you now? Checking up, are you . . . before you risk your very pretty neck with us?"

"No . . . just asking."

"Well . . . they're *very* good. Been with me for a long time." He hesitated. "That is . . . all except the Second Pilot." He paused again. "So you see . . . you'd be well looked after."

"I'm ready . . . any time. You see . . . today . . . I was rather disappointed."

"So was I. Pity! I'd have liked to show you around."

"Oh, well—" Now her expression seemed to soften. "Just one of those things, I suppose."

"That's all it was." The W.R.A.F. waitress took his empty plate away, and again he stretched for the menu. "That bread-and-butter pudding have currants in it? Good! I'll have a basinful. And look . . . let's have our coffee here. I know it's in the ante-room and not really allowed, but I have a hunch that if I asked Aircraftwoman Second Class Stannard nicely . . . she'd bring us a couple of cups." And when the grinning girl had gone, "That mode of address suit you, Durrant? Good! Now about that air test . . . for the first and last time . . . beg pardon."

She had, he noticed, alarmingly candid eyes. His remained on her face expectantly, while the waitress brought the pudding and then put a cup of coffee in front of each of them. When he still went on staring, saying nothing, she hesitated and then rather diffidently began, "Shall you . . . do you think you'll be flying again? Tomorrow, perhaps?"

"Might be . . . probably will be . . . *now*."

"So can I come with you then?"

"Come with me? Flying with me, you mean?" He shook his head. "Sorry. No can do."

She held her chin in her hand, her brows slightly furrowed. After a long pause, she said, "Oh, well . . . never mind." She gave him a brief cool smile. "Thanks at least for *offering* to take me today."

"Look," he said. "It's not that I don't *want* to take you."

She lifted her chin. "I really don't mind."

"It so happens . . . if you *did* come tomorrow . . . you might go a little further than you bargained for."

"I don't mind how far I go."

He moved closer till his arm was against her arm, and half-whispered, "If you get off your high horse for a moment, I'll make you a bargain."

She leaned away from him and helped herself to sugar, not looking at him. "Well?"

"That trip in the Venger I promised you . . . I'll swap it for a half-pint of beer tonight in the Mess. That's fair, isn't it?"

"I never drink beer," she said stonily, lifting her coffee cup. And with no change of voice, "What time?"

A letter was waiting for Helen in the Mess at tea time. Tearing it open in her room, she found a white card bidding her to cocktails in the Group Captain's house at seven.

"Oh, hell!" she said, flinging her cap on the bed. She stared indignantly at her little traveling clock on the mantelpiece as if to discover an extra hour tucked away between six and seven. John Falkner had said, "See you in the bar at six fifteen!"

It required a head much less mathematically inclined than Helen Durrant's to realize that at best, her session with S/Ldr. Falkner would be brief. To make up for it, although it was still only five, she walked down the corridor and ran the bath.

Lying in the warm water, her hair tucked up in a neat little bun on the top of her head, she was still frowning. But now at herself. She was not in the habit of hurrying unduly to meet any man. And her own flurried preparations irritated even herself. Triumphantly, in self-vindication, she decided that she had picked up the A.O.C.'s bug of doing everything at the double today, a sense unusual in the Air Force of time creeping up on one.

Nevertheless, she powdered and dressed herself even more carefully than she had done the previous night. She was wryly conscious that the final garment should have been a Balmain cocktail gown. Instead of which, because she had only brought her dance dress, it had to be the blue shirt, the black tie, the blue barathea and brass buttons . . . all unhappily and unfemininely the almost exact replica of his own garments.

"Except for the skirt and the nylons," she said aloud, pirouetting her slim legs for her own benefit in front of the mirror.

At five to six, there was nothing more that she could do to improve herself, and feeling for some reason exactly as she'd done at Oxford when she'd completed her papers and there was nothing more that she could do except sit back and await the results, she walked into the W.R.A.F. sitting room and sat down.

It was small and bleak and virginal. Managing even with the modernish Air Force furniture to give the feeling of an aspidistra in a pot, knick-knacks, lace curtains, moth balls and repressions. There was a little radio in the corner . . . the Queen Bee had no doubt been wangling the Comforts Fund . . . and she walked over and switched it on.

She felt like music—soft, romantic, syrupy stuff. But only the Home Service worked. And that was just the news. She didn't really listen. The voice was companionable. She sat tapping her long fingers on the wooden arm-rests. She felt like a cigarette, but she didn't light one because she didn't want her hair to smell of smoke. When the news stopped, it would be about ten minutes past, and perfectly all right for her to walk out to meet him.

The usual category of success and disaster flowed over her head . . . a railway accident in New Zealand, yet another take-over bid in the city, British paratroops being welcomed with open arms in Karkarabad, the capital of Kanjistan.

"That is the end of the news."

Music at last. Her foot kept time to it, but her mind lagged behind. She was still with the announcer's voice—an echo as unreal as the aspidistra pot and the lace curtains. Somehow, a fragment in the smooth flow of the news had lodged in her mind. She didn't even know which it was. Yet magnetically, irresistibly, it seemed to attract other fragments, unnoticed or forgotten, enlarging itself.

Again she was conscious of disquiet. The probing female antennae of her mind stirred.

Abruptly she looked at her watch. Almost quarter past. No time to think now. She got up, smoothing her skirt in an automatic gesture, brisk and self-reassuring, looked in the mirror, patted her hair, and opened the door and stepped out into the corridor.

At this time, the Mess was fairly full. People kept opening the door from the parking lot at the rear, coming in, rubbing their hands, smiling. They brought in with them a smell of the cold night air, and a feeling that once inside, all was warm and comfortable and well. The Mess Office was lit up. The secretary was cashing checks, and a queue of officers waited, talking noisily.

It seemed a long time since she had walked this way to the party the night before. Overnight, she had conceived an affection for this Station, so that the thought of their return to Group filled her once more with a sense of urgency. Her feet went clipping the rest of the way in a half-run. When she reached the door to the bar, she was flushed and breathless. She waited a moment, before turning the handle and slowly walking in.

This time the bar was quiet. John Falkner was leaning on the counter, facing the door in an atttiude at once relaxed and expectant. He raised his hand when she came in, and turned to the barman and ordered a gin and lemon.

"Though, mind," he said to her without any preliminary greeting, "if you and I are going to see a lot of one another . . . you'll have to learn to like beer."

He waited till she lifted her glass, and then touched it with his tankard. "Cheers!"

"You know," she kept her eye on her drink, "I don't suppose we shall . . . see a lot of one another, I mean." Pleasure that he should take it for granted jostled with real regret. "That is, after I go back to Group."

"Group isn't the other end of the world, is it?"

"No. But . . . far enough."

"Oh, I reckon if we can fly up to Dundee to get lobsters . . . I might get as far as Group to buy you the odd drink." He lifted his glass. "But beer, mind . . . nothing more expensive!"

He watched the color come up over her face. She was still young enough to reach up shyly and touch her flushed cheeks as if at once apologizing and denying it.

"Besides," he said, not looking at her now, "you're not."

"Not what?"

"Not what!" He imitated her. "You're not going back to Group as soon as you think."

She smiled. Then she eyed him suspiciously over the rim of her glass. "Who says so?"

"*I* do."

Her disappointment made her say tartly, "And I take it you've told the A.O.C. his change of plan?"

"No," he said, matter-of-factly. "*He* told *me*."

"Why *you?*"

"He told other odd bods as well. Like the G.C."

Cautiously: "You're not joking?"

"Why should I? I wouldn't think it funny if you were going."

Partly to cover up her pleasure, she said lightly, "Don't tell me there's another party laid on!"

He gave her a funny wry smile. "Not exactly."

"I wonder why then."

"Maybe I made it worth his while. Squadron Leader's pay isn't all that bad."

"A.O.C.'s is better."

"Neither," he said, calling the barman and ordering another round, "is as good as Section Officer's." He lowered his voice. "Because of the perks."

"Depends on the Section Officer. But I'll buy this one, if that's what you mean."

He gave her outstretched hand a little slap, and grinned. "All I know is, if there's one rank most people'd swap with, it's that."

"You know, I can't help thinking," she said abruptly after a moment. "Odd that he didn't tell *me*."

"Don't you mean"—he gave her a brief glance, teasing and affectionate—"odd that he didn't *ask* you? Watch out! The old boy's getting a bit above himself. Clamp down!"

"I will," she said sweetly. "On both of you."

"If you hurry," he said, "there's time for another one."

"Actually there isn't." She sighed. "I'm supposed—"

"I know. To be at the Station Master's at seven. Cocktails."

"You know just about everything that goes on, don't you?"

"You're wrong. I know everything. No *just about* about it."

She smiled, put down her glass. "It's a bind though, isn't it?"

"Oh, it could be worse."

"I suppose so."

"I think you'll find," he said gravely, "that it has its compensations. I believe they've invited the three most attractive men on the squadron."

"Don't tell me," she said, sliding off her stool and smiling up at him with a peculiarly endearing wide smile, "that you're all three of them?"

Modestly, he said, "No. Only one. *Number* one." He buttoned his jacket, straightened his tie. "In fact, if you're ready, I might start you off on the right foot and escort you in personally."

"Hang on, then! Wait in the corridor till I fetch my hat."

She slammed the bar door shut behind her. He listened to her light quick footfall fading up the corridor. Then he said good night to the barman and walked out into the corridor for the pleasure of watching her from a distance coming to meet him.

When she came up, he took the cap that she was dangling loosely in her hand, and set it on the back of her head. The corridor was deserted, but it wouldn't have mattered if it wasn't. As he straightened her cap, he kissed her mouth.

"I've waited a long time to do that," he said.

She didn't say but-we've-only-just-met. Nor did he expect her to. Had she asked for any explanation, he would not have been able to give it. All he knew was that could he have formulated it into words, there was a perfectly good one.

"Right?" he said. "All set now?"

"All set." She slid past him as he held open the door. "Phew!" she said. "It's cold!"

He took hold of her arm, guiding her out onto the tarmac in front of the Mess and then down the lane lit by the light from the windows, to the roadway. A few stars were visible above the red glow of the obstruction lights, only to be obscured to the south by trails of cloud.

The quick kiss seemed to have silenced them both. They walked along hand in hand, listening to their own footfalls. She was conscious of an almost alcoholic lightness and ecstasy, yet stalked by sobriety. She sought in her mind for a comparable feeling. But only the mildly ridiculous leaped into her mind, schoolgirlish and gauche . . . like nearing the winning post at the annual egg-and-spoon race . . . struggling with a balloon at a party that someone was going to burst. It was like none of these, of course. She was guarding a bubble of imagined love, afraid that an inept word would dispel it, show it to be nothing.

As the lights of the C.O.'s house reached out ahead of them, he squeezed her hand. "I don't suppose," he said, "I'll be allowed much time with you." He smiled ruefully. "You'll get swept off by the old boys, and surrounded by Scrambled Egg. All the same, I'll know you're there."

A few chrysanthemums and still red salvias stood in shadows thrown by the hall light of the Luceys' house. The lawn was neatly cut, and the edges of the flowerbeds had been razored as if for the Inspection. They could hear a discreet murmur coming from behind the long blue velvet curtains. They exchanged glances—companionable, derisive.

Just then, as if all day she had been feeding in scraps of information to some hidden computer in her mind, and now, rather dilatorily it had come up with the answer, she said, "John! What's happening here? Something's on, isn't it? Do tell me, please. Before we go in. Are you on stand-by? And what on earth for?"

But it was too late. Already the front door was open. They were caught reluctantly in a peach spotlight and drawn in.

She saw John Falkner smile at her in a deprecating, almost apologetic way. Then she was having her cap and gloves taken by the batman, being welcomed by Mrs. Lucey. She glanced around the hall, thinking how familiar it looked and because of that, how unreal, how like a stage set!

"Come in! Come in!" Group Captain Lucey hurried out of the lounge, hands outstretched. "Hello, Falkner . . . make yourself at home. There's not many of us yet."

Then to Helen: "The Air Vice Marshal isn't down. He was on the phone a long time." He twinkled. "You hard-working types from Group! But he'll be with us presently. Now let me see"—he led her into the lounge—"quite a fug in here already."

He snapped his fingers for the L.A.C. batman waiter, who hurried over with cocktails at the double. "You know all the rest of these types, don't you?" He waved at them all in red-faced jocularity. She had a hurried glimpse of various men of various high ranks and as many sizes, all in R.A.F. blue.

"Anyway, Helen, if you don't know them"—an arch smile —"they certainly know *you!* You probably haven't met Mrs. Schofield . . . our Wing Commander Admin's wife . . . Mrs. Schofield, may I present Miss Durrant? Helen . . ."

She exchanged how-d'you-do's, was she enjoying her visit, was she being rushed off her feet, and what a part of the world this was—before being led on to another group: the Wingco of a neighboring station and some squadron types.

"Just the girl I want to see," said the Wingco. "I'm in a rut. Could do with a posting!"

Glancing around, she saw John Falkner saunter into the lounge, glass in hand. Meeting her eye, he winked but made no attempt to join her. She engaged in the usual chatter about Group that she could do with one hand tied behind her back, smiling across at the squadron types. The Adjutant joined them. "Was the Air Vice Marshal pleased with the Station turnout?"

"Very impressed."

It was so easy to please, so easy to be generous. Sipping her second martini, catching a rather nice view of herself in a gilt-framed mirror, exchanging remarks, wisecracks, cigarettes, she felt warm and safe. She had almost forgiven John Falkner for not attempting to come over, had almost forgotten that he hadn't answered her question, when she saw the door open, and this time Air Vice Marshal Chatterton came in.

He wasn't alone. Beside him was a man of medium height, conspicuous not only because in this gathering he was the only man not in uniform. He was thick-set, brown-haired, bespectacled, unsmiling. He walked with small steps, keeping his arms glued to his sides, nodding as a few people greeted him. Seeing Helen, the A.O.C. smiled and moved toward her.

Across the room, everyone respectfully made way for him. "Helen." He took her arm. "Come and meet Dr. Zweig!"

At first, the name didn't mean anything to her. Only the wide forehead, the long upper lip, the formal set of his mouth impinged. Then suddenly it *did* mean something. As though a kaleidoscope had been shaken, suddenly all the small fragments of today shivered into shape, to make a definite pattern.

"I've heard of you, of course," she said. "Of course, Dr. Zweig. Are you down here—"

But before she could finish the question, the A.O.C. had carried him off to pay his respects to Mrs. Lucey.

*

Wednesday

ACCORDING to the Air Almanac, dawn at Oakwood on Wednesday, October 14th, was 0621 G.M.T. It was then still quite dark. Not till the village church had chimed seven did the blackness of night turn gradually to gray, and a dim daylight began to reveal over everywhere a solid curtain of continuous rain.

By eight o'clock, the lights were on in all the kitchens and dining rooms of Tedder Avenue. Beams of blurring yellow gleamed silkily against a backcloth of dripping brown. Figures moved in the square windows . . . small television screens reassuringly showing warmth and dryness and light.

As she opened the back door, and took in the sodden newspaper lying on top of the three milk bottles, a handful of rain flung itself in Jean Halloran's face. The water was gurgling continuously down the roof pipe and the drain outside the kitchen window was choked, most probably with dead leaves. She listened for Mick's returning footsteps. Robin had left his pencil box on the hall table, and his father had sprinted along to catch him before he boarded the school bus.

It was lucky they'd been up early. Mick had been padding around long before the crack of dawn, bringing in the coal, doing the boiler.

The back door slammed.

There he was now! Red-faced, a bit breathless, dripping . . . an airman's old ground-sheet around his shoulders.

Turning from the washing-up, she said, "You look like a mermaid! Did you catch him?"

"Just. Meant to tear him off a strip, but he was on the bus before I could. Next time, though, he's had it!"

He pulled out a chair and sat down. "You didn't throw the coffee out, did you? I could use another cup."

She poured him one, put the milk bottles in the fridge, and seeing the wet newspaper still lying on the table, picked it up and spread it on the top of the boiler to dry.

Mick was the usual paper-reader in the family. Normally he hogged it at breakfast, when she was too busy to read it anyway. Besides, she felt that the real news was usually not to be picked up in the papers.

But lying like that, the headlines caught her eye: CRISIS IN KANJISTAN.

And underneath: *Ibrahim Ben Sayid killed in clash.*

From there, her eyes flitted to *British paratroops welcomed in Karkarabad, Service Chiefs again at Number Ten.* She read on. She had the feeling of tiny harmless little links in a chain, suddenly drawn magnetically together, and slowly tightening.

This morning, she had wakened with a sense of something wrong. Just as some people wakened with a hangover or migraine. The airfield in its mist and dampness seemed to be closing in on her. Mick was up and dressed unnaturally early. But it wasn't really either of those. It was just waking to find the door of her Chamber of Horrors not really closed . . . knowing that today it would probably open a little further, and that sooner or later a beckoning hand would appear. . . .

"Jean! That's the third time I've asked you! Pass the cigarettes, there's a good girl! Left mine upstairs." He turned around in his chair and smiled. "What's that you've got your nose in? Last Sunday's *News of the World?*"

She forced a nonchalant little shrug. "Wrong!" She folded up the paper. "It's today's *Mail.* I was just drying it out."

"Let's have a look-see, then. I was wondering where it had got to."

As he glanced over the headlines, she studied his face. The news didn't seem to register with him. Momentarily, she breathed again. Picking up his empty cup, she said carelessly, "There seems to be a spot of trouble in the Middle East."

"Always is!" He was turning over the pages, now leaning over and reading intently. "Hey!" he said and groaned. "Those oil shares I bought last week are down another couple of bob!"

"It appears," she said, walking to the sink, "that they've killed the rebel leader."

"They usually do."

"This time . . . they say the King used the British paratroops in his capital as a rearguard . . . while his armored cars attacked rebel headquarters."

"Smart work!" Mick said. "Smart boy!"

"D'you think it's true?"

"Course it's not true! Propaganda . . . that's all!" He stretched his arms above his head and yawned.

"Mick"—laughingly—"I suppose this wouldn't affect you at all?"

He turned and stared at her gently and thoughtfully. "Why on earth me, Jean?" Smiling, red-faced, reassuring. "Course not! Dont' be a clot! What've we got a Middle East Command for . . . supposing there *was* anything, which there *isn't?* Course it might affect the rest of my shares . . . all twenty-eight bobs worth." He laughed. "Probably lose the lot."

Reassured, almost gay again, she said, "Look . . . it's almost stopped raining! Mick, there's nothing on today and the boys will be home late . . . it's Wednesday . . . football practice." She ran a cloth quickly over the sink, polishing its stainless steel as if it were her own mood. "Let's go out to lunch and do a matinee!"

"Sorry, Jean, but I can't, you know."

"You did the air test yesterday. That's finished."

"We're still stand-by. I can't go off the camp."

Breathlessly she said, "Couldn't you get someone else to stand in?"

"No. Sorry. Maybe we'll manage it tomorrow. All right?" He stretched out an arm. "Not disappointed or anything?"

"Of course not. It was just an idea." She smiled as she fished in the cupboard under the sink for her polish and dusters, humming as if she had no other thought in the world but her household chores.

As she went out toward the lounge she said, softly but clearly, "*Just what,* Mick, are you on stand-by *for?*"

But he appeared to be deep in the paper, and didn't answer.

She did not ask again. The door of her Chamber of Horrors was wide open now. In a little while, she knew, something would compel her to step inside.

Dr. Marcus Zweig was not a morning conversationalist. He was relieved, therefore, that beyond passing the time of day, and commenting rather unnecessarily on the weather, the Air Vice Marshal made no attempt to enliven the ride down to Number One Hangar.

But as if not quite content to leave the scientist be, from time to time the A.O.C. glanced sideways at him, a slight frown drawing together his bushy brows . . . a look that was at once friendly, baffled, wary.

The scientist was unaware of it. He had passed a tolerable night under the Lucey roof. He could have done without the party, however. Too much cigarette smoke, too much reek of alcohol, too little fresh air. At forty-six, without being overanxious or in any way obsessive, he and his wife kept a careful watch upon his health. He could not, after all, afford to neglect his only capital.

Born of poor parents—his father was a World War One Austrian refugee, his mother a weaver in a northern woolen mill—educated by scholarships, he had chosen science because it offered the best prospects and had specialized in nuclear physics because he knew it was the science of the next two decades. He had reached the forefront by ability, hard work, will power, and a touch of genius. But more than all these—the only legacy of his parentage—he had reached it because he was a realist.

It was a popular misconception of the laity, the man in the street, the airman now saluting this car with the reflex of a robot, just because it carried a flag on the hood, that a scientist had his head in the air.

Far from it. He was the ultimate realist, the facer of facts, the discarder of fancies.

It was the men of action who were the Johnnies-head-in-air—regimented, disciplined, handling weapons they didn't understand, swept along by outdated clichés, catchwords, tenth-hand philosophies. The public, soft and flabby and mindless, sucked syrupy sentimentality, seedless sex, and television. The prelates preached a way of life they never lived, a kingdom of God they had never seen . . . the biggest confidence trick allowed by law, he called it. It was they who had their heads in the air, the sand or the mud—whatever you cared to call it.

But he . . . *he* invented no comfortable philosophies to keep him warm, no benign father-figure of God to stretch the cocoon of childhood around him until it became the shroud of death.

At ten, he had thrown away all that. At ten, he had made himself face up to life naked, while most of these men still fastened around them these pitiful remnants . . . part superstition, part habit, part a disbelieved faith.

Even in his work, he was a realist. He could say, I am better than any other scientist in my field today in England or America with the exception of Hobbs, Barnett and Helpmann. He could look at and face his decision to work on *the bomb*. Hobbs and Helpmann had refused to work on it. After a brilliant start, they had retired—one to Cambridge, the other to a provincial university—where they still taught nuclear physics, where they experimented, where their work would eventually lead, just as all roads led to London, to *the bomb*. They salved their conscience. Not my hand; oh Lord! But in a democratic country, it was everyone's hand. Who finally designed the bomb didn't matter, except—and this was where his own logic crystallized into true clarity—that the brain designing it should be the best.

Hobbs and Helpmann had opted out. Barnett had mistakenly gone on to rockets. That brain inevitably *had* to be his.

"Here we are, Zweig!" The Air Vice Marshal gave the scientist an odd smile, as if he had been trailing uncomprehendingly behind him through the labyrinth of his mind. Zweig wondered if he had said something aloud, or kept working his lips, the way he did when he was moved.

"Number One Hangar. I'll get out first. Easier that way!"

The scientist noticed that as the airman got out, he disclosed his age. Chatterton moved stiffly, awkwardly.

"Thank you, corporal. Wait here, will you?"

They both stood for a moment, staring up the slight incline that led to the hangar, as if they had taken that ride in a dream, had now wakened to find themselves in an unknown place.

"Got your pass ready, Zweig?"

Briskly now, Chatterton walked toward the closed door.

A couple of Service Police, thick-booted, with S.P. in red on their arm bands, advanced on them, kicked their feet hard down in salute.

"Thank you, sir."

They glanced perfunctorily at the passes the two men held out to them, saluted again, and held open the hangar door. They had very young faces, red and dull-looking. Those and the bulging revolver holsters somehow nauseated Zweig.

Carefully, he stepped over the threshold, blinking his eyes, unprepared for the brightness. A little unprepared for the scene altogether. As if his mind, used to disappointment and forbidden fantasies, had not allowed his imagination to anticipate this scene, this final culmination of ten years of excessive work.

The hangar was filled with a pure clear light that cast no shadows. In the center stood a Venger bomber—graceful, aerodynamically perfect, giving even on the ground a sense of thrust and speed and life. The light made its anti-radiation paint glow with a white-hot life.

Perfunctorily he noticed the roundels on its wings, the aircraft number 577.

But most of his attention was riveted on a ten-wheel trolley. Upon it—shimmering a metallic blue, fully forty feet long—lay the K6.

"Well, there she is!" The Air Vice Marshal, he had noticed, always spoke the obvious. If a thing was not worth saying, he said it. What was, he forebore to mention.

"Yes, indeed." Zweig could hardly wait to reach the point where he could superintend the loading. White-coated men swarmed around the aircraft. Two were upon the wing. Several, he noticed, glanced down at the bomb. He watched their faces, wondering if he would see awe. But they were quite blank. They might as well have been filling a medieval quiver with arrows, or fitting the spikes on Boadicea's chariot.

Chatterton remained a pace away, almost as if dissociating himself. "I told them to wait till you arrived before loading."

Powell, Zweig's chief assistant, was under the starboard wing, staring up into the bomb bay. He grinned at Zweig. He was the only person in the hangar who appeared to know what this moment meant. Almost, the professor forgave his unfortunate remark at one of the Harwell Christmas parties: that Zweig couldn't believe in God, because he couldn't accept there was any Being who knew more about nuclear physics than he did.

Now Zweig could see his own body, arms upraised, distorted in the shining stainless steel of the warhead.

"All right! *Gently!* No, down again. You're not properly aligned!"

While three men on either side of the trolley moved it carefully, Zweig turned to the Air Vice Marshal. "I'd like a word with the crew who are flying this aircraft."

"That's already been laid on."

"It's not the usual thing they've been carrying, you know."

"Similar in principle."

"But by no means in power." Momentarily, because of his disappointment at the matter-of-fact way they all accepted this bomb, he almost fell into the highly unscientific pitfall of boasting. "Over a hundred megatons. The approximate area of devastation would be forty thousand square miles."

The Air Vice Marshal said quietly, "All the home counties, in fact."

"More. From the Wash to the Channel, if the winds were favorable." He glanced up toward Chatterton's face. He wanted to tell him of the years of patience that had resulted in his new method of generating the thermonuclear explosion. He wanted the A.O.C. to understand something of his triumph.

But the airman's face was stony. This morning, he was feeling old. He was a Rip Van Winkle, waking up to find the Air Force which was part of his blood and his brain and his life had gone on without him.

"I think," Dr. Zweig said, talking because silence here had become heavy and difficult, "that the Minister was extremely wise not to put too much faith in rockets."

"Quite so!" The A.O.C. smiled wryly. The whole manned-aircraft Air Force, mindful of their jobs, would have been entirely *with* the professor there.

"My colleagues working on them are very worried . . . they've had so many failures of components. Somersaults on take-off. And the present available warheads are too small at present. Most important of all . . . we haven't got one of our own that would reach anywhere *near* Russia. Only the American Thors." He smiled. "And we have to get *their* permission before we fire those!"

"They're waiting for you now." The A.O.C. seemed to give him a gentle push forward. The trolley was in its new position. A technician adjusted one of the leads. Then everything was still. The ground crew, their faces blanched by the lights, had turned toward Zweig. Modestly, head slightly down, he stopped in front of the Venger.

"All right, Powell? All right up there? Let's see how she goes this time!"

He lifted his arms. The mechanical hydraulic jacks began whining and lifting.

"No, slowly! More gently! That's better!"

The light caught his face now. His long chin was upthrust, his mouth smiling slightly. A pleasant, ordinary, happy face.

The A.O.C. thought, God, he's enjoying it!

An airman came up behind him. "Sir, the Wing Commander asks if you'd mind stepping into his office. The Station Commander wants you on the phone."

The hydraulic jacks on the bomb trolley went on whining. Zweig's voice echoed from the high metallic ceiling. His own footfalls sounded on the concrete.

The Wing Commander's Office was immediately off the hangar halfway down on the left-hand side. He saluted, as the A.O.C. came in, gestured toward the receiver lying on his desk, and then withdrew.

Chatterton heard Lucey's breathing first. Then: "We've just had Air Ministry on the scrambler." Unconsciously, the Group Captain paused for effect. "After the assassination of their leader ben Sayid, the rebel elements in Kanjistan have declared that they are the government of the people, and have appealed to the Soviet Union for protection."

"Thank you, Lucey."

"Afraid it looks, sir, as though something might be brewing up."

The A.O.C. gave a wry smile at the masterly understatement. "Keep over at Ops, Kenneth. I'll be over as soon as I can."

Carefully he replaced the receiver, adjusted his cap, and opened the door of the hangar.

The same shadowless light ached his eyes. Crossing the concrete slowly, he saw the long cylinder disappear inside the Venger's bomb bay. . . .

And then the metal pods folded gently over it.

"Terry . . . can't you leave the thing alone?"

"Stop fiddling . . . for Chrissake!"

"Canadians . . . go home!"

Flickering dimly on and off, a man's face was making an intermittent appearance on the Officers' Mess television. A group of exasperated airmen were in front. And behind stood Terry McQuade, a great grin on his face and a screwdriver in his hand, adjusting a number of tiny controls.

Suddenly as loud as an elephant, the voice of the B.B.C. announcer trumpeted, "The crisis in Kanjistan continues grave." Then shrinking to a whisper: "Speaking in White-hall this afternoon, the Foreign Secretary declared that Britain would stand fast by her treaty obligations."

Then the voice faded altogether. Sprawled on the arm of the sofa, Mick Halloran took the briar pipe out of his mouth, and said, "Hurrah!"

From a chair by the far wall, John Falkner watched the antics around the television and smiled. His crew were still standing by. They had had supper together, then drifted in here to the ante-room. He preferred them to wait here, rather than letting them go home. As soon as a man got inside his own house, he would either relax or take on the family troubles. Both bad. If there was anything, they had to be keyed up to it. Not that there would be, of course. He'd have got them released before, if the A.O.C. hadn't been so uncommunicative the whole damned day. . . .

His thoughts were interrupted by a screech from the television. "The Vice President of the United States has expressed concern lest this should be what he called 'another Suez adventure.'"

"Turn it down a bit!"

"*Pravda* has been quoted as saying that Russian tanks are massing on the Russo-Kanjistan frontier . . ."

"Jolly good! You've got his face back now!"

". . . the United Nations Assembly in Emergency Session is trying to come to some agreement to form an international police force to fly out to Karkarabad and take over from the paratroops. . . ."

There was a guttering noise, followed by a flash. Halloran said placidly, "Good show, Terry! Now you've gone and bust it!"

Peace fell again on the crowded ante-room. Except for Falkner's crew, there was a general exodus to the bar. Pinkney and McQuade started up a game of shove ha'penny. Halloran picked up the *Lincolnshire Herald*. John Falkner resumed his own thoughts, was wondering where Helen had got to—he'd hardly caught a glimpse of her—when his attention was caught by the solitary figure over by the window, fair-haired head bent a little, apparently looking out into the night.

Beauchamp. Alone as usual. Keeping himself deliberately apart from everybody else.

A frown almost joined together the thick black eyebrows on Falkner's forehead. In the course of eighteen years on almost continuous flying duties, he had had many second pilots. Rogers, Blake, Hannaford—he remembered the three who had flown with him on his two tours of bombing operations during the war with special affection. But the others were just as good: efficient, cheerful, genned-up. . . .

Not that Beauchamp wasn't—the first and the last, at least. A Cranwell graduate, highly trained. Well-mannered, aristocratic background. Born with a silver spoon in his mouth. Had every possible advantage.

No reason at all for him being—well, to be charitable, hardly the best type of Service pilot.

What was the reason? Shy or snobbish? Not keen on flying or just under-confident?

The figure by the window turned. The younger man caught the older pilot's eye. He knows I'm thinking about him, Falkner thought—but Beauchamp didn't look away.

Instead, he came over to where the Squadron Leader sat. Still staring, in a manner half bored, half exaggeratedly respectful, he asked, "How much longer, sir?"

Steadily, Falkner regarded the quiff of fair hair, the white face. "I wouldn't know."

"I'm dry as hell."

"Aren't we all?"

"Be all right if I slipped back home for a bit?"

To that woman? Falkner thought. "No," he said, rather more sharply than he intended, "it *wouldn't* be all right."

Funny little smile. Half a shrug. Starting to move away again.

Falkner relented. "Shouldn't think it'll be long now, Dick. Then you can buy me a pint."

Before Beauchamp had again reached his solitary position by the window, the loudspeaker announced, "Squadron Leader Falkner . . . telephone . . . number one box, please."

"Ah, here we are, chaps," he said, rubbing his hands together as he got up. "Released!"

But it wasn't. On the contrary, Squadron Leader Falkner and crew were wanted in Operations immediately.

Halloran, Pinkney, McQuade—they groaned good-humoredly when he told them. Beauchamp's reaction was quite unfathomable. But together they went along to the cloakroom, collected their coats and caps, and walked out of the Mess main entrance into starlit darkness.

"Stopped raining, anyway," said Halloran.

"Nice night," said Pinkney.

"For England," said McQuade.

Their shoes on the tar macadam echoed around the deserted Sections. They turned left by Number One Hangar, went across the perimeter track to Station Operations.

Falkner led the way down the corridor, shielded his eyes for a moment against the acid-bright glitter of the neons as he opened the door.

He had not expected to see Helen there. She was standing over by the blackboard on which Professor Zweig was already drawing what looked like an outline of the K6 in white chalk. He gave her a wink, was just going up to have a word with her when the A.O.C. and the Group Captain came out of the glass control box and made an interception.

"It's this training trip, Falkner," Chatterton said. "Not definite yet . . . but they want you ready to take off at a moment's notice."

"So they've at last made up their minds where they want us to go?"

"Oh yes . . . yes." The Air Vice Marshal coughed gruffly. "Cyprus. Been there before?"

"Once."

"Good!" The A.O.C. paused. "Now on this particular trip . . . Command's idea . . . just to get used to it . . . you'll be carrying the K6."

Chatterton's blue eyes scrutinized Falkner's face. Seeing nothing but calm acceptance, he appeared to be relieved. "All your crew here?"

"Yes, sir."

"Well . . . you know Professor Zweig, don't you? He just wants to run over a few points on the bomb. *After* the briefing, of course. Now, let's get started. Where's Met . . . where do they go to, these people? . . . oh, there you are! Come on, man! Do your stuff!"

There was nothing much to the weather. A stationary high over the Mediterranean—giving blue skies and sunshine. Route—airways across France and Italy to Athens, then direct to Akrotiri airdrome. Normal Training radio frequencies until otherwise ordered.

"Any questions?" the A.O.C. asked.

The crew had none.

"Well, then . . . Zweig"—he half-turned to the Professor beside him—"if you'd care to—"

But the scientist was already on his feet. Used to lecturing to students, he had a clear, unhesitating voice, just tinged with a trace of foreign accent.

"Now I'm not," he said, smiling, rubbing the chalk between his forefinger and thumb, "going to baffle you with science."

There was a small polite laugh from the crew.

"You've all had a course on the K6 . . . your crew electronic experts a very long one . . . but I just want to get your mind *quite clear* on the new fusing system."

He took a billiard cue and pointed to the nose cone of his drawing.

"Here we are! The fuse! As with other H-bombs . . . an ordinary atomic bomb, filled with plutonium . . . which gives us the necessary hundred million degrees Fahrenheit to explode the tightly packed tritium in the K6."

He expounded on the electrical wires and circuits leading from the nose cone. Then vigorously he brushed off his drawing and, like an old-fashioned lecturer, banged his billiard cue on the ground as though for the next slide.

"Now, as you know"—he said, beginning a lightning sketch of the bomb-aimer's panel with all its dials and switches—"to derive the maximum effect from a fusion bomb, it must be exploded *at altitude,* thus creating an unlimited and horizonless area of destruction. This is effected by an aneroid device . . . an ordinary pressure altimeter really . . . connected to the detonating mechanism of the nuclear bomb fuse. Now you'll recognize this—"

He had completed his drawing of the bomb-aimer's panel.

"Just the same as the old panel . . . *except* for these two fellows." He tapped two switches on the left. "They control a new type of slave motor device, actuated by the aneroid. When they're pressed *down,* two red lights will come on just above them"—Professor Zweig paused dramatically—"which means the K6 is *live.*"

In the brief silence that followed, McQuade asked, "What height is the bomb set for?"

"I was just coming to that. Five thousand, five hundred feet. Two fives, two zeroes. That is already set on the bomb before it's loaded in the aircraft. You have already been instructed that the fusing . . . since it first involves checks on the pressure and radar altimeters . . . must be initiated over the sea *before* crossing the enemy coast. Afterward, all you have to do is to carry out the fusing sequence correctly. It's very simple . . . two master switches on, the usual A, B and C guard switches on, finally the two altitude fusing switches. To defuse, just the other way around. You can't go wrong."

"And the safety height?" Falkner asked.

"The safety height for dropping? Ah, yes—" Zweig wrote it down for them on the blackboard, just to make sure they'd understand. "Fifty-five thousand feet. The shock waves are, of course, intense . . . but as you'll be carrying out the turning escape drill away from the explosion, you'll be quite safe at ten times the explosion height. Easy for you to remember . . . fifty-five thousand feet!"

He looked benignly around at the five aircrew. "Everything else . . . all the other controls . . . bomb doors, release and jettison switches . . . are exactly the same as you're used to. Those two switches"—again with his billiard cue he pointed them out—"energizing the five thousand, five hundred feet detonating height are all you've got to worry about. Not very difficult, is it?"

The aircrew agreed that it wasn't.

"Any more questions?"

But they had none. As though they were an attentive and well-behaved class, Zweig beamed at them, rubbed his drawing carefully off the blackboard, and stowed the billiard cue behind it. He wiped the chalk off his hands, and then looked expectantly toward the Air Vice Marshal, as though he were waiting for a vote of thanks.

Chatterton came forward and gave him rather a curt nod—that was all. He rubbed his eyes, as though they were tired, then said to Falkner, "We've got no time of departure yet. You better all go to bed . . . and Ops'll tell you *if* and *when* you're wanted."

"It isn't definite then, sir?"

"Not completely definite . . . no. They want you fully briefed, that's all. Available at a moment's notice."

"Shall we all sleep in the Mess, sir?"

"I think it would be better, Falkner . . . yes." He began looking around him. "Ah, there you are, Helen! How about organizing us a spot of coffee or something?"

"It'll be coffee or nothing, I'm afraid, sir."

"Ah, well . . . let's have it anyway!"

A W.R.A.F. orderly, eyes downcast, lips smiling, came over with cups of steaming coffee—occasionally, when she had to reach for a spoon, or walk a pace for the biscuits, flicking her hips saucily from side to side.

Reality increased.

When John Falkner suggested, "Over there, eh?" Helen walked to the corner at which he jerked his head, and stood leaning against it. From across the room, veiled now with light-gray drifts of tobacco smoke, she saw the A.O.C. watching her. Then he turned back to the Group Captain and Dr. Zweig. She was forgotten.

"I got you white coffee," John Falkner said. "I thought you'd sleep better on that."

"Thoughtful of you!" She smiled. Yet she was oddly touched.

"Well," he said, mentioning nothing of the briefing or the stand-by, "what have you been doing with yourself all day? Twiddling your thumbs? Painting your fingernails?"

"Around the Station, mostly. There were a few points that the Old Man wanted to check up on." She felt suddenly immensely tired. She leaned her head against a wall lined with maps and notices, arrow-headed with pointing signs.

"You've got yourself into the right category." He pointed to the part against which her head rested. She turned her head and read *Danger Areas*, saw circles of dotted lines all over the map of England.

She shook her head, shrugged. The bright neon lights, the pale painted walls made her eyes ache. She seemed submerged in some solid metallic ocean from which she struggled to free herself, to rise to lightness and laughter.

She was aware that Falkner was watching her levelly, intently. Then he said, smiling, as though he had been reading her thoughts, "We have to lay these things on occasionally, you know. Gives you types something to do."

"D'you think you'll go anywhere?"

He put down his cup. "I don't. I'm sure we won't. We've had these stand-bys before. Quite a number of them. We've never gone."

"Only one," she said sharply. "In the last six months."

He patted her arm. "Just testing your gen. You'll do!"

She smiled.

"Why don't I get some nice civilian girl," he said, "who doesn't know all the answers?"

"There's still time," she said, rallying a little.

He glanced at her. "You reckon?"

She was aware that the A.O.C. had moved nearer to them. She heard Dr. Zweig say, "The disadvantage of lecturing is the effect on the throat!"

Someone was talking about the fishing on the nearby river . . . the Group Captain probably. She hoped that John Falkner would suggest that they go back to the Mess now. She wanted a few moments, just to sit alone with him, a few moments for the world to right its curiously distorted face.

But instead, he looked at his watch. The A.O.C. now was

at her elbow. "Well, Helen," he said. "The car *is* here now. It's been a long day. I'll drop you at the Mess. You'll be tired."

"Thank you, sir." She nodded, and then half-turned to John, questioningly, as though to say *Are you coming too?*

She saw Air Vice Marshal Chatterton glance from her to him. "Falkner will still have one or two things to do here."

He put his hand under her elbow, where it was suddenly personified as a symbol of plump protection.

"Good night, John," she called over her shoulder. She almost added, "Good luck!" Instead, "See you tomorrow!"

"In the bar. I'll buy you a beer."

The night air was cold and sharp after the overheated Ops Room. It seemed to force the air back into her lungs. The earth smelled moist with the dead decaying reek of autumn. Corporal Kidd was waiting, holding the door of the Humber open. She hunched her shoulders, stepped quickly into the back.

It was only a half-mile—but it seemed to take a long time. The airfield was silent, spread out, darkened like a deserted village. There were only a few lights burning in the Officers' Mess.

"'Night, Helen." The A.O.C. turned and watched her get out of the car. "I'll phone you when I want you tomorrow. But I don't suppose it'll be early. Have a lie in!"

In the half-light, she could see the puffy skin under his eyes, the deepened lines between his nose and mouth. "Good night, sir," she said, suddenly almost maternal, wanting to say, "And you do, too!"

The corridor light burned all night. But the bar was closed, the lounge in darkness. The Mess Office was locked, its window shuttered. Her footsteps echoed hollowly. In the W.R.A.F. Officers' wing no edge of light showed under any door. She had left the window of her own room open, and the blind flapped, and the air was cold.

She undressed quickly and lay shivering between the sheets,

turning over, curling herself up, holding her arms comfortingly across her body. A screech owl sounded, a soft piping whirr of sound. She was aware that she was straining her ears, listening. But she heard nothing else, except now and again a truck changing gear.

She must have fallen asleep, because it was just on one when she sat up—alert, awake. It was as if all night this was the noise that she had waited for. She switched on her light, checked her watch. Then she jumped out of bed, threw up the window, and leaned out.

The sky was quite black. There were no stars. But south of the Mess where the main hangars lay was a bright blue glow. And there . . . *there* it came again! Fading, increasing . . . fading again, and then rising up to a fantastic whistling crescendo.

Engines. Jet engines. The high banshee wail of a Venger's engines at take-off power.

*

Thursday

"Warning lights?"

"All out."

"Magnetic indicators?"

"All black."

"Hydraulic pressure?"

"Three thousand, two hundred pounds."

"Throttle friction?"

Beauchamp bent over the four levers to tighten the nut. In the ultraviolet glow from the instruments, Falkner caught sight of his Second Pilot's face, looking like a baby spaceman's under the hood of his plastic crash-helmet.

All tensed up. Whiter than ever. Might just be the ghostly effect of the cockpit lights, of course. Or it might be that he was nervous.

Falkner's eyes returned to the Before Take Off Check List in his lap, and went on with his chanting questions, while in the left-hand seat Beauchamp did the responses.

"Air brakes?"

"In."

"Jet pipe temperature limiter switch?"

"Override."

"Fuel switches?"

"Transfer switches off and guarded. Flight refueling cock closed. All other switches on."

"Oil contents gauges?"

"Fourteen gallons . . . full, on all four."

As the litany proceeded, even the man's voice seemed to hesitate. Falkner began wondering whether he'd done the right thing. It had been intended more as an act of faith than anything else. Bolster him up a bit. Show him he was trusted. That even under these circumstances his captain was letting him do the take-off. When they'd been woken at midnight, after only an hour's restless sleep, thinking about it as he dressed, remembering the boy's isolation in the ante-room and his own abruptness, John had decided he'd give it a try-out. A Venger take-off wasn't difficult, and after all, there were dual controls. . . .

"Oxygen?"

Through the intercom came Halloran's voice: "Checks at the navigator's station."

Now Pinkney, rather gruffly: "Bomb-aimer/Radio checks."

McQuade's Canadian twang: "Blinker operation checked on Electronic Officer's station."

They all sounded faintly reproachful, faintly apprehensive. He could imagine the three of them, sitting side by side at the long table, nine steps down from the flight deck in the tiny compartment Halloran called the "Black Hole of Calcutta." All facing the rear. All aware that the twenty-ton bomb—invisible certainly, and utterly ungetatable—was separated from them only by a duralumin bulkhead. All highly conscious that a Second Pilot—and Beauchamp, at that—was doing the take-off.

"Refusal speed?"

"115 knots."

"Unstick speed?"

"140 knots."

Falkner put the Check List back in its position. "O.K.," he said, "Line her up!"

Rather slowly, Beauchamp maneuvered the huge aircraft into the center of the runway.

Over the V.H.F., Falkner reported to the Control Tower, "577 ready to roll."

"577 cleared take-off."

The words seemed to crackle around the flight deck. Now the double row of yellow lights awaited them—a mile-long springboard into the moonlit night. Falkner could see quite clearly the familiar shapes of the hangars, and beyond, the smaller silhouettes of the Mess and the Married Quarters, dogtoothing the horizon of the starlit sky.

"Come on! Come on!" he said, all at once irritable with the man's slowness. "Let's get it over with . . . for God's sake! Brakes on?"

"Yes, sir."

"Well then . . . open her up!"

As the four throttles were pushed hard against the stops, a roar of noise seemed to explode all around them. Venger 577 shivered and shook.

"6,500 revs!"

The aircraft moved. Ambling at first, slowly she gathered speed. Glancing to his left, Falkner saw Beauchamp's arms stiff and unrelaxed, his hands grasping the control column almost as though it were a lifebelt, the knuckles white under the strain.

He was keeping her straight, anyway. On and on they rushed, the blobs of the runway lamps streaming past them like forty-millimeter flak. Now the nose started vibrating. The red boundary lights were coming up.

"O.K.!" Falkner called out. "140 knots!"

But either Beauchamp didn't hear him, or he took no notice. He hadn't even got the nose wheel off the ground. On and on thundered the Venger. Six lights left—that was all. Now five. Now four . . .

Still the Second Pilot made no backward movement on the stick. There he sat, his wide eyes staring out of the tiny windscreen. Couldn't he see the bloody hedge coming up?

Another light went by.

Unable to wait a moment longer, Falkner was just about

to get hold of his own control column—when suddenly and sweetly he felt the Venger rise.

"Gear up!"

He put down his left hand, and pulled up the lever. Already at 180 knots, the aircraft began to climb steadily at over a thousand feet a minute.

"Nice take-off," Falkner said.

The boy seemed pleased. He gave a slight smile.

"Though you stayed too long on the ground."

Beauchamp said hesitantly, "I reckoned as we were heavy—"

"No need to hold her down beyond the unstick speed."

Perhaps he shouldn't have said that. Once again, Beauchamp seemed to withdraw into a private pool of chilly isolation. Watching him fly with a kind of offended precision, Falkner shifted his body a little on his seat, trying to get comfortable.

There were times—this was certainly one of them—when he ached for the freedom and solitude of a Tiger Moth; yearned above all things to get back to the sheer fun of flying, to roll around the sky, to tilt up the earth, to climb and spin and turn. While right now, here he sat at the side of a difficult co-pilot, plumped up in his pressure waistcoat and overalls, his Mae West like a yellow halter around his neck, pinioned by his parachute straps, trussed up on his ejector seat like a chicken, breathing in air that reeked of oil, paint, duralumin and the rubber around his oxygen mask.

He watched the jeweled brooch of the altimeter needle clocking in the feet. As though he were encircled in some weird Piccadilly Circus, oil pressures, r.p.m. counters, jet pipe temperatures advertised their wares in different-colored designs and numbers. They made little impression on him, for they were all normal. Outside, they had already risen above what pale scarves of cloud there were. There was slight fog in the Midlands: lighted blobs of towns and cities looked muzzy and unfocused, as though deep under water.

As he stared down at them, he was thinking to himself, About that long take-off, maybe it was me, not him. I'm a bit jumpy, on edge, perhaps. He seemed to know what he was doing. There was probably more room than I thought. Maybe I was a bit tired. Maybe I was a bit strung up—things seem to have been happening pretty quickly lately. Or maybe it's just the effect of carrying this bomb. Anyway, he seems to be coping perfectly well now. . . .

"Forty thousand feet, sir. Shall I level off?"

"Yes." And over the intercom: "Cruising altitude, Mick."

"Right, skipper. New course . . . 165."

"Roger . . . 165. Boxes of tricks all behaving?"

"Yep. Radio . . . Doppler . . . radar . . . the lot!"

"So you're all quite happy down there?"

"Happy as sandboys."

On the starboard side of the crew compartment, Halloran didn't particularly look it—but who could in a hell-hole nine by seven, crowded out with men and machinery? And as Mick was always saying, "Never could ride with my back to the engine!" In line with his eyes were the continuously changing ground positions derived from the Doppler Navigator, the squiggles of Loran. To his right clicked the Dead Reckoning Computer. Radio compass dials, radar altimeters, gyro compasses—they overflowed all around him. Above, descending from the roof, was the periscopic sextant, now being kept electrically warm for him. "A highly mechanized navigator," was what Halloran called himself.

Beside him sat Pinkney, and beyond him, on the port side, was McQuade. Between the two of them—for the Venger was a mass of electrical gadgets and veined by wires—they controlled more power than the power-station of a medium-sized town.

Both had had similar training—and were theoretically interchangeable. Both had had similar courses in electronics; both were skilled wireless operators, and shared the radio watches.

But where McQuade was young, quick, university-trained and knew far more theory, Pinkney was considerably older, and through years of flying and two tours of bombing operations had far more experience. It wasn't that they disliked each other. Nobody could do anything but like the perennially cheerful McQuade; everybody was agreed that Pinkney was a good solid citizen. In the bar, they stood each other beers, told stories, were the best of friends. It was just that— now and again—their ideas and opinions would clash on their job in the aircraft. And then even the Canadian's wide white-toothed smile seemed to grate on the Englishman.

As 577, serene and calm, winged her way at over six hundred miles an hour across central France toward the glittering, moonlit Alps, Pinkney was saying, "He used thirty-seven runway lights!"

Diverted for a moment from delving into the intestines of the radio, McQuade suggested, "You shouldn't count 'em, Pete."

"Don't usually. Tonight's different."

"Why?"

"Well . . . Beauchamp doing it."

"Did you expect him to crack us up, then?"

"Don't be so bloody silly, Terry! But with this delicate passenger—"

"She's not fused. She *couldn't* have gone off."

"Don't be so bloody sure! I tell you . . . I'm keeping my fingers crossed."

"Primeval superstitions . . ."

"All the same," Halloran put in mildly, coming in as he often did to intervene and keep the peace, "I see Peter's point. And *my* fingers are crossed right now that the *Skipper* does the landing at Cyprus."

Standing on the balcony of the weather station fifteen miles due north of Zurich, the Duty Officer taking the two A.M. readings watched them go. They were east of the normal civil airway to Rome. He watched the green and red navigation lights carving a straight track through the pale moonlit sky. The belly-light winked down at him, human and friendly. Behind them, the moon silvered their swift vapor trails, which the cold caught and held—four unraveled ruffs of feathery silk.

It was the kind of clear night when the sky seems too big for the mind to grasp. An empty silent eternity against which only the shoulder of the mountains—white-topped, sharply delineated—had substance. Now those same mountains threw back the whining sound of the jet engines, sent it howling down the somber valleys, let it fade only when the lights dwindled and diminished—south, southeast.

Ten minutes later, when the Alps were only a backcloth to the dark, fertile, light-pricked Plain of Lombardy, Venger 577 appeared only as a quick blip on the screen of the Italian Air Force radar station at Chioggia. She was observed, plotted, her flight plan checked upon; sped on her way as a military aircraft of a friendly nation on normal training.

In Venice, a party of American sightseers, returning by canal from a late night party at a restaurant along the Via Salorosa, saw her flying quietly and whisperingly over their upturned faces, before heading out over the calm Adriatic. Her navigation lights, her minute moonlit shape, reflected themselves briefly in the fairy light-edged canal waters. The tourists pointed her out, smiled up at her, as if she were part of the colorful scene, part of the tour. Then the catching-up sound of her jets shivered the air, reverberated around the ancient buildings. And seconds later, she was out over the sea—dwindling.

Fifty miles further, a sardine fisherman, trapping the shoals with his big black-hooded light, briefly glanced up at her. For a moment, he wondered if her noise might disturb the heavy catch swimming thickly into his net. Then he shrugged, looked down again from the tiny, almost phosphorescent shape above him to the million shimmering similar shapes below the surface of the sea.

A Yugoslav soldier on the frontier near Scutari saw her pale light hurtle across the sky some ten miles off the coast. Momentarily he thought it was some comet or shooting star, and he was filled with vague misgivings, until he screwed up his eyes, picked out her port red light. Just another airplane! Now his ear caught the whine of the jets. Reassured, purposefully he continued his pacing up and down.

577 passed from him into the vision of an Albanian coast-guard, a lighthouse-keeper near Durres. Then, obligingly, she turned herself into a green blip to appear on the radar screens of half-a-dozen plotting stations in Albania and Greece.

A shepherd in Crete saw her lights leap up over a pine-forested hill, mirror themselves in the lake he stood beside, and disappear to the east, where the darkness was already beginning to split into a line of pale peach light.

It was almost dawn over the Mediterranean, and a few keen passengers were already up on a white pleasure yacht on a Greek island cruise. They could distinguish the Venger's shape clearly. The pink light from the rising sun burnished her leading edges, flashed along her perspex windows, as she lowered herself toward Cyprus.

By the time her lights finally disappeared from the sky, it was day. But five hundred miles away, thick dark cloud—a black relic of night—lay cupped in the hollow of the mountains around Tamarisk.

Where the silent man had stood patiently three days ago, there he stood again, looking out toward the northeast. Again he saw lights moving toward him.

These were not stars. Nor were they trucks. At exactly the same time as Squadron Leader John Falkner landed 577 at Akrotiri, an endless gray-green line of Russian heavy tanks, clanking slowly forward, crossed over the border, and then moved down into the now sunlit plain of Northern Kanjistan.

"Good morning, ma'am. Seven thirty, ma'am."

Exactly the same time as yesterday, Helen woke up, surprised and a little disappointed that after hearing John Falkner's Venger take-off, she had slept both soundly and dreamlessly. Exactly the same W.R.A.F. batwoman had brought in her tea, which was of exactly the same consistency, with almost to the drop the same amount spilled in the saucer. With exactly the same gesture—head modestly averted from the briefly nightgowned officer in the bed—the girl drew up the blind.

Helen dressed to the same smell of porridge and coffee and bacon, the same rattle of pans from the kitchen, the same intermittent ringing of a telephone bell, the same broken-off voices as doors opened and shut.

Everyone in the dining room looked the same. All of them seemed to be sitting in exactly the same places. A few men had the morning papers propped in front of them. She caught sight of headlines . . . CHIEFS OF STAFF AT NUMBER TEN . . . but then the page was flipped over to the funnies, the scandals, the crosswords, the pools, before she could read any more.

Breakfast tasted the same, too. Eggs turned over American-style; wide, streaky, over-crisped bacon, coffee tinny from the urn. Spills on the table, crumbs, daubs of marmalade . . . all the same as yesterday.

Leaving the dining room, she walked across the corridor into the ante-room. The time was eight thirty now, and the Mess was beginning to empty. She stood by the tall windows, watching the officers disappearing through the glass-front doors, walking past the little potted Christmas trees—leftover decorations from the party—toward their Sections. A few stood on the steps, shouldering their way into greatcoats. A truck drew up, and a group of aircrew clambered into the back. They were laughing. Their cheeks were reddened with the wind. One of them had an oxygen mask hanging from his hand. They seemed suddenly immensely young . . . a crowd of schoolboys off for the day. The cold drew their breath in little wispy balloons from their mouths. Someone ought to have written the words in. They were as far removed from her as figures in a newspaper cartoon.

At a quarter to nine, the older, statelier procession of the S.H.Q. officers began. The Wing Commander Administration and the Adjutant left together, heads close, deep in some orderly conversation. Then the Equipment Officer, wheeling out a bicycle from the concrete stand, propping it up, while he carefully rolled his trouser-leg, fastened on a clip. The ration van picked up the Catering Officer. His W.R.A.F. driver gave him a familiar saucy wink as she flung open the door. Then the Padre—which was he? C. of E. or R.C. or O.D.?—making his way purposefully toward the N.A.A.F.I. with a table-tennis kit under his arm.

Everyone seemed to have somewhere to go, something to do. Safe from thought within the little boxes of their daily routine. The Charge Sheet for the Adjutant . . . the radar let-downs for the air crew . . . inventory adjustments for the Equipment Officer . . . a ping-pong tournament (was it Junior N.C.O.'s against Senior N.C.O.'s?) for the Padre . . . all looming larger, nearer, more imperative than any K6 or H-bomb . . . as a speck of dirt on a telescope might blur a comet.

This Thursday to them all was just the same as any other Thursday.

She glanced at her watch, checking it with the ante-room clock. An airwoman kicked open the glass doors, began sorting the magazines into piles, ostensibly tidying. Overhead, a vacuum cleaner started up. A couple of men on fatigues rattled pails outside in the corridor. She alone had nothing to do. Finally, she was saved by the crackling of the loudspeaker. "Section Officer Durrant. Wanted, Number Two Box! Section Officer Durrant, please!"

The A.O.C.'s voice. Sounding unworried, just the same as usual. "Helen . . . would you join me in Ops? No hurry. Stroll down when you're ready."

She had suddenly joined the ranks of those with a job, those that belonged. As she walked down toward Operations, the wind whipped her face. She had to use one hand to hold on her hat, and another to hold down her skirt. An airman passed, saluted smartly. She had to lift her hand from holding her skirt to return it. Wryly, she thought, He did it for that.

The imprint of last night's doings—the briefing, the bomb, the take-off—was already beginning to fade. She noticed the bare line of birches, their fine branches fretted against a pale ice-blue sky, hangars casting square shadows on the tarmac. As she passed the Control Tower, she saw the black gleam of the runways contrast against the dull green of the grass.

In the Operations Block, it was warm and quiet. No humdrum sounds from the airfield could penetrate in here. Along the polished linoleum, her footsteps seemed muffled and muted.

Pushing open the door of the Operations Room, the first sight that met her eyes was the bulky figure of Air Vice Marshal Chatterton, standing by the side of the Controller's glass-sided cage. And everything must be all right, because he was smiling.

"Morning, Helen. Sleep well?"

"Very, thank you, sir."

He was looking tired. "Well," he said, "the training trip went off all right." A ghost of a smile seemed to cross his face. "You'll be glad to know."

He jerked his head toward the Movements Board. There was only one entry: *577/S/Ldr.Falkner/Landed Akrotiri/ 0425*, and written beside it, under *Remarks*: *Provisional time returning Oakwood 2230*.

"They're coming back tonight, then, sir?"

"Apparently. That's what Command says." He seemed as pleased as she was. "If he's quick . . . you might get a drink out of Falkner before they close the bar."

"Are we staying on here, sir?"

"For the present . . . yes. That's why I wanted you. Make

a true copy of the entries in the Operations Officer's log. And Helen . . . get Group on the tie-line, would you, and tell them to send a dispatch rider with these files?" He handed her a slip of paper. "Oh, and tell them to get onto my wife for a couple of clean shirts . . . and some socks, collars and things. He can bring me those, too."

"Right, sir."

She drew out a chair, sat down at the table and unscrewed her pen. Happy, reassured, on top of the world, momentarily she allowed her mind to wander onto what John was doing now: if he was thinking of her at all, and whether he was the sort of man who might possibly find time to go to the bazaar and buy a small something for her to remember and cherish.

A silence broken only by the small noises of people going about their normal daily work descended over Operations. One of the airwomen was sponging the perspex-covered wall map. The other was pasting new amendments in the Operations Manual.

Now and then, the A.O.C. walked up and down, his hands behind his back, glancing up at the map on the wall, at the red route-tape leading to Cyprus and the little red cross that marked the position on the ground of Venger 577. Inside the glass cage, the Group Captain chatted to the Controller.

And then, suddenly and shrilly, the bell of the scrambler telephone rang out.

It was as though all along they had been filling in time, pretending to be busy, waiting for just that sound.

The A.O.C. had crossed the room in a moment. Inside the box, the Group Captain and the Controller waited for him to pick it up, as though it were too white-hot for them.

"Chatterton."

"Denis . . . it's this Kanjistan business."

"What's happened now?"

"The Russians."

"Oh, God!"

"Taken things into their own hands. Tanks crossed the frontier at dawn."

"How far south now?"

"Two hundred miles from the capital, still on the move. We've protested, of course. They've replied they won't leave till our paratroops have gone."

"That's a hell of a situation!"

"I know . . . I know! Our men can't budge, of course. Bound in honor to remain."

"But they can't cope with tanks!"

"Quite! The Russians have got to be stopped somehow. That's where we come in."

"I don't quite understand, sir. D'you mean—"

"The K6 of course, Denis. Astute move of Duggane's to get it positioned out there."

"But it's not really operational!"

"Theoretically . . . no. But under the present grave circumstances . . . it's all we've got."

Chatterton drew a deep breath. "Is it war then, sir?"

"Oh, no. Deterrent. Bluff, if you like. But it'll make those tanks think twice about entering Karkarabad."

The hush that followed seemed like the stillness of the end of the world. Have they all gone mad? Chatterton thought. Don't they realize where this dangerous game will lead?

"Are we going to threaten to drop it on them?"

"No. Not so crude as that. A threat to Moscow. Backed up by ten squadrons of V-bombers at readiness here. We can't use the Thors . . . because we can't get American permission. But you'll be receiving deliveries of more K6's within a matter of hours."

The Air Vice Marshal kept silent for a moment. When he spoke, he chose his words carefully. He had the feeling that he was walking through a minefield, as indeed he was. He had passed the age for heroism, passed maybe the age when one threw away one's own security for a principle. But he could throw it away if necessary for something that in his opinion was unsound planning, dangerous to the country and detrimental to his Service.

"Sir . . . the proposal has certain obvious drawbacks."

There was no invitation to continue from the other end of the wire.

"One . . . the crew have had insufficient handling practice. Two . . . in a highly inflammatory situation, the presence of the K6—"

"Chatterton . . . it's the only thing we can do. A top-level decision has been taken. A Cabinet decision."

"I see, sir."

"This is nuclear tactics . . . the 1960's, not the 1940's—"

You are old, Father William, the young Chief said, thought Chatterton. "Have the United Nations organized that volunteer police force yet?"

"There is still considerable disagreement."

"Well . . . I hope to God they hurry up!"

There was a short silence. Then in the Air Marshal's most frigid voice: "For your information, Chatterton . . . these orders are being sent direct to Middle East Command from Air Ministry, if you'll have them taken down. . . ."

Chatterton beckoned Helen over. At his dictation, she started to write. "*Venger 577 . . . Full tanks . . . Armament K6 . . . take-off time 0300 hours G.M.T. . . . Patrol in area 42 30 North 35 30 East . . .*"

Two thousand miles away, in a Transit Crew Mess on the cliffs near Limassol, the crew of 577 were still asleep. Falkner was the first to wake; and by that time it was past noon. He rubbed his eyes, looked out of his window at the vineyards growing on the mountains, at the dazzling blue sparkle of the sea, and grunted to himself, "Bit of a change from England!"

Then he jumped out of bed, and pattering along in his bare feet to Halloran's room, banged on the door and shouted,

"Hey, Mick . . . you lazy bastard! Want to buy a battleship?"

A sleepy voice answered, "Oh, go to hell!"

"Come on, man! Bloody marvelous outside! Let's go and have a bathe!"

"O.K. . . . O.K.! Anything for a bit of peace!"

In shorts and sandals they went down the winding mule-track, past the cypresses, oleanders and olive trees to the golden sands and the sea. The water was warm. They stayed in for an hour. Then full-length they lay stretched out on the beach with their eyes closed, drying out.

"Wouldn't mind if all training trips were like this," Falkner said.

"You can say that again!" Halloran paused. Then, elaborately casually, "John, this *is* a training trip, isn't it?"

"As far as I know . . . yes." Falkner shut his eyes a little tighter. "Why?"

"Nothing. You can't help wondering . . . that's all."

Deliberately, neither of them explored the situation any further. Their Air Force training had drilled their minds into obeying an order, never looking beyond it or below it. If sometimes, with family pressures and worries, unanswered questions appeared to beckon them down haunted alleys, they must be resolutely squashed and killed. Live for today only—that had been the R.A.F.'s triumphant watchword during the war. If in peacetime it was more difficult, all they could do was to bring their blinkers down quicker, trusting their superiors implicitly, never admitting the presence on their doorstep of the ogre that stalked the world.

Now, all Halloran said was, "Christ . . . but the water was wonderful!"

"Bloody marvelous!"

"Only wish the family was here. Especially Jean."

"How is she?"

"Oh, she's fine." Halloran propped himself up on his elbow, searching in his shorts' pocket. "But sunshine's what she needs." He found a packet of cigarettes, lit one himself, said, "Smoke?"

"No, thanks."

"She enjoyed the party." He looked sideways at Falkner. "So did you, eh?"

The lid of the pilot's left eye opened warily. "What d'you mean by that?"

"You know."

"Certainly don't."

Halloran blew a blue puff into the cloudless sky. "The girl with the initials."

"Initials?"

"A.O.C.'s A.D.C."

"Oh . . . Helen." He had, as a matter of a fact, been thinking about her. "She'd enjoy this, too."

"Send a signal to Daddy Chatterton that we're organizing a dance. He wouldn't be able to resist coming here to Inspect."

"It's an idea."

"Tell him to find a small corner in the plane for Jean."

"We could have quite a party, couldn't we?"

They lay in the sun discussing it, before having a late lunch at the café on the beach. It was past five when they walked up the cliff path again; and the vine-poles were sending long shadows over the parched earth. Together they sauntered through the Transit Mess garden with Falkner saying, "Better give Ops a buzz, I suppose, and find take-off time back home," when Beauchamp came out onto the veranda and saw them.

"Skipper . . . they've been screaming for you." Somehow, his face was even whiter in the sunshine. "Middle East Command."

Suddenly Falkner felt his heart beat faster. But all he did was to unwind the towel from around his neck, shake the sand out of it, deliberately appearing far more casual than he felt. "What's the flap now?"

"Some trip or other, Skipper."

"Say where to?"

"No."

Falkner laid out his swimsuit on the brick wall of the veranda to dry. "It's probably just our return flight to Oakwood."

He didn't really believe that; but the other alternative was best not thought about. Going along to the hall, he picked up the phone, asked for Middle East Command.

It was the Senior Air Staff Officer who gave him his orders. His crew were required in Operations at two A.M. Local tomorrow morning. Transport would be sent. Further details would be given at briefing.

In a casual voice, Falkner told the others. They heard the news in silence, asked no questions; but at supper that evening, no one had much appetite. Afterward, they all went to their rooms to lie down. Falkner couldn't sleep. It was just like being back in the war, waiting to go out on a raid. When he moved on the narrow bed, he found he had to unlock his limbs first, they were so tensed up. For most of the time, he lay on his back, his hands behind his head, his eyes wide open, staring up at the ceiling.

It was a relief when the transport came for them. To be doing something stopped him thinking. As though this were the most natural thing in the world to be doing, everyone chatted quite cheerfully as the van took them slowly along the coast to Episkopi.

"Well . . . here we are!"

They had stopped outside a low white-painted building, marked OPERATIONS, MIDDLE EAST COMMAND. After being checked by the guard, John Falkner led the way in. At the end of the corridor, he pushed open a door labeled DUTY PERSONNEL ONLY.

His eyes were highly trained from past experience for a moment like this. Immediately, they went to the huge wall map. He saw a single red tape going up from Cyprus over

Turkey and into the Black Sea, becoming a long rectangle off the Crimea.

He felt better. A certain relief came flooding over him. A patrol off the Russian coast. Not nearly so bad as it might have been.

Almost the whole of the high brass appeared to have assembled to watch their briefing. Not that it was much different from any other: Met, Code and Cipher—it was remarkable how very similar these officers were to their counterparts throughout the world.

"Radio silence will be maintained at all times. That includes all radar navigational aids." The Signals Officer was speaking now. "Patrol ninety miles off the Crimea coast at thirty-five thousand feet. Their radar isn't too good down there. We don't think you'll be picked up—on the plot."

"If we are," Halloran murmured to Falkner, "then I suppose it's just too bad. . . ."

"Russian fighter airdromes!" said the Intelligence Officer brightly. "Few and far between. Two squadrons at Krasnodar . . . three squadrons at Sebastopol, but we're pretty sure they're training. Anti-aircraft rocket bases at Bazaluk and Vatkinsk, so don't get too close to the coast. A reconnaissance squadron here"—he pointed to a town close to the southeast end of their patrol—"who do tactical exercises. But as Met told you . . . there's bags of cloud cover in the area. . . ."

Pinkney whispered to McQuade, "Wish they'd all stop trying to make out it's a trip to Southsea!"

It was the Navigation Officer's turn now. "You'll be off the ground at three hundred G.M.T. Half an hour to get there. Nine hours on patrol." He beamed at them. "Back here in nice time for tea."

McQuade whispered to Pinkney, "I think he wants to come with us."

"I'll tell the skipper to send out an invitation."

"Load," said the Armament Officer. "One K6 thermonuclear bomb. You'll know more about that than I do . . . so I won't say any more. Unless you receive orders to the contrary, it will, of course, remain unfused."

The Senior Air Staff Officer, Middle East Command, was the last to speak. He gave them a brief appraisal of the military situation, told them their vital role, warned them of the importance of avoiding detection. "Information on which area you are to devastate . . . should the need arise . . . will be sent to you in code." He finished by asking, "Any questions?"

"Sir," Falkner said, "I take it that the Russians aren't being told of our presence?"

"Oh, no . . . most certainly not! A Note's been sent, that's all. Telling them that unless they halt their tanks, we will be compelled to take 'certain measures.' "

Falkner kept silent for a moment. Then he said, "I see."

The next hour was taken up with plotting tracks on their Mercator map, studying the latest orders and Intelligence information, getting the frequencies and the code books, organizing their equipment. When they left the Operations Room, the S.A.S.O. said, "Good luck . . . chaps!"

Nobody made any comment on their way back to the airdrome. But as they assembled under 577, queuing to clamber up the ladder into the crew compartment, Pinkney suggested that this really *was* a basinful.

Halloran asked, "What d'you think, Skipper?"

Falkner said shortly, "I don't."

Twenty minutes later, a white ghost in the black early hours of Friday, Venger 577 roared off the runway and, leaving the lights of Akrotiri far behind, slowly became lost in the stars to the north.

*

Friday

VERY EARLY on Friday morning, a man in a dark overcoat, wearing a soft trilby hat and carrying a brief case, came down the steps of the Russian Embassy in London, climbed inside a waiting Zvinsk limousine, and was immediately whisked away.

Through Knightsbridge. Down Piccadilly. The car turned right into Whitehall. Right again into Downing Street. Outside Number Ten, it slid softly to a stop.

The man got out. Already the front door had been opened. There was a short consultation. A long envelope was handed over. Then the man returned to the Zvinsk—and was gone.

Another Note from the U.S.S.R. had been handed to the British Government.

All through Thursday night and early Friday, Notes had been continually passing between the two countries. This particular Note was carried up to the same third room on the second landing. Here they all sat—Cabinet and Service Chiefs—as they had done for hours now, around the same mahogany table. The same green-shaded lamps cast similar pools of light over the neat piles of papers and dispatches.

The Note was laid beside the map of the Mediterranean, spread out in front of the Prime Minister.

For a few moments, there it remained—unopened.

He could hardly be blamed for his hesitation. All around him now, the atmosphere was tense and strained. This particular crisis was getting rapidly out of hand. He had expected sympathy from the Americans, not this cold wind of disapproval that was blowing in from the West. He had not expected world opinion to be on the whole so much against his action in Kanjistan. Even the more kindly NATO powers said the British had been duped into the King's trap. The less kindly declared they had been in the plot all along.

This was the man who now starred in all the newspaper caricatures.

An anarchist with a bomb in his hand (*Pravda*). A skater on extremely thin ice (*New York Daily News*). An Imperialist with a whip (*Cairo Herald*). David with a stone in his sling, facing a Goliath of a Russian Bear (*Karkarabad Mail*).

If the artists could have seen him now, they would all have drawn one picture: a well-meaning, not bad-looking, rather elderly human being, worn out by too much worry and not enough sleep.

Now at last he stretched out his hand. He took the Note. He opened it. He read it. As though he could not trust himself to speak, he handed it over to the Foreign Secretary.

There was a whole minute of dead silence. Then the Foreign Secretary said, "Gentlemen . . . this is grave news."

They were all watching him—the Admiral, the General, the Air Chief Marshal. . . .

"This is an ultimatum. Our paratroops . . . the Russians tell us . . . are to be removed by midnight tonight."

The General said, "Impossible! What about their tanks?"

"They say their tanks will also be removed. *Afterward.*"

"How do we know they will?"

"That's just it . . . we don't!"

"It is utterly unacceptable, sir!"

"They say that the situation is so explosive . . . in the interest of world peace, they cannot allow it to continue."

Air Chief Marshal Duggane inquired ironically, "Do they mention their atomic rockets?"

"It's implied."

The Admiral suggested, "Bluff."

"They wouldn't dare, sir," the Foreign Secretary said. "World opinion—"

"Undoubtedly they're risking it this time on account of our unfortunate difference with America and the NATO powers."

"My paratroops," the General said firmly, "are on police duties . . . at the invitation of the ruler. They *cannot* be removed under threat. Therefore they *must* be protected."

The Prime Minister nodded. "Yes . . . but *how?*"

"Of course," the Admiral suggested, "there's *Scipio, Scorpio* and *Centipede*—"

"And what can they do?"

"Sir," asked Duggane, "what's the present situation in the United Nations?"

"Still hope, of course. But still disagreement."

"Do you think perhaps"—it was the Admiral who made the quiet suggestion—"that our intervention was a little hasty? In view of what it's led on to?"

There followed a somewhat heated discussion. In the end, it was agreed that they could have done nothing else. Immediate action had been necessary to prevent civil war. Treaty obligations had to be fulfilled.

"And now we agree that the paratroops have to be there," the Prime Minister said. "To come back to my former question . . . *how* are they to be protected? And protected *immediately?*"

There was a long silence. The General had no suggestion. Neither had the Admiral.

It was Duggane's moment, and he savored it to the full. Only the Air Force could in this atomic age be called the protector of the nation. He leaned forward right over the mahogany table, and clasped his hands very tightly together. "Sir . . . as you know, our rocket radar at Fylingdale gives us four minutes' warning. Four minutes only! Against a thermonuclear threat, there is no alternative but a similar threat in return."

Nobody disagreed with him. He was very much aware that faces all around that table were turned toward him.

"Since we cannot use our American Thor rockets, we shall, of course, get the V-Bomber squadrons airborne. But"—he could not keep a note of triumph from ringing in his voice—"in this crisis . . . we shall rely mainly on our very own K6. That weapon . . . far more powerful than any other in the world . . . is our greatest defensive asset. As you know, one is already positioned below the soft underbelly of Russia. At present, it is, of course, unfused. But, sir, under these circumstances, when immediate readiness is absolutely *imperative,* I would suggest . . ."

At the sudden noise of clattering behind him, quickly Falkner turned his head. Then he saw what it was and smiled.

Halloran and McQuade were coming up the companionway onto the flight deck.

That was a relief. Since they started the patrol, there had hardly been another sound, except the shrill whining of the jets. As they went around the area, Beauchamp had said very little. Outside the tiny windscreen, there had been nothing to look at but the cumulonimbus tops and the stars. Now and then, a light had jerked him up into a tense alertness: this was it, this was where they were discovered. But it would only be from some town; a lighthouse; or a lamp in a faraway home.

Not that, in this hide-and-seek game, they could escape forever. Sometime or other, Falkner was sure of it, the Russians would catch on, come up and investigate. And here 577 would be just waiting for them—a huge white butterfly, limelighted by a bright moon. And without guns, all they could do was to switch the pressurization from *Cruise* to *Combat*—so that one bullet hit wouldn't make them explode like a balloon—and then fly for their lives.

Beside him, Beauchamp had spent his time keeping a sharp

watch out of the window. The Second Pilot seemed nervous: when he moved, he moved jerkily. More to give him something to do than anything else, Falkner had taken out George, and put him on hand-flying. Gradually, as the time passed and they were still unseen, the tension in the cockpit had relaxed.

And then slowly, the instrument lighting became less bright. The stars began to disappear before a milky tide. Beauchamp pointed out the glow in the east. "Dawn."

"So I see."

They turned ninety degrees starboard, onto the tiny northern leg of the patrol. Beauchamp kept looking over his shoulder. "Sir . . . I can see our vapor trails."

Falkner turned east. "Can you?"

"We're fairly sky-writing." Beauchamp had hesitated. It had been on the tip of his tongue, Falkner knew very well, to add, Now they just won't be able to miss us—

When up came the navigator and the electronics officer and made their appearance.

The sight of their smiling red faces and their bulky bodies was one of immense reassurance. Whatever they were thinking was disguised by cheerfulness. They literally shone with confidence and solidarity; giving off a wave of well-being that was picked up by others, and again reflected. Which was how morale, as Falkner well knew, was kindled and maintained.

"We've been in that bloody Black Hole too long," Halloran said, pushing his way up behind Falkner. "Got our tongues hanging out to see a little bit of daylight. Ah, the sun"—he stretched out his hands toward it as though to warm himself— "the sun!"

"Have you also seen what we're towing behind us?" Beauchamp demanded.

But Halloran didn't appear to have heard him. "Where is it?" he demanded.

"What d'you mean, Mick?"

"The Russian coast. According to my calculations, I should now be getting my first glimpse of it."

Falkner screwed up his eyes. "There's something on the port bow. . . ."

McQuade bent over the throttle box to have a look. A dark tongue was projecting below a gap in the heavy cumulus build-up. "Yes, Skipper . . . that's land, all right."

In a disappointed voice, the navigator said, "Doesn't look much different to me."

"Has it got a name?"

"Cape Sarych. Apparently a seaside resort."

"Sort of Russian Blackpool, eh?"

"That's it, Skipper. Probably got a tower, too."

"So long as it hasn't got a fighter airdrome," Beauchamp put in. "I don't care *what* it's got!"

But Halloran was not to be put off. "You've got five o'clock shadow, Dickie! Out of bed the wrong side! Not using Amplex! Blood sugar's low, too! Here, Skipper . . . what about some breakfast?"

"Good idea, Mick!"

Halloran bent down to pick up a tin and a thermos on the floor behind the pilots. "Couldn't be better!" he said, as he took off the lid. "Catering's surpassed themselves!"

"What've we got?"

"Caviar . . . Black Sea swordfish . . . Russian boot and virgin sturgeon."

"My mouth's watering."

"What'll it be then, Skipper?"

"Sturgeon."

"Now Terry, what's yours?"

"Caviar, Mick."

"One sturgeon . . . one caviar coming up!" Reverently, Halloran unwrapped a napkin and took out a cheese sandwich for Falkner, a ham one for McQuade.

"Better than the wife's cooking, eh Terry?"

The navigator poured out tea from the thermos into two

cardboard beakers. "Vodka." He handed them over. He passed a ham sandwich to Beauchamp. "There you are, Sunny Jim! And I'll pour out your poison in a moment."

The Second Pilot stared down at the sandwich and said, "Christ!"

"Something wrong with your caviar?"

Beauchamp snorted, "Practically sitting on the Russian border . . . you'd have thought the Air Force might have lashed out with a bit more than this!"

"Don't bind, Dickie! That's not all! You're getting a banana, too!"

Beauchamp grinned sourly. "I know now why you're not worried about retirement, Halloran. With your sense of humor . . . you'll make your fortune on the stage."

In reply, Halloran passed around the tin for a second round of sandwiches. There were times, Falkner reflected as he ate, that he wished Beauchamp had the remotest idea of leadership. How the R.A.F. expected to make a captain out of him, God knew! Didn't he realize that all this was a front? Beauchamp might think he had a problem with that wife of his, but Mick had a far tougher one with Jean.

As the Venger slid majestically through the air, a white silhouette against that bright blue sky, as the minutes ticked past and nothing at all happened, while the others talked and ate and Beauchamp kept peering out of his window, Falkner was turning over in his mind the responsibilities which the others had physically left behind at Oakwood, but which mentally must all the time be close to their consciousness.

He supposed he was fortunate himself in being an utterly free agent. Sometimes at cocktail parties, out to tea or coffee at their houses, he would be aware that one or other of the wives was looking anxiously at him, scrutinizing him, perhaps trying to sum up whether or not he could be trusted to look after such a precious cargo as her husband. He knew them all fairly well—Mrs. Halloran best, Mrs. Beauchamp least. But whereas the beautiful and wayward Diana might well

become a perfect Air Force wife—once she had diluted her
affairs into just attractive and sociable flirtations, and provided her husband received promotion—Jean would never
be satisfied till Mick was out of what he had given his life to.

Falkner had never been to the Halloran house without
feeling Jean's nerves screaming at him. Fears, probings, leading questions poked through the polite smoothness of conversation in the same way as her thin bones poked through
her silk skirt. He liked her as a woman. She was nice as a
friend; and sometimes he'd have given his eyeteeth to be able
to take her hand and promise her, *swear* to her that everything would be all right . . . *always.*

Val McQuade on the other hand—now there was a sensible
little body if ever there was one. Always bright, always neat,
always smiling. Ask her how she was, and even if she was at
death's door, she'd answer—he'd guarantee—in that not un-
attractive Canadian drawl . . . *fine, just fine!*

And now he was on the subject of marital problems . . .
what about Peter Pinkney's, for God's sake? Five motherless
children to cope with by himself for years. How he had managed to do anything else, Heaven only knew. Falkner began
wondering why the man hadn't married again, whether he
would even now perhaps sometime. . . .

And that brought him naturally to Helen Durrant.

In his thirty-six years, he had had a number of affairs with
women, had fallen in love two or three times—and then out
of it. He always meant to get married—hadn't deliberately
avoided it. And now he had met Helen—from that very first
moment it seemed when first he'd seen her—he didn't know
how he could avoid it.

Quite what it was that was so attractive about her, he didn't
know. Pretty? Yes, of course . . . but he'd known prettier
women. She had attractive blue eyes. That fair hair was nice;
so was her figure. But there was a sparkle about her, a kind
of cheeky challenge which was irresistible. That one day
soon he would ask her to marry him had somehow never been

in question. She was in his fate, in his hand, in his stars. Just as this trip was—inevitable.

But sitting up here, with nothing to do now George was in but twiddle knobs, with nothing to see, and only the crew's gossiping to hear—for the first time the thought occurred to him that it might not seem quite so inevitable to her. She was twenty-four, good-looking, clever; the world, or anyway, the R.A.F., at her feet. A day or two spent in his company at Oakwood might be neither here nor there in her young life. . . .

"Dreamin' oh my darlin' love of thee, dreamin' of thee—"

He was suddenly conscious of a body leaning right over the throttle box, and Halloran's grinning face looking up at him.

"For the third time, Skipper . . . turn! Unless, of course, you want to cross the Russian coast—"

"Eastern end of the patrol already?"

"Too right! Beyond it now."

Falkner took out George and, swinging the Venger ninety degrees, momentarily caught sight of the dazzling white paint on the lifted port wing.

"Well . . . at least you don't seem worried."

"Not now."

"But you were once?"

"A bit . . . to begin with. Weren't you?"

"Christ . . . petrified! Still am. Can't you see me shaking? Tell me . . . what's the cure?"

Falkner smiled. "They'd have come up by now . . . if they *were* going to come up."

"You think that? And what if we bump into anything accidentally?"

Falkner had already worked out all his tactics long ago. The only way, he had found, of keeping his mind clear and steady, free from imagined emergencies, was to know exactly what he was going to do in any foreseeable situation. Now he pointed to port. "See that dirty great cloud over there, Mick?"

"Yep."

"If anything comes along . . . I'll turn 577 up on her wing-tip and dive. Certainly . . . at seven hundred knots . . . we could beat a fighter into it."

"Well . . . thank you! That's a comforting thought to take down the Black Hole. Have some more sturgeon?"

"Thanks, Mick . . . no."

"Well . . . you know what you're missing." Halloran pushed back his sleeve and looked at his watch. "Time to submerge now. You coming, Terry?"

"Better. Should have relieved Pete on the set five minutes ago."

"We'll take his food along as well." Halloran bent down and picked up the ration tin and thermos flask. "Oh, and before I go, Skipper . . . time to turn again!"

Then, with the Canadian behind him, he clumped off down the companionway.

Once more there was silence on the flight deck. Left on his own again with his second pilot, Falkner moved the control column, marveled as always at how lightly the heavy aircraft swung over to starboard, steadied on a westerly course.

The hours went by, one by one. They went around and around the patrol area, and still they saw nothing. The sun climbed higher in the sky, but now, instead of making things seem more dangerous, taking away the cover of darkness, illuminating all sorts of suspicious objects, it just painted up the scenery with warmth and friendliness. Not the faintest trace of another aircraft. Not a single solitary ship on the glimpses of the sea below. Just the cumulus tops, bubbling over like cauliflowers well below them. And above, the inverted blue bowl of the sky with everything shaken out of it—but 577.

The trip was going to be a piece of cake, after all. Falkner stretched his legs off the rudder pedals, lay back in his seat

and relaxed. The clock on the instrument panel said eight
o'clock. That was G.M.T. Half the patrol gone already. With
a look almost approaching benignity, he looked over to the
right, where Beauchamp—his Cranwell training had at least
made him technically genned-up, accurate and punctual—
had begun to make up the Engineer's Log of all the instrument readings, exactly on the hour.

He was leaning over the starboard console, checking the
cabin temperature. Next he started on the instrument panel
proper, peering at the Machmeter, noting down the jet pipe
temperatures, oil pressures, the engine revolutions.

"Cruising at eighty-five per cent power, Skipper?"

"That's right."

"And what's your altimeter reading, please?"

"35,100 feet."

"Mine's a couple of hundred feet short."

"Pressure altimeters aren't all that accurate . . . up here."

Beauchamp began busying himself, pressing the buttons
beside the twelve fuel-tank gauges on the central console, and
writing down their readings. Then he turned his attention
to four tiny dials just above the throttle quadrant—the oil-
contents gauges of all four engines.

That was the end of his check. He made no comment,
seemed just about to put the Engineer's Log away, when almost as an afterthought he said, "Number Four Engine, sir."

A certain amount of Falkner's present peace of mind evap-
orated. "What's the matter with Number Four?"

"Using a lot of oil."

"How much?"

"Twice as much as the others."

"Which is what?"

"Half a gallon an hour."

"Christ, man!" Falkner's voice was raised in irritation.
"That's nothing! The tank holds fourteen gallons. What've
we got left? Eleven and a half?"

"Just over eleven . . . yes, sir."

"And we'll be back in Cyprus in another five hours . . . so what's the worry?"

Beauchamp replaced the Log in its holder beside his seat with an air of injured innocence. "I wasn't worried, sir. Just pointing it out to you."

Falkner grunted. Venger 577 whistled onward unconcerned. The somewhat strained silence in the cockpit was resumed.

Down in the crew compartment, Pinkney was chewing away on another sandwich. He had just changed over with McQuade on the radio. Now he watched the Canadian fiddling and fussing with the set as he always did. He took a swig of lukewarm tea, and sighed to himself.

McQuade was a man who could never let well alone. Always trying to get things just a little bit better. Now he had taken off the front cover of the W/T receiver and was delving inside among the valves and the wiring.

He said, "What's up, Terry?"

"Distortion."

"I didn't notice it."

"Background crackle, too."

"Perfectly all right when I was on."

McQuade gave a good-humored grin, which Pinkney interpreted as, *what's all right with you isn't all right with me*. Stonily, he watched the Canadian take out a valve.

"What the hell are you doing now?"

"Changing a T12 valve, Pete. That'll do the trick."

"Trouble with you . . . your Dad never gave you enough Meccano to play with."

"Could be."

Pinkney took another sandwich and chewed at the ham resentfully. McQuade wasn't a bad chap at all, cheerful and all that, but he was always throwing his knowledge around. Technically a perfectionist—that's how he tried to act. Giving the impression that the Englishman was second-best. Not quite up to *his* standard. And certainly sometimes the man overplayed the part.

Pinkney had spent all his watch listening eagerly for the slightest peep from Control. This trip wasn't exactly a comfortable one. He had been on several not dissimilar—looking for rocket sites in the islands off North Russia—and had invariably been recalled.

And he was expecting a recall on this trip. They had, in his opinion, been quite long enough off the Crimea coast. A man when he gets older loses any ambition to do anything reckless—especially when he has five childen. Pinkney resented every minute that the receiver was in bits.

"McQuade . . . they may be trying to contact us."

The Canadian went on working. "Doubt it."

"We should keep a continuous watch, you know."

"Shan't be a tick, Pete."

Nevertheless, he took his time. His headphones lay on the table between the two of them. It was Pinkney who first heard 577's call sign faintly coming through, when at last McQuade switched on.

"Told you! Told you! For Christ's sake, man . . . they're calling us!"

McQuade shoved the headphones on, and began rapidly writing in his log.

"Recall, eh?"

"Don't know. In code." McQuade leaned over for the Code Book, and began leisurely interpreting a confused hieroglyphic of numbers and letters.

"They're recalling us, eh?" Pinkney demanded eagerly.

"Well, if they are"—McQuade slid a piece of paper over to the man beside him—"they got a damn funny way of doin' it!"

Pinkney looked down at six capital letters in the Canadian's rather straggly handwriting: FUSE K6.

The church clock at Oakwood had sent the chimes of the early hours of Friday over the flat quiet lands of Lincolnshire.

Elsie Pinkney had gone to bed, dog-tired after turning out her father's room. Her ears registered to her mind that one of the twins had gone along to the bathroom to get a drink of water, and that Margaret had used paper but hadn't pulled the chain, without these observations pulling her out of a deep and dream-filled sleep.

But Jean Halloran had never once been unconscious for her to be wakened by anything. She had taken two sleeping pills and a glass of hot milk. Yet she had heard every hour strike, had heard and tried to identify every vehicle that hummed along the distant perimeter track. No aircraft had taken off. Except for the perennial illumination around Operations, the Control Tower, and one lit square in S.H.Q., Oakwood bore a normal night face, as if indeed nothing more unusual than a training flight had taken place.

But it had, hadn't it? The quick air test, the long-drawn-out briefing and preparations, the secrecy about the flight, the A.O.C.'s continued presence here, the crisis in Kanjistan . . . worst of all Mick's face, red and bland, his don't-be-silly-little-woman face . . . as he kissed her good-by . . . had he kissed her extra hard? . . . did he really not trust Beauchamp? . . . was there something wrong with Venger 577? . . . what *had* happened to Williams? . . . in these small hours, on this silent night, her horrors seemed to come alive like wind-up toys, jostling big ones with little ones, old ones with new ones, screaming for her attention.

It was a sudden relief to hear a taxi turning along Tedder Avenue. From inside came muffled giggles, a man's voice. Jean Halloran bet herself she knew who was inside. If she crossed the landing from her bedroom and stood on the bath, she could catch a glimpse of the back of the Beauchamp house. The sound of the taxi disappeared. Yes, sure enough, immediately afterward, a light came on in Diana Beauchamp's hall. Well, Jean thought, that was one way of killing time while your husband was away. She sighed and shrugged.

Yet when she returned to her bedroom the horrors had re-treated slightly. She thought that now if she lay down awhile she might just snatch an hour or two before the boys were awake.

Five miles away in Ilminster, Val McQuade had done everything except stand on her head. And if she didn't get a bit of shut-eye soon, that was precisely what she'd do, or whatever else Yogi recommended. She'd counted sheep; she'd told herself dull stories; she had said over and over again, *Valerie McQuade, you are very, very tired, and are just about to drop off to sleep.* But as the clock chimed six, she had sat up and said, *Valerie McQuade, you've got it all wrong, you've never felt more peppy in your life.*

It was not that she was worried. It was just that she missed the sight of his tousled head on the pillow beside hers. It was cold, too, that's what it was! With no central heating, you needed a husband beside you in bed of an English night. She reminded herself to make a crack about that when the boys got back.

At six thirty she felt as wide awake as if she'd been on a couple of weeks' vacation. And at seven, telling herself she had been feeding herself too many vitamins, she got up and dressed and simply put the clock forward and began doing her household chores a couple of hours early. Just at eight thirty, when she was washing the ornamental flower pots on the kitchen windowsill, she heard the front door of the flat below open and shut. Leaning forward, she saw their land-lord, wearing what she and Terry had christened his *impor-tantest face,* let himself out of the garden gate, mount his cycle, and head for the airport road to the north.

After breakfast on Friday, when he heard the news of the fusing of K6, Air Vice Marshal Chatterton had been furious. Though he said nothing on the scrambler, all the time his shoulders were stiff with suppressed rage. He demanded of the Group Captain, "What the hell are they playing at *now?*"

Lucey shrugged his shoulders.

Out of the glass Controller's box tore the A.O.C. Helen had been chatting to the two airwomen on duty, asking them how they liked Oakwood, was there enough entertainment, when she was interrupted with his roaring.

"Get me the Engineering Officer! I want every available Venger serviceable! Rout out the Armament Officers! Tell the Squadron all aircrew are on immediate stand-by! Get hold of Zweig and his team . . . tell 'em to load up the new K6! Oh . . . and Christ, get hold of a flight-refuelling tanker! And I want it now! *Now*, I say! Come on, get cracking! *Get cracking!*"

He stumped around, glowering at everybody. Oakwood was only one of six stations under his control. Ahead of him today lay the superhuman task of trying to get them organized from this Station, where he had been ordered to remain. In his present red rage, nobody dared approach him for the moment until the Controller asked timidly, "The tanker's asking . . . who's it going to refuel?"

"577, of course."

Helen felt a sudden sharp stab of fear. "Where are they going now, sir?"

"Nowhere. Staying put."

"But, sir . . . Squadron Leader Falkner's crew has been flying for hours!"

"I know! I know! Orders. A signal's been sent them from Air Ministry. They're to remain on patrol."

"How long for, sir?"

"God knows! But one thing *I* know . . . we've got to get some kerosene into Falkner! And very quickly, too! Come on! *Come on!* Haven't that tanker crew turned up *yet?*"

"Just coming, sir. Flight Lieutenant Erskine and crew."

"Tell 'em to get a bloody move on! This is a damn crisis . . . not a Sunday School treat!" He swung around on his heels as the door opened, and a Flight Lieutenant with a thick black moustache came in, imperturbably leading his crew into the Briefing Room. "Ah, there you are! At last! Now I want you off the ground in twenty minutes!"

He had better than his wish. Erskine was off in quarter of an hour. With Chatterton's exhortation *And don't bother to come back if you don't find him* ringing in their ears, most of the crew were still clambering into their flying suits, stowing their parachutes and arranging their gear, while the huge jet tanker climbed up to cruising altitude. In this model Venger the bomb bay had been converted into a vast tank holding nine thousand gallons of fuel. In addition, another four thousand gallons would be transferred from the wing tanks. After rendezvous with 577, they were to proceed to Cyprus for refueling themselves, before returning home.

On over France, across the Alps and Italy, they followed almost the same route as 577 on her flights to Cyprus. Then they doglegged across Greece and Turkey. And just over three hours after leaving Oakwood, they were flying over the Black Sea.

They were descending now to 35,000 feet. Another twenty minutes, and they should be over the patrol area. In the tanker's crew compartment, the navigator shifted restlessly in his seat. With jaundiced eyes, he peered out of his tiny window into the cloud-filled world below.

Layers of cirrostratus now. How the hell the A.O.C. *expected* them to make an accurate rendezvous with 577, God knew! Jenkins was a Scot. Very conscientious, and very hardworking. But this was just about impossible!

No radar, no radio, no Doppler—in case the signals gave away their position. Out of Loran range. Daylight certainly, but lots of cloud. And to help him, only a tiddly little Russian beacon, which was causing the needle on the radio compass to swing twenty degrees either side, as if it, too, couldn't make up its bloody mind.

577 had been sent the position of the rendezvous, sure. But had they got it? Might well not have. They weren't

allowed to acknowledge. And even if they received it, Halloran had been stooging around for hours, with practically no navigational aids available. His position might easily be miles out. . . .

And when the tanker had reached the rendezvous, and there was no sign of 577, what then?

At the thought of it, Jenkins shuddered. That was his own private nightmare, a vision that sometimes woke him up in a cold sweat. No thought of the crisis was now in his mind. Russian fighters seemed nothing in comparison. If they didn't make the rendezvous, 577 would not have the fuel to get back to Cyprus and God knows what would happen to Falkner and his crew.

Turning his head, Jenkins glanced sideways at his altimeter; they were down at 35,000 feet. Straight and level, thank God. He reached up his hands and took the cover off the periscopic sextant, opened the Air Almanac, looked at his watch, and then began to take a shot of the sun.

He managed to focus the little yellow spark quite easily in the center. Then just as everything was all set, it swam off to the right.

"Hey!" he called crossly through the intercom. "What's the matter with George?"

"George is out." The second pilot's voice—quite casual, not at all worried. "Been acting up."

"Well . . . don't act up yourself! For God's sake, keep her steady!"

"I'm not flying the thing!"

"Oh." Jenkins paused. "I see." He paused again to stifle some of his exasperation. Then he said, "Skipper . . . I'm trying to take a sight. Need a fix badly. Can you keep her dead steady?"

"Roger! Will do!"

Erskine's voice—bright and cheerful. All right for him, Jenkins thought sourly. He didn't have to do the interception. The navigator's jaundiced eye returned to the rubber eyepiece. That was better! He looked at his watch, pressed the two-minute button, grimly hung on.

Altitude 24°59'. Mean Time 12:34:21 G.M.T.

Five minutes later, at least he'd got a fix. When Erskine asked airily, "Navigator . . . when's our E.T.A. for the rendezvous?" he could reply quite confidently, "1250, Skipper."

At that moment, though there was still ten minutes to go, he ached to climb up on the flight deck and have a look. But he steeled himself to stay down. . . . It'll be there, he told himself. No need to worry. We'll be able to see him all right. He stayed at his work, making last additions to his plot.

At 1246, purposely casual, he picked up his microphone. "Any sign yet, Skipper?"

"Nope."

At 1248, in a rather higher tone of voice: "You should be able to see 577 now."

"We can't."

At 1250, very anxiously: "Skipper . . . rendezvous time."

"Well . . . there's not a sausage here!"

In a flash, Jenkins was up the companionway and standing behind the pilots. He scanned the horizon with his own eyes —forward, up, down, port, starboard. Surely there must be some trace! Surely they should see his contrails?

"You're sure your position's right?"

"Quite sure."

"Well"—Erskine's voice had gone somewhat irritable now— "what d'you want to do?"

So it had come at last into reality, his nightmare! On the most important mission that he had ever flown, he hadn't been able to rendezvous with the other aircraft. For a few moments, he said nothing, still gazing around the sky, hopefully trying to construct vapor trails out of bits of scattered cloud.

All at once, the second pilot said, "There, over there—"

"*Where?*" Jenkins shouted.

"No . . . no." His voice trailed away. "I was wrong."

"Christ!" Erskine turned to look balefully at his navigator. "Looks as though we've missed them!" His voice was really angry now, with just a trace of panic behind it. "We've overshot the rendezvous now! Come on, make up your mind! Is this where we meet them . . . or isn't it?"

Jenkins was conscious of the high heartless whining of the jets, carrying them along at ten miles a minute. With a loud clatter, somebody in the crew compartment dropped something heavy, and swore. The navigator shielded his eyes, looked once more from pole to pole. Then miserably he said, "Circle, Skipper . . . would you?"

Immediately, up on its port wing went the tanker, and began a sedate merry-go-round.

After ten minutes, Erskine said, "I'm getting giddy. We'll go around the other way."

As Jenkins scrutinized the sky, all sorts of ideas were passing through his head. 577 might have been shot down. She might not have got the message, and returned to Cyprus. She might possibly—

"This is no good!" Erskine was saying. "Better get cracking along the patrol track. See if we can find her ourselves."

"We wouldn't have a hope, Skipper."

"We're doing a whole lot of no good sticking here!"

"They'll turn up."

"You don't sound too confident!"

The second pilot asked, "What the hell's happened to them?"

Nobody answered him. Sweat had begun to form on Jenkin's forehead. It ran over his brows, into his eyes, salty and stinging. He blinked. Then he closed his eyes, for they were still painful.

When he opened them, it was to a hopeless sight. A cloud desert, a foreign wilderness of white vaporous hills and black shadows. It was impossible that another Venger could ever materialize from that panorama.

Hopelessly, Jenkins turned his eyes to port, was just looking down toward a glimpse of the sea, when suddenly he saw a long white thread, a frail gossamer rope as though spun from a spider, apparently joining one cumulus head to another.

He looked again, to make quite sure. Then, gulping with relief, he shouted, "There she is!"

577 had seen the tanker, too. Gradually the familiar triangular shape dissociated herself from the cloud, and came climbing up toward them. In a wide turn, she swept around them. Then skillfully, she formated close to their starboard wing—her huge eight-foot probe sticking forward on her nose like a gigantic sting.

Both aircraft now straightened out. Though both crews were imprisoned in their own particular hunks of metal, they all crowded at the windows, gesticulating to each other, making V signs and waving.

"Nice to see old Falkner again!" Erskine had recovered his equilibrium. "Seems very cheerful, doesn't he?"

Beauchamp's head could just be seen over the Squadron Leader's shoulders. Halloran's face was pressed flat against the crew compartment pane of perspex. For three minutes, against the background of the vast cumulonimbus anvils, the two Vengers flew side by side. Then, through the intercom, Erskine called out, "Flight Refueling Operator!"

From the nose came the answer: "Yes, sir!"

"Standing by the panel?"

"Standing by!"

Erskine turned a switch on the port console. "Bomb doors selected open! Stream the drogue!"

"Streamed!" On his dial, the Operator watched indications of hose length. "Twenty feet . . . sixty feet . . . ninety feet!"

Now Venger 577 started slowly to drop astern and below. From the belly of the tanker aircraft, the long rubber hose streamed, with the cone-shaped drogue like a target at its end.

Falkner maneuvered 577 a few yards behind it. Cautiously,

inch by inch, he crept forward, using the long probe on the nose as a sight.

Gradually, it connected with the drogue. There was a clunking sound as the steel probe tipped the fuel valve; then was itself gripped by claws inside the rubber cone. Under pressure from 577, now thirty feet of the hose was pushed back onto the drum inside the tanker bomb bay.

The Flight Refueling Operator watched for the yellow band on the reel length, indicating optimum refueling position. He opened up a cock, called out, "Fuel on! Number One Tank!" Then he switched on the green traffic light below the aircraft that would indicate to Falkner that the fuel was flowing.

577 started to suck at over six hundred gallons a minute.

Joined in the Gargantuan mating, the two white Vengers, one slightly below the other, flew steadily forward high in the sunshine at 35,000 feet.

The fuel poured down the hose. No red light was received to tell the receiver to break contact. No hitches, nothing to disturb them. Smoothly and almost silently the flight refueling proceeded. The Operator switched onto the belly tank; when it was exhausted, onto Number Two Tank in the wing. All the time, he was watching the fuel gauges on his panel, as they rapidly went down.

Twenty minutes passed. Still in this perfect formation, the green light under the tanker changed to yellow.

"Fuel tanks closed!" the Operator reported. And shortly afterward: "Refueling complete!"

Erskine asked, "How much did you give him?"

"Twelve thousand, eight hundred gallons."

"Quite a suck! That'll keep him going for a while!"

"Winding in!"

They felt a slight jerk as 577 broke contact.

The receiver rose up, drew level in formation with the tanker. Falkner could be seen waving his hands in thanks.

Then the two Vengers parted. Gradually the distance between them lengthened.

And 577 resumed her lonely patrol.

The two pilots in 577 kept their eyes on the tanker—till she disappeared over the southern horizon.

"Lucky bastard!" Beauchamp said.

Falkner said nothing.

"Going home."

"Mmm."

"And leaving us here to go around and around and around!"

Finding his captain was not disposed for further conversation, Beauchamp started fishing around at the side of his seat for the Engineer's Log. Falkner stared through the windscreen at the now empty sky. It was not so much the metal presence of the other Venger that he was missing—it was the number of unanswered questions she had left behind.

Why had the K6 been fused? That was the most important one. When at first they received the message, a kind of fatalistic calm had come over all of them. This was it! This *must* be war! The next message would be an order to a Russian target, to drop their fantastic load.

And return . . . *where?* Where in the world, after the inevitable Russian retaliation, would be in existence? But they were bound by orders. They had to do what they were told. So Pinkney had crawled into the nose and taken up a position at the bomb-aimer's panel. Very carefully checking all the time with the radar altimeter, he had carried out the fusing sequence. Then, over the intercom, in a sepulchral voice he had reported; "K6 fused, Skipper. Two red lights."

Sounded as innocent as an undercarriage-up warning, Falkner had reflected.

Half an hour later, when they had seen McQuade again writing in his log—this time a much longer screed—Pinkney and Halloran had exchanged significant glances, and had tried to look cheerful. This was the logical sequence: they were about to be told where they were to go, and when. They had watched the Canadian's face as he began decoding it, saw his usual smile gradually come back.

"O.K. . . . you guys! Relax!"

"What is it, Mac?"

"Rendezvous with refueler. Maintain patrol . . . that's all."

The tension then had broken. This was an anticlimax to what they'd expected. Though they'd all been aching to get back home . . . now it didn't seem quite so important.

Quite cheerfully, they had resumed their eternal roundabout. Meeting up with Erskine had provided some excitement. The sight of the other Venger had been immensely cheering. Somehow, more than fuel had been injected into 577 by the tanker above her.

But now she had gone, all the unanswered questions returned. *Why* had their patrol been extended? How much longer would they have to stay here? What was going on at Oakwood?

To be so near and yet so far from the answers had been tantalizing. Falkner felt he had been shut away from the rest of the earth—allowed only a tiny useless spy-hole, which he could not point or focus. He stirred restlessly in his seat, caught sight of 577's shadow, a tiny black arrowhead ringed by rainbow colors, crawling across steamy cloud five thousand feet below. It looked very like a fighter—but fighters and all Russian opposition had completely gone from his mind. The U.S.S.R. didn't appear to mind in the least. By this time, anyway, 577 had become part of their scenery.

"Skipper!"

Lost in his own thoughts, Falkner did not hear.

"*Skipper!*"

He turned his head, looked at his Second Pilot, now sitting with pencil poised over the Engineer's Log. The man looked tired. More white-faced than ever.

"It's the oil."

"What oil?"

"The oil in Number Four."

He remembered it. "Still using half a gallon an hour?"

"Yes." Beauchamp paused. "Pity they haven't devised a flight refueling for oil as well!"

"No need to. We've still got bags. How much now?" He made a lightning calculation. "Eight gallons . . . enough for another sixteen hours! Christ, man . . . they won't keep us up *that* long!"

In the top flat of 22 Lime Street, Ilminster, Lincolnshire, England, Valerie McQuade had gotten herself bitten by the work bug. She didn't know what it was, but all day she hadn't been able to stop doing this, doing that, washing this, ironing that. She'd fixed a chicken and left it cold in the larder for Terry's return. She'd baked a lemon meringue pie, a blueberry cake, Chocolate Indians and his favorite simnel cookies.

She'd scorned to listen in to the crisis on the radio—though she'd have been a dumb bunny if she hadn't heard the tanker aircraft taking off. She had read her morning paper headlines, and they had done her a lot of no-good. But if she wanted to know anything, she was not the sort of gal to beat about the bush and listen into this and look at that.

No, sir! She went straight to the horse's mouth.

So when she'd heard nothing by lunchtime she lifted the receiver and dialed the number of R.A.F. Station, Oakwood. "Operations, please," she told P.B.X.

When the Controller answered, she said without preamble, "Say, you borrowed a husband of mine a day or so back. Have you finished with him yet?"

The Controller's voice smiled. "Is that Mrs. McQuade?"

"Sure."

"Hang on, Mrs. McQuade. I'll see if I can find anything out."

She listened with her ears flapping; but she heard nothing but a muffled footfall, a distant voice, the rustle of papers.

"They're still doing flying training, Mrs. McQuade. As far

as the program is at present . . . they're not expected to land for the next few hours."

"Wowie!" she said. "Some training trip!"

"If you like, I'll give you a ring when they land."

"I'd be glad. Do that . . . will you?" She wrinkled her smooth forehead. The friendly voice was firm, kind, vague, off-putting. "Bye now," she said to the already empty line.

When she put the receiver down, she stood for a long time with her hands on her hips, staring around the flat as if hypnotizing it to give her a job to do.

"Valerie McQuade," she said aloud. "You're growing a neurosis! Do something about it! You aren't the only pebble on this goddamned beach!"

Immediately into her mind leaped a vision of the wives of Falkner's crew, as she knew them: from dances, teas, cocktail parties, occasionally bumping into them out shopping. Not that she was exactly well acquainted with any of them—which hadn't been her fault. British stand-offishness she and Terry had put it down to. A pity, all the same.

And then, least of all known—not a wife but a bunch of assorted kids. She'd seen them, fastened around Pinkney like grapes around a thick stem, at the Group Captain's garden party last August. Terry had been sweet with them, had brought each of them a Coke. The kids! Now for land's sakes, why hadn't she thought of them before?

She walked into the kitchen, opened the larder, and took out the chicken and the Chocolate Indians and wrapped them carefully in grease-proof paper. "Don't sentimentalize, McQuade!" she said, as she packed a little basket of goodies, "No Community Chest visiting, *please!* You're doing this to help your own sweet self!"

She put on her coat, pulled a woolen cap over her hair and, not bothering to lock up, walked down the stairs and out to the garage. The place looked empty without *Angelique*. Over in the corner was her three-gear two-wheel velocipede. She wheeled it out, down the garden path and onto the roadway. Then she mounted and headed toward the airfield.

There wasn't much traffic at this time, and she pedaled as fast as her tough little calf muscles would take her. The wind was cold on her face, and the feeling that she was going places did her more good, she was sure, than a half-hour session with a head-shrinker.

She didn't have any difficulty getting onto the camp, but she did have a bit of a time finding Portal Street . . . and then Number Six. Finally successful, she dismounted, took her basket off the carrier, walked up the path and rapped on the door.

Elsie Pinkney answered it. She looked at once surprised, gratified and suspicious.

"Hi!" Val said. "Remember me? I'm Val McQuade . . . Terry McQuade's sidekick. Can I come in? Thought I'd just drop in and see how you kids were making out."

Through the open lounge door, she saw that Beauchamp's wife . . . of all people, Diana Beauchamp . . . no doubt impelled by the self-same mixture of emotions as her own, had already arrived.

Parked in front of Number One Hangar, through the window of his Humber, Air Vice Marshal Chatterton watched the refueling tanker slide home out of a graying sky. It was a sight that, middle-aged as he was, unemotional as he was, hardened as he was, never failed to stir him.

All around the topmost buildings glowed the red blobs of obstruction lights. Everything was switched on . . . a harlequinade of lights and colors. And over the fenland, with a silent inevitability, the mist was coming up. He could feel it in the bones of his back, in his shoulder joints. This was the time to be coming home. From the immense yellow-lit runway, the throttled-back engines seemed to sigh it.

As he did. One more operation in this tricky business over

and done with . . . *safely*. They'd had the signal in four hours ago. *Contact made. Refueling completed.*

He had waited around in Operations until that message had been received, and decoded. He had held Lucey in a seemingly relaxed, interested conversation about quail, and duck-shooting on the fens, and Madge Lucey's abhorrence of blood sports, until he knew for sure that 577 had got its injection of fuel and could stay up another ten hours.

Then he had spent all the rest of the afternoon checking continually with Bomber Command.

Now, as the refueling aircraft taxied toward dispersal, he turned to Corporal Kidd and said, "The Group Captain's house, Corporal. Time's getting on! Have to hurry if I'm to change for dinner."

He was looking forward to nothing so much as a hot bath, a drink, and a good meal. It had been one hell of a day and he for one was damned glad it was over. Or nearly over. Necessity dictated these measures, he supposed. But he was always glad for the days when necessity did not arise. Not given to introspection, he tried painfully and with clumsy honesty to probe his own motives and reactions in this day's doings.

He still smarted from his phone calls with Thane. He was still convinced that sending 577 into the area, let alone fusing the bomb, had been a major tactical blunder. Yet his reasons were slight, easily brushed aside, overriden. Wasn't, after all, the real reason an inexplicable sixth sense? As if his long partnership with the Air Force, like a long marriage, had given an instinctive know-how of what would work out for the best in the end? A tactical equivalent of flying by the seat of your pants?

Or maybe the Chief of Bomber Command was right, and mentally he was outdated. Never quick, never adaptable, maybe he brought to bear now a sort of cavalry mentality . . . like the blimps of the twenties who had tanks scrapped and replaced with horses.

When he came to think of it, there was a lot in that. He had heard earlier that Oakwood had taken delivery of the second K6 with a deepening of his misgivings. Why? Bomber Command was committed to these weapons. And he was the chief of the most important Group in that Command.

Or, to be fair to himself, had he become increasingly aware of the political mentality of the most senior Air Force officers? Were they not playing out their political ambitions too hard, with the stakes too high?

Since Thane had phoned this morning, Chatterton had had the feeling of being committed to impending disaster. Once 577 had gone to Cyprus, the steady build-up of events had not altogether surprised him. It was as though he had heard the first few bars of some forgotten tune . . . and each new event was another note, not recognized till heard but then immediately familiar . . . and each note was carrying on, building up to some terrifying crescendo.

When his mind reached the Russian ultimatum—due to expire in just over five hours—he deliberately clamped it shut. It was impossible to allow himself to think of that. Thrusting out his chin, leaning forward, he concentrated on the Station around him. It was busy at this time . . . crowds of airmen coming out of the Mess carrying their irons . . . cycles everywhere, swooping out of side roads, far too fast. Some, he was sure, had no rear lights. Because such small duties were a solace to his mind, he made a mental note to speak to Lucey about them when all this was over.

The Humber swept past S.H.Q., outside which a couple of heavily made-up airwomen were obviously waiting for their boy friends, turned off by the Officers' Mess, and then up came the lights of Group Captain Lucey's house.

Mrs. Lucey was prodigal of lights. Tonight when he saw them, he had the most extraordinary feeling . . . for the first time in God knew how many years, he was homesick. He suddenly wanted to be sitting at this moment by his own fireside, while Lillian knitted for their new grandchild . . . and ease off on her some of the burdens of the day. And now, oddly, he was able to identify the feeling inside him. It was nothing comparable to leading a bombing operation. It was nothing comparable to the sending of someone else to do one, against heavy enemy opposition. It was worse than that. It was like the time thirty years ago, when he was twenty-two and Lillian was pregnant for the first time, and both of them knew she wasn't strong . . . it seemed as though by one small act he'd started off something that must carry on to an inevitable and unforeseen conclusion . . . and that conclusion might be the end of everything he loved.

He got out of the car, and walked slowly up to the front door. He saw Mrs. Lucey flit across from the brightly lit lounge to the hall. He prepared his face and his mind for the polite exchanges of everyday conversation that she would expect of him.

Madge Lucey said solicitously, "You must be exhausted! Which shall it be first? Drink or change?"

"Change, I think, thank you, Madge."

He laid his cap down on the hall table, peeled off his gloves. The ornamental grandfather clock showed close on seven.

Its cheery chimes caught him halfway up the stairs. He could hear the sound of the batmen's voices in the kitchen preparing dinner. It smelled capital. Duck! And some sort of spicy sauce. From the lounge came the rattle of ice in a shaker . . . the comfortable background noises of a comfortable family.

An odd contrast to the clock, gabbling off the five hours to midnight. . . .

In the bathroom, he turned on the water. Then he undressed and lay wallowing. It was wonderfully warm. Madge had fixed up the décor with considerable taste. There was a plethora of soaps and crystals and lotions. He could hardly imagine Madge indulging herself like that. Responding to the comfort and cosseting of his body, his mind became quiescent, lulled in well-being.

At first, he thought he must have dozed off. Someone was hammering on the door. Probably Lucey, summoning him hurriedly for dinner.

Leaning forward, quickly pulling out the plug, the Air Vice Marshal called out, "Yes? I'm here. What is it?"

"Lucey, sir. Sorry to drag you out like this. Ops have just phoned. Command on the scrambler, sir! Thought I'd better get you at once!"

He sluiced off the soap from his armpits, and said, "Phone them back and tell them I'll be right over. Tell Kidd to bring the car."

He said nothing else. But over and over in his head, to the sound of the water gurgling out down the drain, to the sound of his hasty movements, his labored breathing, were the words: "God, this is it!"

The sight of Madge waiting in the hall, good-hostess-like, to be told, "Don't wait dinner! We may not be back!"; the sight of Lucey holding open the door for him, incongruously sucking a throat-lozenge; the sight of Corporal Kidd waiting by the Humber . . . they all struck him as unreal . . . as the figures in a world which might already be half-dead.

Inside the car, neither of the men spoke. If they did, it would only have been to hazard a guess as to which way the international wind had blown. And neither cared to do that.

Instead, Chatterton watched the concrete of the roadway unwind under the Humber's powerful headlights. They passed a girl in W.R.A.F. uniform. Her face was momentarily spotlighted: cheeks scooped out, lips slightly apart, eyes staring, blinking a little, wondering who was inside the car and where they were going. Momentarily, she seemed a disembodied mask of all the people that he had in his charge. The thought twisted his stomach. He thrust it away, drew deeply on a cigarette.

The last turn before Operations, the gentle slowing up of the car in front of the long line of square lights. He didn't hurry out when Corporal Kidd held open the door. He waited for Lucey to get out first. Then casual, smiling: "Hang on, would you, corporal?"

It was warm and stuffy inside Operations. He could smell the air, dehydrated as cardboard. Coming out of the cold, it made his mouth feel dry. He walked briskly down the corridor.

Lucey kept exactly in step with him. Tonight he found the habit annoying. It gave a sinister underlining to his own footfall.

He thrust open the door of the Operations Room.

He was aware that everyone was watching him—but he was used to that. This time, however, they were watching him in a different sort of way. Even more than usual, he thrust out his jaw and walked with added ponderousness and purpose.

He said, "Good evening," to the Controller, murmured, "And now what, I wonder?" Then he took off his gloves, lifted the scrambler and drawled, "Chatterton."

In the second before the Chief of Bomber Command spoke, Chatterton deliberately brought to his mind that this might be the announcement of total nuclear war, that the world hung like some child's yo-yo at the end of this wire.

Then the Air Marshal's voice came over loud and clear. "Thane here." His bright successful voice . . . that might mean anything from relief of international tension to a K6 having been planted straight on top of Moscow.

Which?

"Good news . . . very good news! Chatterton . . . we've got the United Nations moving *at last!*"

In the Halloran house, the children were taking a long time about going to bed. They always did when their father was away. Crossing the hall to the bottom of the staircase, Jean Halloran shouted, "For the last time . . . get out of that bath and into bed! The bath isn't meant to play in!"

From the landing, Robin's voice floated down. "We *are* out. Will you come up and hear our prayers?"

"Oh, all right."

She didn't like hearing their prayers when Mick was away. She was always afraid that they'd forget to pray for their father's safe return. And that would be an omen. And when they did pray, the very necessity for those words made her ache to throw herself across the bed and cry on their shoulders and have their young arms comfort her.

She bustled around, irritably tidying their clothes, drawing back the curtains, while they gabbled through their prayers.

She stood staring out across the airdrome, at the lights of the houses and the lights of the hangars and the lights of the fields.

They did remember.

"There now!" She turned when they'd finished, tucked them in, kissed their foreheads. "No more talking! Goodnight! God bless!"

She left the door ajar, so that they could see the glimmer of the landing light.

Walking down the staircase, she looked at her watch. Nearly seven twenty-five. Almost time for the news. She went into the lounge, carefully closing the door behind her. She poured herself a stiff whisky from the cabinet, lit a cigarette, and turned on the television. She crossed to the chair immediately opposite it, and perched on the edge.

Her watch must be a little fast. She was at the tail end of some silly minstrel show. She stared at it blankly, puffing her cigarette. Unlike some of the other wives, she was not a fool. She hadn't missed the fact that Erskine had taken off in a tanker aircraft. Nor had she missed his return. That might well mean that the trip was being extended. But where— north, south, east, west—had they gone?

Kanjistan? Probably—though she couldn't be sure.

There it was! The announcer's well-known face.

First item: crisis in Kanjistan. She waited breathless, while the stupid man licked his lips, smiled benignly.

"At a special session of the United Nations, a resolution

was passed earlier this evening to send a United Nations force to Kanjistan immediately. In London, the Foreign Secretary said he would be willing to hand over as soon as adequate police protection arrived. Troops have already emplaned from Holland and Sweden, and are due to arrive shortly—"

She switched off then, and sat for a long time, with her head back and her eyes closed. Another crisis fizzling out! Thank God! Even if he didn't get back tonight, Mick would be home early tomorrow. She'd cook him a special lunch . . . chicken, maybe . . . and she'd make up her mind never to get worked up about these trips again. Impulsively, she crept upstairs and into the boys' room. Then she knelt down and pressed her face against young Tony's cheek.

He stirred quickly. "What's up, Mum?"

"Nothing, darling. Everything's fine!" She stroked his hair. "I was just saying good night again . . . that's all. Now go to sleep!"

Not long afterward, Helen Durrant returned from a brisk but aimless walk around the airfield. She had hesitated outside the camp cinema, wondering if she should get inside and escape, if only for half an hour. But the feeling that she should be available in case she was wanted, in case news came through, drew her back to the Mess. Then back to the anteroom. And then back to the television set. She turned it on just in time for a special announcement of the news.

There was hardly anyone in the room. Nearly all the officers were in the bar, except for two elderly men in the corner. At the sound of the unwelcome noise, they dropped their papers, protesting silently.

She missed the opening phrases . . . then there it was! The first contingent of United Nations troops—from Turkey—had already landed in Kanjistan. The Foreign Secretary had given the order to the British paratroops to withdraw immediately.

She glanced around, willing to share the unutterable relief of this moment with anyone and everyone. But not a flicker of interest stirred the newspapers of the men in the corner.

"Troops are also on their way from Holland, France and Scandinavia. Now here is a film of the Dutch contingent emplaning at Schipol. . . ."

Suddenly, a result, no doubt, of the day's tension, she felt an unaccustomed emotion thicken her throat. She remembered her mother telling her of the day that the Second World War was declared. How one after another came the rallying of the forces of the Commonwealth. Now something like that, a fleet of little nations was surging forward to save the world and to allow Great Britain to withdraw with grace and dignity. The paratroops would be whisked out of Kanjistan before the Russian ultimatum expired at midnight. A Cinderella over-estimating her riches, her strength, the intelligence of her politicians, would return to her kitchen before the last stroke sounded.

The world, black all day, seemed to have righted itself. On a wave of emotion, tonight God did indeed seem to be in His Heaven, all indeed right with the world.

Sitting unseeingly in front of the television, she became aware that the A.O.C. was beckoning to her through the glass swing door. She got up, and as she crossed over toward him, read the confirmation of the good news in his face.

"Hello, Helen."

"I was just watching the news." She said it apologetically, as if he had found her out in some discreditable occupation.

"Thought you might be. Come and have a drink. Don't fancy dinner . . . not just at the moment."

He smiled down at her benignly as they walked along the corridor.

"Well, Helen . . . we've just sent a signal to Falkner to return to base. *That* should please you!" He held the door of the bar open. Warm noisy air encompassed her. "The thing's over now. We'll all be able to sleep tonight."

It suddenly crossed her mind that God had shared His Heaven with a hydrogen bomb capable of destroying a huge section of His beloved world. She dismissed it as an exercise in philosophy, not to be admitted at this moment.

Yet it remained. A tiny persistent gnawing at her feeling of well-being.

Long ago, silence had settled over 577.

For hours, there was not a sound from the crew compartment. Out of a kind of understanding tact, nobody used the intercom. The possibility of having to report an order to a target was still there; and the first *click* as a mike went on could make any heart miss a beat. In the war, Falkner had had a rear gunner with a weakness for nattering; over the target, there would be a crackle, a pause—then a grumble about a lost glove or the cold in the turret.

Nobody was like that in this crew. Only the jet engines of 577 kept up their eternal sibilant whispering, as for the umpteenth time, the Venger rounded the eastern leg of the patrol.

Remembering the war made Falkner think nostalgically of the old heydays of Bomber Command. The roar of piston engines was somehow stronger and sweeter than this shrill high whine. He liked the big, cussed, unstreamlined strength of a Halifax: the way you got to know how she behaved, and learned to humor her. There was a monstrous majesty in a big night offensive—the rattle of the Brownings, the squirts of red tracer, the smell of cordite and of their own fur-lined flying jackets and the reek of the sweat down their faces. He remembered the clammy excited approach to the target; the sight of the flares wallowing down, the slow rising of the heavy flak, the bright arms of the searchlights reaching into the sky. Then . . . bombs gone! The lightening of the aircraft and of everybody's spirits—and the wide-throttle dash back home.

You were conscious of the companionship and the danger— the risks taken at the drop of a hat, gladly and with enormous exhilaration. You didn't think of the destruction. Your blinkers came down, sure; but they were also part of your armor-plate. Somehow, you had found yourself in this situation—and because you were a man, you had to go. But at least, by and large, it was a war of man against man, in the company of men. While now . . .

He looked sideways at his Second Pilot. Beauchamp would never know. That was why the spirit in this supposedly peacetime Air Force could not reach the tremendous morale of the war.

Now it was a struggle of machine against machine. Nothing left for the human spirit. Just a job for the human thumb —and weapons like the K6.

He grunted, pulled himself up. No point in going along that avenue of thought, especially now. Different circumstances, anyway; a completely different world. He pulled the blinkers hard over his mind. Putting out his hand to the automatic pilot, he turned the Venger three degrees to starboard. The clouds were lessening. Evening was coming on. Falkner looked down at his watch. It would be just after four at Oakwood now. Idly he began speculating what Helen Durrant would be doing at this moment. Probably with the Luceys. Probably having tea. Probably twisting the A.O.C. around her little finger, flirting in a nice demure and decorous manner with the G.C. and all ranks down.

He grinned a little sourly at himself. Here he was, off the Russian coast with a fused thermonuclear weapon of enormous proportions; and here he sat—dreaming as any other man would, in a similar nightmarish situation, of a little blonde twelve years younger than he was, and promising himself how he'd make her toe the line when he got her.

There was a sudden clank of the metal rim around the Engineer's Log. Beauchamp's voice said, "Still using half a gallon."

"O.K. . . . *O.K.!*"

Now night was coming up toward them—not falling, but gradually coming up from the ground. In the cooler air, the higher tops of cumulonimbus were crumbling. The sun changed color from yellow to red, as it began slipping behind a thin gray bank of stratus. Shadows lengthened, deepened, multiplied—till the air below became one vast vat of purple. Caught in the limeshine of the last uptilting sunbeams, the Venger still glittered against the blue background of the universe; till slowly this light, too, went out. The level of the shadow came up to engulf them, slowly smothered the radiance of the white paint.

And 577 became part of the night.

Beauchamp turned up the rheostats of the red fluorescents; the numbers and needles of the instruments glowed like tiny candle-flames. Now they were under cover of darkness, he seemed more cheerful.

"Must be used to us by now, Skipper!"

"Yep! Russians'll be sorry to see us go!"

"How much longer . . . d'you reckon?"

"Your guess is as good as mine."

The patrol went on in darkness. Falkner gave up counting how many times they went around. The moon came up. Deneb gradually climbed higher in the sky. Capella swung above the horizon. Of them all, only the Pole Star stayed where it was.

All at once, Falkner was conscious of someone standing just behind him. Turning his head, he was surprised to see all of the other three crew members merged close together, wide grins on all their faces.

"Message, Skipper!"

The sight of the slip in McQuade's hand momentarily made his heart thump. He took it and held it under the instrument lighting. He read, *"Return to Oakwood. Defuse K6."*

So it was over! Whatever had been going on since they became airborne had somehow peacefully been sorted out. Now all those questions of his had suddenly been answered. He breathed again with delighted relief. "Thank God for that!"

"Goin' home!" McQuade got hold of Halloran and did a grotesque elephant dance around the flight-deck floor.

"What's the course? I want to get the hell out of here!"

"Hang on a second, Skipper. . . ."

The three of them clumped down the companionway to the Black Hole. Then Halloran's cheerful voice: "236."

Falkner leaned over to put it on the compass grid ring. "236 it is! Now let's get cracking! Seen enough of this place to last me a lifetime!" He swung the Venger to port. "Climbing to forty thousand!"

"O.K., Skipper"

The crew returned to their own individual jobs. Everything became lighthearted and easy. As rapidly they left the Russian coast far behind them, now they could use their many navigational aids. Pinkney switched on the radar, watched the time base come up bright and green, detected the irregular scribble that was the Turkish coast.

"Istanbul, thirty degrees starboard . . . thirty miles, twenty-nine miles—"

"Thanks, Pete." Halloran plotted the fix. "Piece of cake from now on!"

Shortly afterward, now at altitude and with everything settled for the return journey, Pinkney arranged his pencils in a neat row, made sure the radar was working well, and then picked up his microphone and said, "Just going forward to defuse, Skipper."

"O.K., Pete."

He got out of his seat. Following the beam of his torch, his bulky figure penetrated into the narrow darkness of the bomb-aimer's position. He saw his face in the perspex of the floor panel; and beyond it, the moonlit sea.

He felt for the lamp switch, found it, pressed it down. Then he squatted on the floor, opposite the two round red lights on the bomb-aimer's panel.

As methodically as ever, he picked up the Fusing and Defusing Check List. He read it twice. He touched all the switches lightly with his hand. The expression on his red face—the round black eyes, the tongue just peeping from the large lips—was a study in concentration.

Then he started.

First, he checked the radar altimeter on the intercom with Halloran. Then he turned off the two large switches just over the red lights. Next, the guard switches—off in the reverse order: C, B, A. Finally, he took hold of the two master levers on the bottom of the panel, and pressed them up.

Then he sat back, and took another look at the panel.

All the switches that should be off were in the *off* position. The sequence was right. And yet there in the center, like two bright sores, the two FUSE ON lights still glittered malignantly.

He frowned. Putting out his right hand, he tapped them.

Nothing happened.

He tapped them harder.

Still red.

He took up the Check List. He read out each item aloud, verifying the position of each relevant switch.

Everything was exactly as it should be. Except that the fuse lights still showed red.

Very slowly, a look of horrified astonishment came flooding over his face.

What the hell was the matter with the thing?

He put out his hand and gingerly touched the master switches. Then he thought better of it. He was acutely conscious of the fantastic power of the K6. He was also acutely conscious of how comparatively little he knew about it.

The two red lights seemed to be boring into him. All his muscles had tensed up. His mind would not function. He sat there, hypnotized.

Sweat started up on his brow. Hunched in his flying kit like a great big teddy bear, he felt hot. His mouth was as dry as sand.

Of course it was ridiculous, he tried to tell himself. No

need to get flapped up. Probably just a sticking contact. Better not touch anything. Better get Terry. For once he was grateful for the Canadian's knowledge. He'll know.

As though he were breaking a ju-jitsu grip, he jumped up on his feet and groped his way back to the crew compartment. Looking up the companionway, he saw the silhouettes of Falkner and Beauchamp—close together, obliviously talking —against the red fluorescent lighting.

"Terry?" He took one of the phones off the Canadian's ear. "Can you come forward?"

"What about the W/T?"

"Leave it for a moment."

"Something up?"

"Spot of bother on the fusing circuit."

"Told the Skipper?"

"Not yet. It's nothing much." He tried to pump confidence into his voice. "Defective switch . . . I think."

"I'll come and have a look."

McQuade reached down for his box of tools and equipment. Pinkney led the way back into the nose.

"There, you see! Those bloody fuse lights! Still on!"

"All switches off?"

"Yep."

"In the right sequence?"

"Of course."

The two of them knelt on their knees as though before some strange altar. McQuade studied the panel. Watching him, Pinkney heard the hum of the jets, felt the slight vibrations through his body. Momentarily, he was thrown off balance as the Venger slipped to port. He put out his hand to steady himself.

"Pete . . . you've really balled it up this time!"

He felt his face go fiery. "What the hell d'you mean?"

"*Sure* you got the sequence right?"

"Told you I did!"

"Don't look like it to me." McQuade took hold of the master switches. "Better try again."

Pinkney grabbed the Canadian's hand. "No . . . you don't."

"Let go!"

"You'll explode the thing."

"Relax . . . relax, man!" McQuade shook himself free. "This won't do any harm!"

He had put the switches back on the ON position. For one terrible moment, Pinkney had the impression of being trans-figured into thin air. Then he was conscious of McQuade saying, "Now we're back at the beginning . . . we'll start again."

Then, carefully calling the sequence from the Check List, he switched them all off again.

Unmoved, the lamps stayed red.

"Damn bastards!" McQuade shook the panel vigorously. "What's the matter with you?"

He rooted around in his tool box. Then, with a screw-driver, he began to take off the panel. Petrified now into silence, Pinkney watched while he delved into the red and yellow intestines behind. At any moment he expected the whole thing to go up, as McQuade's hands pulled at the wir-ing, checked for a loose connection.

"Aw . . . hell!" The Canadian sat back and wiped his forehead.

"Is it a contact?"

"Christ knows!"

"What else could it be?"

"I got a hunch it's in the bomb bay."

"But *what?*"

McQuade screwed up the panel, stared at the lights—still red and unblinking. Then he said slowly, "Whatever it is . . . we can't get at it."

An icy fear struck into Pinkney's heart. "Mac . . . you reckon . . . it's still set . . . to detonate at five thousand, five hundred feet?"

"Yep."

"*Christ!*"

The Canadian got up off the floor, glared at the switches. "So much for them!" Savagely he threw his tools back into the open box. "Now all we can do is tell the Skipper!"

*

Saturday

In Kanjistan, at last it was quiet. All Friday night, the country had crawled with movement. In the towns and the villages, the inhabitants had turned out to see the Russians and the British going out, and the United Nations coming in.

Frequently-changing flags had been waved, friendly cries exchanged. The *Daily Mail* correspondent had got an excellent shot of a British sergeant-major being presented with a basket of fruit by a small dark-eyed Kanjan. *Pravda* had taken a picture of a Russian tank garlanded with the yellow daisy-like flowers that grew in Kanjistan's northern province. And most papers of most nationalities had got photographs ready for the morning's edition of cheerful troops marching to their bivouac in the old Palace, and of the welcome accorded them by the citizens of Karkarabad—especially by the King.

His Highness, after a long and formal banquet, had retired to his bedroom . . . while up in the hills, the arms were laid away oiled and wrapped . . . till next time. The oil fields began functioning normally. The few trains ran. From nearby Turkey, the French and American residents prepared to return. All around the Mediterranean, the countries seemed to relax, to let tension escape and the atmosphere become as calm and quiet as the sea.

In the Kremlin, the attitude was one of smiling self-congratulation. *Pravda* had prepared a political cartoon, showing the Russian eagle as a dove of peace. In Downing Street, all was quiet: the Prime Minister had retired early for a good night's rest. Only the usual lights burned in the Air Ministry, the War Office, the Admiralty. The Chief of Air Staff had dined with a few close friends. His high spirits had been most marked. At Bomber Command, Air Marshal Thane had been idly turning over the pages of the R.A.F. Seniority List— and had gone home to bed, well pleased.

And in Lincolnshire, R.A.F. Station Oakwood had sunk back, without a sigh, into complete calm and normality. At ten fifteen that night, the shaded lights of the guardroom, the yellow windows of the Telephone Exchange and the barrack blocks, the subdued green in the Control Tower, and the brilliance behind the bars of the Operational Block, were all placidly home-like.

Inside the Operations Room, in contrast to the almost hard efficiency of the neons, was a scene of domestic bliss. Gone were all traces of the last few terrible hours. The tapes and pins of the Black Sea patrol had been removed. The Movements Board held one chalked announcement: *S/Ldr Falkner E.T.A. Oakwood 2329.* Of the two airwomen on duty, the pretty one . . . a chocolate-box blonde . . . was reading the advice to the lovelorn at the back of a woman's magazine, and the plain one . . . a plump brunette . . . was placidly knitting the foot of a man's gray sock, and drinking a mug of cocoa. Inside his glass cage, the Controller was writing home to his wife.

And then suddenly the phone shrilled. The Controller sighed, put down his pen, picked up the receiver. "Duty Operations Officer. Yes?"

"Message from 577."

Idly he glanced across at the clock. "What is it? Revised E.T.A.? Well . . . fire away!"

"Sir . . . it's in code."

"In code!" He pursed his lips, glanced from the clock to the Movements Board. "Better bring it along then." He replaced the receiver, opened up his little glass panel. "Betty!"

The blonde looked up from her magazine. "Yes, sir?"

"Wake Section Officer Jones, will you?"

Within a few minutes, the sleepy contentment of Operations had gone. Side by side with the Signals Officer, the Controller was staring down at a meaningless jumble of figures and letters.

Neither of them spoke. The plain airwoman had put away her knitting, and the pretty one could be heard through the open door of the Cipher Office, tactfully murmuring, "Ma'am . . . Ma'am."

Five minutes later, the Controller and Signals Officer were still staring down, but this time over the Cipher Queen's shoulder, as slowly she transformed the jumble to: *K6 fuse warning lights both remain red . . . repeat RED . . . after defusing procedure complete. Request instructions.*

There was a hideous persistence of sound in his ears. He had gone to bed early, dead tired. Now in his dreams, a shrill noise whirled itself into the whining of jets, the scream of an aircraft diving into the ground, the ringing of mammoth alarm bells. He jerked himself up. It was the phone beside his bed. Penetrating the softness of his sleep, boring into his brain.

God, what now?

The A.O.C. reached out a hand, raised himself on his elbow and grunted into the receiver, "Chatterton."

He blinked the sleep out of his eyes, ran his tongue around his lips, as the voice said, "Sir, it's Operations . . . Duty Controller here . . ." The man's voice was full of urgency and irritating alarm.

"Yes. What is it?"

"We've just had a message from 577—"

Well, at least she hadn't pranged.

"In code. It reads . . ."

The A.O.C. closed his eyes as he listened. That sixth sense, that seat-of-the-pants know-how, squashed down by discipline and the fear of being out of date, now seemed to shout *I told you so*.

Into the phone, he said sharply, "Get my driver over here. I'll be right over." He glanced at his watch: 2230. Screwing up his eyes, he could see in his mind the route map of 577's return flight. Should be over Switzerland. "And get the stand-by crew of the tanker out of bed, and the aircraft ready to take off. Send a signal to 577 . . . tell Falkner to do nothing . . . repeat *nothing* . . . till he hears from me."

He put down the receiver, and grabbing his neat pile of clothes, banged first on the Luceys' bedroom, and then on all their other bedrooms, because he couldn't remember where the hell they'd put Zweig.

Lucey's face appeared around the open door—rosy, alarmed, rather righteous.

"Get Zweig up! Message from Falkner to say they can't defuse K6." Chatterton pulled on his shirt. "I want to know what's wrong. Ring the hangar. Get Zweig and his team working on the new K6 there. *Got* to find out what's wrong! And *got* to find out fast!" He shouldered himself into his jacket. "He'll probably need some of the factory people. If he does, get 'em! Get him any damned thing he wants! But tell him . . . for Christ's sake, find out! And find out soon!"

He paused to put on his cap. "I'll be over at Ops for the next twenty minutes. Then I'll join Zweig at the hangar."

He ran down the stairs. Through the hall window, he could see the lights of the Humber. As he shut the front door behind him, the village church was chiming a quarter to eleven.

Three minutes after, he was in Operations. Five minutes after, he was on the scrambler to Command.

Waiting for Thane, he thought . . . Had he forgotten anything? He watched the Controller busy with arranging the take-off of the tanker aircraft. What had gone wrong? A short in the wiring? Maybe the bomb was not really fused, but the lights still showed in error . . . was it a risk worth taking? Well, he shrugged, only Zweig could tell.

But *could* he?"

"No," in reply to the W.R.A.F. operator, "I'll hold the line. This is *most* urgent."

Should he have phoned Air Ministry direct? No, better get Thane. He probably had more technical know-how, was slightly less the politician. With so many people knowing . . . a security leak was a definite risk . . . might cause one hell of a panic . . . and if it got known internationally . . . *Christ!*

Opening the panel, he said, "Get the Station Adjutant on the phone! Tell him I want to speak to him when I've finished with Command . . . and get me the Station Security Officer . . . tell him to come here. . . ."

The receiver in his hand clanged as the line re-opened.

"Thane." The voice cool, wary.

He made no greetings, no apologetic preamble. "Chatterton speaking. We've received this from 577." He read aloud the message he now knew by heart. He made no comment, letting it fall cold and hard and bare for Thane to pick up.

A long pause. Then, in a different voice, controlled and quiet: "What went wrong, Chatterton?"

"I don't know, sir."

"Well, you'd better find out."

"Exactly what we're trying to do."

"You still got Zweig there?"

"Yes."

"Can't *he* tell you?"

"He's just started working on it."

"Then tell him to get a move on." Another pause. Then: "Which crew took it, Chatterton?"

"Squadron Leader Falkner's, sir."

"Very experienced?"

"Experienced, yes. There's no crew *very* experienced on the K6."

"But they were very experienced on the standard bombs?"

"Yes."

"Same thing."

"Not *quite*, sir."

The C-in-C's voice was edgy. "You know what I mean. Could they have done anything wrong? Bungled it somehow?"

"No."

"But it must be a possibility."

"A faint possibility."

"And is it possible . . . have you asked Zweig . . . that K6 isn't fused at all? That the lights are wrong . . . and it's all a false alarm?"

"It's possible. I haven't seen Zweig. He's at the hangar working on it."

"Then find out . . . get on with it! I'll have to phone Air Ministry. I must have all the facts. . . ."

"Sir, we've had approximately twenty minutes—"

"D'you realize what this means?"

"I realize what it *might* mean."

"Then get on! Find out! I'll let you know Air Ministry's reaction, of course. But find out!"

Find out, *find out!* His own blood seemed to pulse the words. They underlined every movement that he made, every breath he took, every word he uttered. They underlined his talk to the Adjutant . . . to the Security Officer . . . his instructions to Ops. They underlined the humming of the tires as Kidd sped through the darkness to the glaring lights of Number One Hangar.

But inside, under the shadowless lights, all seemed in contrast. The high fluted roof echoed the sounds of footsteps, the clang of metal on metal. A Venger stood in the center, as though on some gigantic operating table. Her bomb doors were open; the blue metal of another K6 tucked inside her could just be seen.

Men in white coats worked all around her. Wires connected from her to banks of instruments and dials. A vast mobile X-ray apparatus was standing by. Arc lights poured down over her. Three assistants were checking with analyzers and oscilloscopes. And at a long bench, Zweig himself was poring over drawings and circuit diagrams.

Vibrating over everything was the hum of electrical power.

"Well, Zweig?"

The professor did not look around. "Well what, Chatterton?"

"Found out anything?"

"Give me time." Zweig walked over toward the aircraft, watched the flickering movements of needles on a dozen meter dials. His eyes traveled from one to the other. Then, returning to the bench, he made an alteration to the check calculation in front of him.

The A.O.C. went on staring at the figures and formulae, as though willing them to impart the same knowledge to him. Baffled, he turned away. He was more aware than he had ever been of the limitations of the human brain. It could ordinarily specialize in one thing only: a comparatively minute field. What he knew, he could never impart to Zweig— nor the scientist to him. Nor could they really communicate with each other on their specialties. Only trust each other . . .

Around him, silently, Zweig's assistants checked and checked again. Chatterton watched Powell, the chief scientific assistant, clamber up into the Venger. Now he could see him through the perspex in the bomb-aimer's position.

"Could it be a short?"

Zweig's impatient shrug implied that a *short* was all A.O.C.'s ever knew about electronics.

"Or is the fusing design defective?"

The scientist bridled at that. "Why should it be?"

"It's not impossible."

"Every part's been tested a hundred times."

"Something might still have gone wrong."

"It's *not* defective." Zweig paused. "It was probably wrongly handled."

"I'm quite sure it wasn't! I'm quite sure my crew—"

"We haven't got time for loyalties." Over his shoulder Zweig called, "Rathbone . . . want you a moment." And when the assistant hurried up: "This capacitor, if it's at the low end of its tolerance, might not be sufficient to provide enough decoupling. Then any surge in voltage might send the amplifier into self-oscillation."

"Yes, I see."

"And so this overloading would prevent any control signal from getting through to the slave motor and disengaging the plunger on the detonator." He lifted his head. He shouted out, "Powell! How are you getting on?"

Muffled by the metal, back came Powell's lilting voice, "Nothing . . . not yet."

Chatterton said impatiently, "What's he trying to do in there?"

"Trying to reproduce what's happened in 577. Red lights on . . . when the fuse switches are off."

"And he's had no luck?"

"You heard him. Not yet."

Chatterton walked a few paces away. If Zweig concluded it was only a wiring fault in the indicator circuit, that the bomb was safe, defused, and only the red lights defective . . . would he have the courage to order Falkner to land? Would he . . . dare he . . . risk the chance of Zweig being wrong?

A signal was sent to 577 to try fusing the bomb again, and repeating the defusing sequence. Back came the immediate reply: *Have tried that three times. Same result.*

Suddenly the waiting, the weighing of alternatives, became intolerable to Chatterton.

He took hold of Zweig's arm. "Have you made up your mind?"

"Give me time!"

"There isn't the time to give!"

Zweig ran his hand slowly through his hair. His face in the light looked blanched and lifeless. Chatterton had the impression that the professor was going to decide nothing, to make no decision, to leave it all—on his inadequate scientific training—to him. He would have to say *do this, do that, risk this, risk that* . . . yet without fully understanding *why*.

Almost with a feeling of relief, he heard Zweig say, "So far . . . everything points to the fact that if the red lights show on . . . the bomb is still fused." He half-closed his eyes. "They must be told not to descend below five thousand, five hundred feet. If they do, there is every likelihood that the K6 will detonate. . . ."

Helen Durrant had not yet gone to bed. Had she gone, tired though she was, she would not have slept. It seemed impossible to contain within herself this airy upsurge of relief.

577 was estimating Oakwood around twenty-three thirty . . . that much she had found out from the A.O.C. And she had no intention of allowing the aircraft to slip home unwelcomed. These last days she seemed to have traveled emotionally from pole to pole. Now the only solid, sane thing she could think of would be the sight of John Falkner coming across the tarmac to meet her.

Yet already the crisis was beginning to fade from her mind. When she heard eleven strike, she had to remind herself that this was the hour before the Russian ultimatum expired at midnight.

She listened to the sounds dying away in the Mess. The last footsteps clumping up the stairs to the first-floor rooms, the last few phone calls, the slamming of doors, the restrained little sounds as the W.R.A.F. officer in the next room prepared herself for sleep.

She filled in a few minutes cleaning her cosmetic tray, painting her fingernails, brushing her hair, changing her stockings.

Finally, she switched off her light, opened her bedroom door, closed it softly behind her, and walked down the cor-

ridor. It still smelled a little of tobacco smoke, like the ghost
of a party. Her footsteps echoed, but in a friendly way. The
long windows mirrored her trim figure, handing her reflection over from one to the other all the way down the corridor
till she reached the hall.

The big glass doors were unlocked. Always, they stayed
open, waiting, as the airfield itself waited, for the ever-
expected returns.

The night air was sharp in her throat. She stood for a moment at the top of the steps, blinking her eyes. As far as she
could see, there were no clouds in the sky. It domed above
her—blue-black now, pricked with thousands of stars. She
walked down the steps, feeling her cheeks tingling, hunching
her shoulders a little under the stiff epaulets of her greatcoat.
For a short distance, the lights from the Mess lit her way.
She trod down a shaft of artificial sunshine that reached to
the first half-dead rose bush, then she turned right toward
the dead darkness of the main camp.

No one stirred. A few dead leaves crackled along the concrete of the road. Behind her, one white light burned in the
guardroom, proclaiming its round-the-clock duty. The woods
beyond the football pitch were an interwoven, almost solid
mass against the starlit sky. The same old screech owl
whirred.

She was never afraid of walking alone in the dark, but even
had she been, she could never have been afraid on an R.A.F.
Station. It was like a benign village, where there was much
more fun and much more life than any village in England,
where the only really unpleasant characters were safely
locked up at Air Ministry. And where always someone
watched, someone guarded.

It was quite a way to the taxi track. She hummed to herself in time to her own footfall. She wondered what John
Falkner would say when he saw her. What should *she* say to
him? A picture floated in her mind of the aircraft coming
down, of 577 taxiing, coming to a stop, of John Falkner

climbing out, looking around—and eventually, after a moment, of her stepping out of the shadows.

Another square of light glowed in the M/T Section . . . the Duty Crew's room. The hangar was a huge hunk of blackness. There! Now she could see the whole airfield stretched in front of her. Obstruction lights, lead-in lights. The flarepath was on.

Her heartbeat quickened. They must be due any moment.

She continued past the big Number One Hangar, past the old disused hump of wartime air-raid shelters toward a slight rise which commanded a full view of the sky and the airfield. The blood pounded in her veins. The walk had warmed her so that every part of her seemed wonderfully alive, alert and well. Sometime, she must come out like this and walk in the middle of the night again, just for the sheer joy of it.

But she knew that no walk would ever be the same as this one.

Reaching the place she had decided upon, at the edge of the taxi-track, near to dispersal, she stood scanning the sky. The light wind whipped the loose strands of her hair beneath her cap.

Nothing yet.

She made a little circuit of her place, treading on the wet grass, smelling the peculiar yearning smell of an airfield at night . . . the moist earth, the grass, the faint haunting reek of exhausts and gasoline and kerosene.

Half past eleven. She stood on tiptoe. Nothing! Then ahead, straight out of the southwest, two new stars. Not the delicate icy fragments of the others, but two bold baubles of red and green.

Moving in homeward. Navigation lights!

She wanted to jump up and down with relief.

Nearer! The space between the red light and the green light widened. Now she could just glimpse the winking of the white belly-light. Now they were sweeping above her, a high shrill whistle of engines, their great dark wings blotting out the sky. They were in the circuit. They were home.

There! She swiveled around. They were turning, banking gracefully on the port wing, the red light tipped toward the earth. She waited for 577 to line up with the runway, to lose height. . . .

But instead, the Venger began orbiting in a wide circle of the field. They were coming back again. They could not have been properly lined up before.

"Come on!" she called up, laughing. "Do hurry! It's cold down here!"

She stamped her feet. Overhead again, the belly-light winked. Down went the port wing, banking again, still high in the sky.

Once again along the same circuit, around went the Venger. Back again, banking. Once more, 577 continued full circle—losing no height, maintaining a steady altitude.

She watched for seven circuits. And with each circuit, her alarm and bewilderment increased. Behind her, the station of Oakwood seemed oddly silent. The Control Tower's lights still glowed. What was the matter? Was there radio trouble? Why then didn't they flash him a green? Why didn't someone *do* something? Didn't they *realize* he was trying to land?

The Station seemed deserted, a kind of *Marie Celeste* on which the aircraft had homed. Rapidly, despite the cold feeling of dismay creeping up inside her, she made her mind go through all the logical reasons why the aircraft didn't land. Perhaps they couldn't get the undercarriage down and locked. Perhaps they were using up fuel before attempting a belly-landing.

But no sooner had she begun to fear that explanation, than she heard the high whine of jet engines. She looked up quickly, thinking that by some odd blind spot, she had missed the landing of the Venger. But no! There was 577 now, at the southerly tip of the circuit, turning toward Oakwood.

And then around the taxiing track, from dispersal came

another Venger, its landing lights like antennae, probing the ground ahead.

As the ghostly shape flashed past her, she realized that this was the tanker aircraft. From the end of the runway came the sudden roar of full power. A terrible, bodiless, gray-white visor lifted itself steeply off the earth.

She put her head right back on her shoulders, and stared up into the night. Now two pairs of red and green lights, very close together, floated among the stars.

Not using up fuel, taking on fuel . . . yet the crisis was over, the patrol finished. Blinking back tears of disappointment, anxiety and bewilderment, she half-turned away from the airfield.

And then, immediately, her eye was caught by a bright shaft of light, where before had been darkness. She wiped her eyes with the back of her gloved hand and looked again. There it was! A cold steady blue-white light. She looked around for landmarks, struggling to place it.

A door was open in Number One Hangar. Where the new K6 was temporarily housed.

Immediately, without reasoning why, she began hurrying toward it, taking the short cut over the mud in front of squadron dispersal. She could hear nothing now but the sound of her shoes slushing through the wet, and her own breathing.

Back on the roadway again, she ran up the slope that led to the entrance.

The front of the hangar was visible now. Outside, as she had known it would be, was the A.O.C.'s car. Behind it, several others that she did not recognize. Leaning through the window of the Humber talking to Corporal Kidd were the two S.P.'s guarding the hangar. She saw them straighten up, look behind them, as they heard her coming. And immediately she calmed her footfall, walking the last few yards unhurriedly.

As the diffused light from the side windows of the hangar fell on her face, the S.P.'s recognized her and saluted.

"Ma'am." One of them smiled wryly as if to say, *Fine-how-d'you-do-at-this-hour-of-the-night*. He stepped back and opened a small door in the huge front shutter of the hangar.

Stepping inside from the darkness, she had to pause for a moment, till her eyes adjusted themselves to the brilliant neon light.

Then she stopped by the door—quite still.

In the center of the hangar, yet another Venger stood—bomb doors open. From the K6 just visible in its belly streamed wires to test-bed panels of dials and switches. Men in overalls were working everywhere. At a long bench, Dr. Zweig was standing with the A.O.C. She could see a similar expression clearly illuminated on each of their faces: exasperation, perplexity, mistrust, almost hatred. . . .

It was then that the Air Vice Marshal became aware of the figure by the door. He looked up. As though inviting her to join their nightmare in this dream-enchanted wood, he called out, "That you, Helen? Come in!"

High in the clear sky, for hours a twinkling satellite of red and green had been circling Oakwood.

In the village, a policeman on his beat had identified it to his own satisfaction as an aircraft on exercise. Residents of Avondale who telephoned the R.A.F. to complain of the noise found that no incoming calls were being accepted. Getting the same response, anxiously Valerie McQuade had set off on her bicycle to the Station main gates, where to her fury she had been courteously but firmly refused admittance. Hearing the eternal whine of the jets, and instinctively knowing what it was, Jean Halloran lay tense and rigid on her bed, staring dry-eyed up at the ceiling. Two hundred yards away, Diana Beauchamp was being told for the sixth time by P.B.X. that all Operations numbers were engaged. From the window by the telephone, she could see the runway—lit and waiting.

Yet the aircraft did not come down. And there seemed to be tremendous activity down Trenchard Street. The sound of trucks and cars was continuous. For that time of night, the airdrome seemed unnaturally alive.

And alight, too. Though it was hidden from her eyes, a slit of acid-bright neon spilt from the main hangar. Yellow oblongs showed from the workshop. The whole of the Operations Building glowed. But this gala of illumination was not a welcome but a warning—the flashing *keep-aways* of a lighthouse.

An infected outcast to be kept at a distance, a giant white leper in the night, 577 whistled around and around its own forbidden airfield.

Below, Zweig and his team worked feverishly to find out the cause of the trouble. In the shadowless, echoing atmosphere around the second K6, tempers flared. Scientists in white coats desperately tried test after test, working through each circuit in succession, checking the effects of varying voltages, temperature and vibration.

Nothing, no result.

There was a curious sweaty whiteness over Zweig's face as he pored over the circuit diagrams. Again and again, the phone rang out for him—

What was the matter?

How much longer?

He knew that aircraft couldn't stay up there forever?

Had he any clue at all?

"We're coming to the idea"—his voice to the A.O.C. sounded breathless—"that the slave motor which disengages the plunger has failed in the live position . . . which leaves the altimeter detonating device still connected to the bomb. The cause looks like a poor capacitor."

"What could they do about it then?"

"We're not by any means certain that's the trouble," Zweig snapped back. "But if it *is,* they can do nothing."

The A.O.C. said grimly, "*Something's* got to be worked out! And *soon!*"

Chatterton had been continually harried by the C-in-C. The C-in-C had been harried by Air Chief Marshal Duggane. Duggane—caught in the trap of his own ambitions—had been harried by the Army and the Navy at yet another Cabinet Meeting in that same room at Downing Street.

All down Whitehall, lights blazed—giving unheeded evidence of this new silent crisis that threatened the sleeping nation. In a hundred places, men's brains struggled to avert a calamity, the mechanism of which they had themselves devised.

And as they worked—the clock ticked.

One hour passed. Then another, and still *nothing yet* was the only answer on the Oakwood scrambler. In high political and military circles, the usual blind faith in scientists was waning. The possible causes of the bomb's behavior became less and less discussed.

Finally the Prime Minister said, "We can give them no more time."

"Sir," Duggane pleaded, "just a little longer! I'm sure—"

"The country cannot be subjected to this horror hanging above them. We must get it away! Get rid of it!"

"But the consequences would be considerable."

"They would be far more considerable if it stays where it is!"

Duggane said nothing. In its own way, this was the nemesis of an Air Chief Marshal.

"Immediately, Duggane! Oakwood must be told immediately!"

Around that airdrome, half an hour later, the whistling was still going on. Softly, reproachfully, patiently—as the five men in the Venger awaited their orders.

Standing inside the greeny glow of the Control Tower, momentarily Helen closed her eyes as she listened to it, an endless reminder of John Falkner's nearness and farness. This place—which should have resounded long ago with cheerful instructions for him to land—was quiet and subdued. Group Captain Lucey stood over by the wide glass windows, looking out at the pattern of the flarepath. The W.R.A.F. watch-keeper sat wide-eyed at her desk. In the center was the A.O.C., his legs slightly apart, his great bull-jaw projecting over his chest.

The Flying Controller spoke into his microphone. "577! Blue Jay calling 577!"

Blue Jay! Now the sound was incongruous. Small, feathered, pretty, puny. Six months earlier, when Group had decided to give all their airdromes bird names as call signs, it had seemed so appropriate. She could remember other suggestions of senior officers at the conference . . . Cuckoo for Cuckfield, Pippit for Penstone.

"577 . . . this is Blue Jay. Are you receiving me?"

Like statues under water in this sea-like light, they waited silently for an answer.

"Go ahead."

John Falkner's voice suddenly filled the room. From the loudspeaker near the ceiling, it came blaring out—clear and strong and abundant with life. He seemed closer than any-one here; and yet he was unreachable. She felt a lump come up in her throat, blinked quickly to keep the tears away. This was so like stories of men trapped in submarines; of divers tapping the hull to communicate with them, and hearing the tapping back. Already, it seemed, he was in some other world than theirs.

"577, I have a message for you."

A sudden eager note, the voice louder than ever: "Have they had any joy?"

"Not yet."

Efficient again now, unemotional, undismayed: "577 stand-ing by for your message."

Chatterton walked across the room, and took over the microphone.

"577 . . . this is Blue Jay. I have your orders. Proceed to Jettison Area X. Repeat . . . X."

"Jettison Area X." A pause. "Stand by . . . Blue Jay. We're checking the book for its location."

"Blue Jay standing by."

There was a full minute's silence, broken only by the sound of the aircraft outside. Then: "Roger, Blue Jay. Jettison Area X located."

"577 . . . you are to jettison immediately on arrival."

"577 understands jettison immediately on arrival. 577 standing by."

There was a pause. Then: "577 from Blue Jay, your safety height remains unchanged."

"577 understands safety height remains unchanged."

"577 . . . confirm you are fully serviceable."

"Fully serviceable, except—" A long pause. "Number Four Engine's using oil. But we've got enough for X and return."

"Roger . . . good . . . proceed immediately then. Straight there, straight back. The weather will be sent to you."

"Understood."

Echo and counter-echo vibrated around the hushed Flying Control. The A.O.C.'s voice and John Falkner's from the loudspeaker merged together like swirling waves.

"Send a signal . . . operation complete."

"Will do." A second's pause in which the whine of the jet engines swelled above their heads. "577 climbing."

"Good luck, Falkner!"

"Thank you, sir."

A moment of human recognition between Squadron Leader and Air Vice Marshal—the only one allowed. Then the loudspeaker held no more trace of him. The figures in the Control Tower remained as they were. The Group Captain still stared out of the window, now scanning the sky to catch the last glimpse of the Venger's lights. Then he looked away, as though they had already disappeared. Only the sound of the jets remained awhile. Then that too faded. The Controller walked over to the Movements Board, and picked up the chalk. The A.O.C. leaned over to say something to Group Captain Lucey.

And then suddenly, unexpectedly, his voice again . . . faintly as though from high up and from far away: "577 at altitude. Setting course . . ."

A Yorkshire engine driver called Mr. Jackson wiped the sweat off his flushed forehead, and peered through the left-hand port. The milk train was laboring up the long straight stretch leading up the East Riding incline. Through the foggy darkness, right in the distance he saw a twinkling red light.

"Looks like the Ecclestone signal, Joe," he said. "Against us!"

"Ugh!" said his fireman. "Tck!"

Behind them, the forty old trucks and the guards van clanged and clattered along the rails. They were running late; this fresh hold-up was the last straw. But as he blinked his eyes at it with a hating ferocity, the red signal moved far faster than their miserable closing speed warranted. It appeared to climb toward the smudgy moon. A little white light was now added on to it.

"Either the Ecclestone's turned into a ruddy firework," said Jackson. "Or 'tisn't the Ecclestone, after all!"

"Tck!"

"What the hell is it?" He craned his neck forward to get a little nearer, felt the sting of fog and smoke in his eyes. "Bloody star?" He watched it growing fainter. "Got it, Joe . . . an airplane!"

"Ugh!"

Mr. Jackson watched the tiny spark with envious watering eyes. Ahead of him, the grimy funnel chuffed furiously. He could hear and feel the driving wheels slipping and skidding on the icy rails. Up there, everything was fast and clean and sweet. It was only down here, with milk churns banging behind you, and the dark dampness of early morning and the smoke off bad coal choking your lungs, crawling along at five miles an hour, late and tired, that there *were* any troubles.

The future, that's what was up there; while down here, he slaved in a very dirty past.

"Going . . . going," he said of that tiny red future, fast disappearing to the north. "Gone!"

From 60,000 feet, no trace of Mr. Jackson or his engine could be seen. Only bright splodges of towns under the fog, and the peaks of mountains sticking up into the moonlight like volcanic islands. As he looked down at them, Falkner rubbed his eyes. He was dead tired. His whole brain seemed to have sunk into a muzzy haze. Down there *could* be some dream landscape; a kind of man-in-the-moon world, his sense of unreality was so increased.

"You must be shagged out."

Falkner turned his head away from the moonshine outside, and saw the red rims around his Second Pilot's eyes. "You don't look exactly fresh yourself."

"I'm all right."

"If you lie back in your seat . . . you might get some shut-eye."

"No . . . I'm not sleepy."

"Come on!"

"I feel fine."

Falkner gave Beauchamp a quick smile. In the past few hours his opinion of the Flying Officer had begun to change. As things got worse, Beauchamp's attitude and morale had got better. When the bomb would not defuse, and Pinkney had got a bit hot under collar, Beauchamp had not turned a hair. He had even, in that tense atmosphere, managed a joke —which, though not very good, had brought a sane slant on a difficult and highly charged situation.

The Venger hummed on northward. Slowly, the cloud below her thinned. A brief glow suddenly came up well over to port that Beauchamp identified as Edinburgh. Not that he could miss it: the close-packed glitter of the city, the thinning of clustered lights down the Firth to the sea. Then, looking at his watch, he saw it was on the hour, and leaned forward yet again for the Engineer's Log.

"Don't worry . . . I'll do that!"

The Flying Officer turned around and gave Falkner a look. One that Falkner had recognized immediately after eighteen years of flying. Appraising, unconsciously appealing . . . assessing the state of the captain's mind. Beauchamp was looking into the Squadron Leader's eyes for all the answers to his unasked questions.

Is he worried?

What about the oil situation?

Are we going to make it?

What went wrong?

Is anything else going to happen?

Falkner had neither grinned in reassurance, nor yawned in feigned nonchalance. He had met his eyes, let the younger man stare till he got what he wanted.

The look had vanished. If he isn't worried, why on earth should I be?—that was Beauchamp's reaction. Reassured, he had looked away. Falkner's trained eyes had reflected back at him nothing but equanimity. It was one of the disciplines of leadership—this all-radiating calmness, whatever the situation —that Beauchamp himself would one day learn.

"Why not have some shut-eye, Dick . . . while you can?"

"No, thanks."

Falkner had already started on the Engineer's Log. His eyes swept over the instruments from left to right—but none of the needles moved. All those familiar faces stared back at him: well behaved and wearing exactly the right expression. Jet Pipe Temperatures—all 590°C. Oil Pressures—all 55. Oil Temperatures—all 78°C. They had changed very little throughout the hours. Great blocks of figures in the log were all identical.

Fuel gauges, he had got to those now. All the tanks were

showing reasonably full—thanks to the second refueling operation, completed over Oakwood; more tricky than in daytime, with the light on the streaming drogue a will-o'-the-wisp dancing before 577's nose probe.

Now he came to the oil contents. Number Four was using if anything rather more than before.

He was not exactly worried. Jettison Area X—a vast sheet of Arctic Sea in Latitude 73 North, Longitude 8 East, three hundred miles from any land—was less than two hours away. And once they were rid of the weight of K6, he didn't mind going onto three engines, if necessary.

All the same, he was a little uneasy. He had seriously considered stopping Number Four, and starting it up again when it was needed. He had not done so, lest when he had wanted the engine, he wouldn't be able to get it going. Such things did happen not infrequently on the re-light system, and he wasn't prepared to take the chance. To maintain the safety height of 55,000 feet, he would need all four engines. . . .

With his pencil, he wrote the reading down, outwardly dispassionate: 2¼ gallons. There was still over four hours' life in that engine yet.

Then he put the Engineer's Log back in place, and sat back.

It was times like this, sitting as he was now in the absolute calm of a cold northern night, that small chinks of thought escaped the disciplined blinkers of his mind to trouble him.

Had Pinkney done the defusing sequence wrong? No . . . he was sure he hadn't . . . he'd back Pinkney's accuracy anywhere. Was the fuse duff? There'd be a hollow laugh if the thing didn't go off anyway—just slid into the Arctic like a dead fish. Damned good job if it did, though. How much radiation would just the jettisoning of the thing hurl into the earth's atmosphere for how many years? How much disease how much suffering, how many cases of . . .

Resolutely, he closed the blinkers tightly over his mind. Once more he contained his imagination within the armor of his Air Force loyalty and obedience. He had been given an order: he obeyed that order. His was the loneliness of command *here*. The crew must automatically look to him. But behind Falkner, absolving him morally, spiritually, and politically, were Group Command, Air Ministry, the Government, the combined conscience of the people of Great Britain.

He opened and closed his eyes hard three or four times to get the blood moving over his face. Glancing to his right, he saw that Beauchamp, after all, was asleep. He lay huddled in his seat, his left cheek against the head-rest. His mouth was slightly pouted, and his lips looked red and child-like.

Right now, Falkner envied his second pilot three things: his youth, his ability to be reassured into unconsciousness— and his subordinate position.

He heard a step behind his seat. Halloran's voice said, "Shetlands over to port, Skipper. New course . . . 021."

Falkner set it up on the grid-ring of the compass. "Can you see 'em?"

"Just. Port beam."

He looked. A tiny hump ringed by surf as white as snow. "Stormy."

"Yep. Southwesterly gale." He saw the sleeping Beauchamp. "Dick looks nice and comfortable."

"Are we doing all right?"

"Doing fine. Thirty-knot tail wind."

"E.T.A.?"

"Three hundred fifty-nine."

"*Really* moving!" Falkner smiled. "Thank God! Helluva way north, isn't it?"

"Yep. Wonder they didn't make it the North Pole . . . while they were about it."

"Maybe thought we'd knock the earth off its axis!"

"Could be." Halloran grinned. Then softly, after a pause: "Wonder what it *will* do, though?"

Falkner said evenly, "We'll make a big bang. A bigger

bang than ones we've made before. That's all. Only this time there won't be anyone but us to hear it."

"Making damned sure we get high enough. Fifty-five thousand feet!" He turned his eyes upward. "They must be expecting a godalmighty crump."

"I'm keeping her at sixty thousand . . . just in case."

"Good show! Never did like getting too close to the ones that bang. I always get the kids to light the rockets on November Fifth. Play safe! That's me!"

"Ever been into the Arctic before, Mick?"

"Nope. Nor wanted to."

"Nor me." Falkner yawned. "How're Terry and Peter?"

"Terry's out for the count. Head on the table. Pete's on the W/T. Thinks they may change their minds again, and tell us to drop it on Moscow . . . while we're about it."

Falkner smiled dutifully. "They won't like wasting the tax-payer's money . . . certainly."

"No election coming up . . . so that won't matter so much." Halloran leaned forward, propping one knee on Falkner's seat and resting his hand on it. "There's one compensation in all this, you know."

"What's that?"

"Keep thinking of the flap there'll be down there . . . Group, Command, Air Ministry. And then a *beautiful* smile spreads over my face."

"*Bet* there is! Can-tossing from one to the other! Someone up the creek without a paddle."

"Oh," Halloran grinned. "That's probably *us*, come to that!" He shook his head ruefully. Without smiling, he said, "It's bound to contaminate the air quite a bit, isn't it? I wonder what the effect *will* be?"

"Circular westerlies around the Pole . . . the prevailing winds. That'll keep the stuff isolated to a certain extent. . . ." Then: "Any more tea?"

"No tea. Plenty of water, though. And stacks of sandwiches."

"No, thanks."

"Here! Have an acid drop! I've got some somewhere." Halloran felt in his trouser pocket and produced a cellophane bag. "Got them weeks ago for the boys. Must have forgotten them. Found them in my brief case." He tasted one himself. "Not too bad." He handed the bag over.

"Thanks."

"They're a bit sticky, you know. But they'll liven your mouth up."

They sucked and chewed companionably, not bothering to talk. It was so steady within the aircraft that they might have been on the ground. Below them, thin clouds like strands of pale sand in the moonlight came out of nowhere ahead and floated noiselessly past. Outside, their own white paint had taken on a ghostly iridescent tinge. Tiny tinkles of frost, like the spangles on a party frock, glittered and flashed on the windscreen.

Halloran said, "Certainly gone places this trip . . . Cyprus, Black Sea, Europe, Arctic Ocean . . ."

"Your log must look like something out of Jules Verne."

"So it does. Around the world in twenty-four hours!" He paused. "Sounds all wrong. *Too* quick!"

"Or the world's too small." Falkner smiled faintly. "Especially now."

"You can say that again!" Mick jerked his thumb over his shoulder. "Especially with one of these things tucked underneath your arm! Bit hard now to live by the old Air Force maxim regarding sewage disposal on other people's doorsteps. They're all too close! Or too well watched!"

"Well," Falkner stretched, "thank God there's still the Arctic!" He straightened, leaned forward and tapped the instruments. "And so long as the aircraft's going all right . . . fair enough!"

There was a pause between them. All the time, it was as though antennae, not of fear but of sympathy, were stretching out of Halloran's mind toward Falkner's. Falkner could feel them. He saw, too, the look on the navigator's face, as he asked casually, "Suppose the damn thing *will* jettison?"

"Hope so, Mick."

"Hope so too! Be a hollow laugh . . . if we have that thing stuck up our arse. For ever and ever . . . Amen!"

"We'll shake it off somehow!"

"Good." Halloran paused. "And the oil? Number Four bearing up?"

"Enough for a good many hours yet." Falkner crunched his sweet noisily. "And it'll make a nice difference to our weight when the bomb's off!"

"Sure."

"And the weather forecast's clear in the area."

"Fine. We'll get a ringside seat."

They drifted back into silence.

Halloran pushed the bag forward. "Want another?"

"No, thanks."

Falkner pushed back his sleeve, looked at his wrist watch. Another forty minutes and they would be in the jettison area. Seeing the gesture, Halloran said immediately, "Shall I wake Terry?"

"I reckon. Might as well get all set."

Halloran smiled, looked up toward the dark roof of the Venger. "Our big moment, eh?"

And then, resting his hand momentarily on Falkner's shoulder, he moved his big body to the back, and his boots thumped down the rungs.

Five minutes later, everyone in the aircraft was awake and alert. From the right-hand seat, Beauchamp was looking out into the moon-filled night. Behind, in the crew compartment, Loran was still giving Halloran position lines, for which he was grateful. On the table now, instead of the usual Mercator map with its oblong blocks of latitude and longitude—quite useful in these regions—was the bicycle-wheel type of projection called "Zenithal equidistant," the lines of longitude radiating from the pole like spokes. McQuade sat at the wireless, listening to the weather at faraway places, while Pinkney watched the endless revolving time base of the H2S radar.

The minutes passed. Now that they were getting close to the area, nobody spoke. Their bodies were quickened by some magic energizing fluid injected into their blood by the excitement of this moment. They were more awake than when they had taken off, over twenty-four hours ago.

For some time past, Pinkney's thoughts had been concerned with wondering what was happening in Number Six Portal Street, whether his five children were all right and if they were alseep. Now he passed his plump hand over his slightly damp forehead, mindful that the time was rapidly approaching when he would be taking the leading role. Concentrating on the green radar screen, there was nothing there to occupy him, even on the hundred-mile scale.

And then suddenly, right at the top, he saw a minute little pip like a scratch on the screen.

This pip was followed by others. Every time the time base swung around this part of the screen, they were illuminated, became larger, moved down toward the center.

"Skipper . . . radar here!"

"Go ahead!"

"Getting echoes . . . eighty miles ahead. Lots of them!"

"Strong ones?"

"Fairly strong . . . yes!"

"Any idea what they might be?"

"Difficult to tell, Skipper."

Halloran interrupted to say, "Probably icebergs. Been wondering when they were going to turn up. Latitude's 72 North."

It was generally agreed that they would be icebergs. Identified thus, Pinkney lost a certain amount of interest in them, as they came nearer and nearer toward the center of the screen. He looked at his watch: 0352.

Time to go forward. E.T.A. was in another seven minutes. Handing over the radar to Halloran, he pointed out the blips. The navigator whistled when he saw them. "Phew! Pretty big, eh?"

There was a great spiny mass of them now—all around fifty miles away.

"Wonder why they're all together like that, Pete?"

But Pinkney was too occupied in getting ready to go forward. He took up his torch, groped his way into the bombaimer's compartment. The two red lights, like bloodshot eyes, stared at him malignantly.

Kneeling down at the panel, he began to unfasten the wire around the Jettison Lever.

Over the intercom, he reported, "All set, Skipper."

"Roger, Pete. Slowing down now. Four more minutes to go."

Pinkney sat back on his heels. One of the metal strips along the heating pipes was vibrating—ever so slightly. He could hear its tambourine tinkling above the hum of the jets. It was always worst—waiting. Especially now. No opposition—no flak, no night fighters, no searchlights. Yet somehow this was far worse than any raid over the Ruhr. Of course, there was no reason why the jettison *shouldn't* work perfectly satisfactorily. It was just that—

"Skipper, these blips. Still dead ahead. Looks as though we'll be dropping the thing on top of 'em."

Halloran's voice on the R/T. Pinkney's hand was already on the Jettison Lever. Now he frowned with impatience.

Falkner's voice now: "Should do icebergs a bit of good . . . shouldn't it?"

"Mmm . . . maybe."

A whole minute's pause. Then: "Opening bomb doors."

"Roger, Skipper."

The high hydraulic whine of the motor drowned all other noise around him.

"Bomb doors open. Stand by to jettison."

"Standing by."

Throughout the Venger now, there was a stillness as

though everyone was holding his breath. Even the aircraft seemed to feel the tenseness. The jets had gone lower. The whole of the ten and a half miles of freezing air down to the cloud-flaked moonlit sea—which Pinkney could see through the clear-vision panel—appeared to have crystallized for this one moment. . . .

And then suddenly, just before he pulled the lever, Pinkney saw the night beneath him criss-crossed by pale illuminated fingers, moving up and down from the horizon to the stars.

For seconds, he gawped at them—disbelieving his eyes. Then frantically he called out, "Christ . . . *searchlights!*"

"Yep . . . I've seen 'em! Hang on! Don't drop anything, for God's sake . . ."

Tiny gray shapes could be seen now, each towing a white wake. "Ships . . . Skipper! Two long lines of them. Got lights on, too!"

"Get onto V.H.F., Dick . . . they may be calling us! And close the bomb doors!"

Again the hydraulic motor howled out. The jets went up to full power. Pinkney felt the G urge pressing him down on the floor as the Venger swung violently over to port.

"Skipper," he called out furiously, "who are they? What the hell are they doing up here?"

Lieutenant Mikhailovitch, Officer of the Watch on the destroyer-minesweeper *Potemkin,* wiped the spray off his binoculars and tried to focus them once more on that red-and-green spot in the sky. He had been watching it for some time past, ever since the radar had reported it. If only this damned open bridge would keep the spume off! If only the damned deck would stay level just for one instant!

Leading the port formation, the *Potemkin* was bucking and rolling, doused every few minutes by an ice-cold splatter of green sea. On the starboard, the larger and newer *Ziakov* was more fortunate, was riding the swell more steadily. Behind each of them, in varying degrees of roll and pitch, forty-one destroyers, their gray paint made paler by the moonlight, were following their leader's line astern on a dancing, tossing southerly course.

Ah, there it was! Momentarily Mikhailovitch had managed to focus on it. An aircraft . . . yes, of course. The type . . . certainly a jet. He could see the long white trail scintillating like a snail's track across the sky. It might, of course, be a bomber as the Commander had suspected. But why then had it got its lights on? And why now, instead of shadowing, was it going back the way it came—the lights all the time getting fainter and fainter?

He heard the *click* of the searchlights going off forward of the funnels. Over on the right, the bright triangle of the *Ziakov's* searchlights went out, too. Mikhailovitch gave a grunt of satisfaction. At least now they were all satisfied that this aircraft meant no harm.

He spoke to the Commander, now up on the bridge with him and, receiving his permission, went aft to the radar cabin. Inside, there was still excitement. The unknown aircraft had retreated a hundred miles away, was circling around and around.

For a while, the Lieutenant's bright black eyes watched the rotating green dot. Then he looked away, and said to the Commander, "Lost."

The Commander shrugged his shoulders. A discussion followed. The Lieutenant made his opinions known regarding this speck that had momentarily caused panic-stations to the Archangel Destroyer Squadron on Arctic maneuvers. A civil aircraft on the Polar Route. Certainly in trouble. The nationality, of course, it was impossible to know. . . .

Six minutes later, speaking Russian very slowly and clearly, Lieutenant Mikhailovitch was sending sounds across the ether on a wavelength of 118.1 megacycles which part of the world would understand to mean, *Your position 72 North, 8*

East. If you listen out on the International Distress Frequency 500 K.C.'s we will . . .

Up in the Venger, Beauchamp almost had his ears blown off.

"Hell of a racket on the V.H.F.," he reported. "Russian . . . I reckon. Sounds as though they're swearing at us!"

But Falkner did not hear him. He was already calling out over the intercom: "McQuade . . . send a signal . . . in code. Emergency priority . . . *Jettison Area X contains units of the Russian Fleet. Where shall we go now?*"

577 circled clockwise over the Arctic Sea.

Falkner watched the port wing-tip light buzzing like a busy red bee from Dubhe to Benetnasch, from Vega to Deneb, as though trying to pollinate their paleness. He tried not to think of the situation in Number Four Engine. The emergency now was graver than ever before. At least, it was for the crew. He had warned Control of the oil crisis.

Wait . . . stand-by had been his answer.

He knew what would be happening. They would be trying desperately to find an area of at least 40,000 square miles— free from human life, and close enough to his position.

He had to trust them to find one. Now, it seemed to him, all decisions were out of his hands.

He was used to dealing with the snowball, that collection of tiny troublesome particles that grew quietly into an avalanche for airmen. Stamp on it straightaway! Break it up! Or if that was impossible, be cautious, go back. But this one was different. His advance had been dictated by orders from the ground, his retreat now was cut off. Stacked hard with icy difficulties, already he could hear this avalanche thundering down the mountainside toward them.

"Anything yet, Terry?"

"Nothing, Skipper."

For the last half-hour throughout the Venger it had been unnaturally quiet. Hardly a word had been spoken. Only the four jets endlessly gave out their symphony of shrill mechanical music as a permanent reminder of the thought uppermost in all their minds. Not long now, and one of those jets would have to be shut down. On three engines, their altitude at this weight would inevitably sink to 40,000 feet— well below the safety height for dropping the bomb. And then, wherever the jettison area, they would still not be able to save themselves.

"Anything yet, Terry?"

"Nothing, Skipper."

Around them, the Arctic night had flowered golden in all the fullness of its icy glory. The moon now was overhead. From its round fatness poured a blizzard of moonflakes, making everything they fell on yellow and luminous, transformed into something unreal and transparent. The instrument lights were diluted by the moon's thin strength. On the body of the Venger itself, the massive white wings shone like dragonfly gossamer. And the faces of the crew became pale shades in limbo—flesh and blood no longer, but a material that could almost be seen through, of the same consistency and make-up as the milky moonlit air.

"Skipper!"

"Go ahead!"

"Message . . . proceed 68 North, 05 West and jettison."

"How far?"

"Only four hundred miles . . . thank Christ!" It was Halloran's voice on the intercom now. " New course . . . 221."

"That's better!" Falkner turned the aircraft immediately. "221 it is!"

Now that they were under definite orders again, their spirits rose. They could see a horizon at last. As they flew onward, again conversation started spasmodically on the intercom. Halloran could be heard identifying the symptoms now apparent in his right hand as "log-keeper's cramp." Up to the flight deck were passed the last of the stale sandwiches and a mug of water.

"Estimate five hundred thirty-one."

The moon seemed to have lost its powers of transformation. To Falkner, now it had a certain aimless cheerfulness. He had seen it in many roles: over the Mediterranean as a burning ship; twice over the target as an airplane on fire; many times like a sliver of fingernail or a Punch in a horn-shaped hat. At present it looked like nothing more than a yellow balloon, tagged on behind them by a long piece of string.

He looked at his watch. Twenty minutes gone already.

"Not long now." Beauchamp beside him was being determinedly cheerful. But inside himself, Falkner could feel the suspense building up. Every second, he seemed conscious of the oil dripping away, relentlessly, inevitably . . . like life ebbing away. His mouth felt dry, and in his body there was a gnawing ache. Like being sick. He was breathing faster, too; could feel the pounding of his heart. There was a fierce urge inside him to get rid of this burden he was carrying—before it thrust them all down. The disappointment of Jettison Area X had made him wary, fearful of what now he would find. A shiver went through him every time the radar spoke.

His mind started wandering again. Down forbidden avenues. Disciplined as always, he brought it back under control. This area will be all right, he kept on saying to himself. No trouble at all. It'll be quite all right.

"Skipper . . ."

Pinkney's voice. He held his breath. "Yes?"

"McQuade's got a message."

"Yes?"

"Weather in the area . . . clear."

He could have laughed. The air burst out of his lungs in relief. "Good!"

More minutes went by. It was five fifteen. Now that the zero hour approached, the conversation had again died down. Falkner was just about to order preparations for the jettison operation when he heard Pinkney's voice cry out suddenly from the radar: "Skipper!"

The note gave him the clue. There was no need for Pinkney to go on. "Blips?"

"Yes, Skipper."

"Many?"

"Many . . . *very* many! Tiny ones, though."

"Where?"

"Twenty-nine miles ahead . . . a few to starboard."

"First time you've seen 'em?"

"That's right."

"Must be *very* small."

"Oh yes, Skipper." A pause. Then—louder-voiced, determinedly confident: "Too small for ships."

Falkner was thinking, Surely they can't be. Not again! And all the time, loud and strong, his heart thumped out the same rhythm through his body: *Surely it's not true, it's not.* . . .

"Lights!" Beside him, Beauchamp was shouting. "Christ, lights . . . look at 'em. Skipper! *Look at 'em!*"

He turned his eyes to where the Second Pilot was pointing.

He saw them—dotted all over the sea, bobbing up and down, tiny yellow prickles, as though someone had spread pepper over the moonlit calm of the sea. North, south, east, west—they were *everywhere*. They would have come, he knew, from many lands: from Norway, Greenland, Iceland, from Ireland, England and Scotland, led there by the wandering shoals of plaice and cod.

"Yes," he said, "I can see." He paused. "Fishing trawlers! Hundreds!" He picked up his microphone. "McQuade . . . send another message . . . S.O.S. priority . . . *send alternate jettison area immediately. Otherwise* . . ."

Turning the selector box of the intercom to the W/T position, Falkner listened to McQuade's Morse, as in unemotional dots and dashes their story went out on the ether. "Dit-

dit-dit . . . dah-dah-dah . . . dit-dit-dit. S.O.S. . . . S.O.S. . . . Save Our Souls . . . *save our souls.*

And then the answer: *Stand by . . . wait.*

Again, in obedience, around they went. The long hand of the instrument panel clock struck off the seconds. Each one was a drop of erosive acid, eating away at the metal of 577. On the hour, as usual, Beauchamp filled up the Engineer's Log. But he said nothing. He made no mention this time of the oil situation in Number Four Engine.

Falkner looked out of the perspex beside him, keeping his eyes on the endless lights below. To his tired brain there was something hypnotic in those patternless sparks: swelling sometimes, diminishing again as they rode the crest and trough of the waves. Horizonless down there, where black sky merged with blacker sea, they might have been another constellation in a completely different universe to his own.

Certainly he had had no message to remind him that he was part of this world. Nothing since the stand-by signal; only a stunned silence from Oakwood. His body ached with sitting in the same position for so long. It was hours since he had eaten. Not that he was hungry. He felt only a curious light-headedness. A detached feeling of elevation—as once he had felt at the height of a heavy raid over Berlin, and once at school, when he'd gashed his hand and lost a lot of blood. For the present, he was conscious neither of the bomb, nor of how to get rid of it. No image of what was going on back at Oakwood disturbed him . . . no feeling for himself nor for his crew. Only detachment, a sense of impending revelation, a heightened perception of all things around him.

The sound of the jets whistled out over the Arctic night, the starlight caught their wings. But always, his eyes went back to those lights.

He counted them again: *ninety-four, ninety-five, ninety-six, ninety-seven* . . . Each one as he counted it seemed to expand and fill his eyes, and the counting made him drowsy, like counting sheep. In the clear air, the Venger moved only slightly, but it was a gentle rocking, a lullaby motion. All around, darkness cradled him. It was as if he was dozing off in black powdery snow. Lifting his eyes slowly, heavily, as though his lids were weighted, he looked through the perspex at the true stars above his head. But apart from their brittle flicker, they were indistinguishable from the lights beneath. And sinking deeper into unreality, he was not sure where he was, whether the sea lay above him or below. Persistently sucking him down into some dark mad funnel came the conviction that they had dropped the bomb, that reprisals had followed, that there was nowhere for them to return to, that the world was burned out. He was looking down—immensely slowly, not caring much—to see which of those burning stars had once been his world.

He had deliberately to steel himself to take his eyes away from the torches below. Clenching his teeth, he tore his mind out of this defeated woolly half-consciousness. On the instrument panel, just above the throttle box, a phosphorescent needle had started to move downward—anti-clockwise around a tiny dial.

The oil pressure was dropping on Number Four Engine.

"Still nothing from Control, Skipper." He was suddenly conscious of Pinkney's voice beside him. "They'll have to get a move on, won't they?" He heard the faint fraying edges of panic, and glancing up, saw Pinkney's face: controlled still, but lined and now very old.

"Give them time."

Time? *Time?* There was no more time to give! Now in his own comfortable words, meant as morale-raisers, he heard an unnatural note, a ring high, angry, fearful. A red tide was rising inside him like the crisis of some illness. His mind had swung wide awake. Triggered off by Pinkney's voice, Pinkney's face—panic consumed him.

"Get me a sandwich, eh?"

Just to get rid of him! Just to stop seeing his own face—the leader's face—mirrored in those round trusting black eyes!

And when Pinkney had clumped backward, deliberately now he kept the Venger straight and level—northward, away from the lights below.

He'd find some vast black space and drop it. He couldn't wait for any jettison area now. Nobody would blame him. Orders had got him into this. Now there were apparently no more orders forthcoming. It wouldn't be his fault if the area where it exploded wasn't big enough for human safety, if a number of people were killed, and the winds took the noxious dust elsewhere. Forty thousand square miles—where could you find an uninhabited strip of the world *that* size?

A black space—that's all he wanted.

And yet, wherever he went, lights came up in his path. Lights ahead, lights to port, lights to starboard, lights below him and above him. He was haunted by lights. Now they were at him again—singly and in pale clusters—hypnotizing him.

A shower of sparklers, the light of forty torches, a few old bicycle lamps, nothing of value. They were only lights laid out like a runway. They could have been the lead-in lights. Or target lights—for bombing practice.

That's what they were! For bombing practice. Where should he drop it? Bang in the middle? Or on that collection there? Of course they would *all* go out. But what were a few odd lights?

He'd dropped bombs on lights before. On tiny lights and huge lights, on fires and on marker flares.

Then it was them or us. And now what was the difference? His eyes caught the oil-pressure needle, down ten pounds more. A red-hot whirlwind roared in his mind, sweeping up fantastic images from its half-consciousness. His duty was to his crew, wasn't it? He had no responsibility for those unseen lives down there.

It was *them* or *us*.

Drop it while you can—it was as if someone had said it aloud in the aircraft. In another few minutes, you won't be able to—the engines seemed to shriek it, his own blood thundered it out.

Now he was clutching hard on the control column. He could feel sweat trickle down inside his helmet. Struggling up, as though through deep water to consciousness, he forced himself just to look at the readings of his instruments, clinging on to the discipline of his life.

And then, back to those lights. . . .

Aboard each, there would be a crew, as his up here, navigating their way through another element, struggling now with bitter cold and a heavy sea. All over the world there would be clusters of lights like these, lit by warm human hands. From this height, London would look like some vast star, all her lamps coagulated into one immense illumination. Fly over New York or Peking, Berlin or Paris, Rome or Moscow—it would be the same. Cities were stars of the first magnitude, towns second magnitude, villages third magnitude. Yet even the single pricks of light—a farm, a lighthouse, a ship—could still be seen up here.

Emerging as though from a nightmare, now he felt calm and tired. He knew that wherever he flew, there would be lights—from cities, towns, dwellings, ships. The world was too small for the K6. Shrunk by speed, the world was no larger than a village—a village of stars.

"Skipper . . ."

Beauchamp was speaking to him.

"Yes, Dick?"

"Oil pressure on Number Four. It's twenty pounds."

The boy's voice was quite unemotional, cool and collected. All he meant was . . . hadn't we better stop it now? Otherwise it would blow up, probably damage Number Three. Not the least hint of panic; no suggestion of *this-is-our-last-chance-to-drop-it*. Not a thought like that, it was obvious from his face, had crossed Beauchamp's mind.

Falkner had a guilty feeling that his Second Pilot might not be so lacking in leadership, after all. Pulling himself up, he slipped into the automatic role of routine.

He called out, "Closing throttle!"

The r.p.m. sagged back on the indicator. Reaching forward, he closed the H.P. cock, and then switched off the L.P. cock.

He said to Beauchamp, "Turn off the booster pump!"

"Booster pump off. Fuel tank off."

That was all. A stranger, coming up forward, would not have noticed—there were so few indications—that 577 was now flying on three engines. But gradually, the speed started dropping. At 60,000 feet, now the Venger was wallowing. The altimeter began unwinding.

55,000 feet . . . 50,000 feet . . . 48,000 feet, still she was uneasy, flopping slightly, nose up and vibrating. The controls seemed mushy and sluggish. Down and down she went, the needle moving all the time anti-clockwise, further toward the sea.

Till eventually Falkner was satisfied she had found her level. He sent another signal to Oakwood: *577 now on three engines. Can maintain 41,000 feet.*

Far out on the eastern horizon, the night sky now was washed by white. One by one, the lights below were changing into black lozenge-shapes, ringed by smoke and spume. Pinkney and Halloran stood behind the two pilots on the flight deck, looking down at the fishing-boats as they chugged peacefully about their business.

In the crew compartment, McQuade was on the W/T, on watch for the message from Control that did not come.

"You can turn the instrument lights off now, Dick."

Two clicks, and there was no cockpit illumination. Nor was there need of it. From a smoky explosion of black, red and yellow, the sun had broken clear to send long shafts of light through the perspex windows. As though on a stage, the faces of the four crew were lit up in brightness and shadow: Halloran's still red, but now with a thick beard around his jaw, making him look more pirate than airman; Beauchamp's paler still, the only color there the bloodshot eyes; Pinkney's cheeks plump and cherubic, but the skin wrinkled and dry.

None of them mentioned the fact that was uppermost in all their minds. Nobody said, "Where d'you think they'll tell us to drop it?" Nobody looked at the altimeter, as 577 continued to circle.

"Skipper, message—"

At last, something had come through. It must be something, some remedy. Four pairs of eyes brightened, then went dull again as they heard McQuade say: *Proceed 63 20 North, 12 45 West for rendezvous with tanker.*

"Going to fill us up again," Halloran said.

"Bringing us back toward the U.K., too," Beauchamp pointed out.

Rubbing his hands together as though this really was good news, Falkner purposely pumped cheerfulness into his words. "The boffins must have thought of something."

He did not really believe it. For all their smiles and nods of agreement, neither did his crew. As he flew the Venger on a southerly course, Falkner was turning over in his mind what could now be done about their situation.

They were, he was quite sure of it now, not exactly abandoned, but almost. To the politicians, to the Air Ministry they were more a source of continual embarrassment than anything else. His own summing up of the position was that after refueling they would be sent out into the Atlantic, as far from the shipping lanes as possible; all traffic would be diverted; they would then receive their final orders: and over that fantastic acreage of lonely graveyard would disintegrate the K6, Venger 577—and themselves.

The explosion would either turn the aircraft on her back, shredding off her wings, sending her crew hurtling into the center of the mushroom, or, more likely, the detonation itself would be so intense as to pulverize them all immediately into radioactive dust.

Now they were left on their own, just as he had held his hand to keep destruction away from the unsuspecting fishermen, now it seemed to Falkner that it was his duty also to save as many of his crew as possible. It wasn't just themselves: the wives and families had to be thought of. There was no point in them all going down with the K6. . . .

"Hey, Skipper!" Halloran's voice from the crew compartment. "The course is 225!"

"I want to go via Iceland, Mick." And then: "What's the wind now?"

"Light easterly."

"Thanks."

Purposely, as soon as the jagged gray skyline had appeared on their starboard bow, Falkner had turned the Venger toward it. They could manage with two, he had decided. And in selecting the other one besides himself, he had chosen—as always in this world it *had* to be—the strongest. Halloran and he could cope perfectly well between them.

The coastline—white, green and gray colored—was coming closer now. He could see a fair-sized white-timbered town. That must be Svalbard. If he dropped them fifteen miles beyond, they would be all right. They would be blown neither into the sea, nor the mountain range.

He throttled the engines back, and pushed the nose down. 577 began easing down toward the sea.

"Listen," he said, "I'm dropping three of you . . . Dick, Peter, Terry . . . over Iceland."

He looked around to see the effect. Just behind him, Pinkney's face seemed suddenly relieved—understandably, of course; not for himself but for those five children. He had half-expected McQuade to say some protest—even a halfhearted one—over the intercom, but none came.

"Get your parachutes then!"

Instead of an answer, he heard Beauchamp—the one who

a day ago he would have sworn would be the first to accept escape from such a situation—say almost flippantly, "Those umbrella things are far too dangerous for us, Skipper! Never did trust 'em! We're staying put."

If he had said it in any other sort of way, it wouldn't have worked. It was the understatement somehow that made it clear that he spoke for the other two; only in the background, unexplored, was the conviction that to leave now was unthinkable.

Back into the corporate spirit, now Pinkney said, "Course we are!"

And McQuade chipped in with, "Those boffins have got something up their sleeves . . . don't worry!"

Falkner paused, thought for a minute in silence. Then he said, "Well, I'm not going to force you out. . . ."

As he altered course away from Iceland, Falkner gave Beauchamp a quick smile. An atmosphere of human warmth and mutual protection spread over the aircraft now, making the doom that hung over them less terrible, far more remote. After all, before the oil in the other engines was used, 577 could fly for a good many hours. There was still hope yet.

"New course 215," Halloran advised over the intercom. "Estimate at seven hundred forty-five."

Already McQuade could hear the wireless operator on board the tanker calling him. He had transmitted a long dash, so that they could take a bearing with their radio compass. Sooner than expected, John Falkner saw the Venger fifty miles away, glinting in the bright morning sun.

They made contact. The two aircraft flew level in formation. It was Erskine again, smiling still, looking just the same as he had yesterday over the Black Sea.

But this time, there was no need for radio silence. They chattered continually to each other over the R/T as the two aircraft linked up.

"What're you think you're trying for, boy?" Erskine demanded. "The long-distance record?"

"Tell those boffins at Oakwood to pull their finger out!" Falkner retorted. "We want a bit of sleep!"

There was never a hint that of those two aircraft, joined by the hose, one was already mortally afflicted. Except that, just as they broke away, after passing nearly 12,000 gallons, almost wistfully Erskine said, "Wish I could pump in some oil too, chum."

And then, rising up in formation again, everyone waved at each other, till the tanker waggled its wings in salute. Off she moved southeast, becoming bit by bit a tiny white spark, and then nothing in the sky.

"Goodbye 577! Good luck!"

Air Vice Marshal Chatterton watched the Ops Room door open, and Helen lead the scientist in.

"Helen told you?"

"Yes." Zweig took off his spectacles and rubbed them carefully. "Yes. She told me."

"Then come over here. Sit down. We've very little time. And what we have got, we must use."

He drew out a chair from a square table covered by a map, around which already sat the Group Captain, and two other senior officers.

Zweig watched Miss Durrant take her place beside the A.O.C. He watched her with a curious dislike. He had not yet recovered from the sight of her cool-looking pale face bending over him as he knelt under the bomb, mathematical probabilities, factual theorems, diagrams of circuits and fuses, revolving around his brain in orderly precision. Till she had shattered and dispersed them with, "The A.O.C. wants you in Operations, Dr. Zweig. At once, please! It's terribly urgent! I've got the car outside."

She had laid a small irritating hand on his arm to hurry him, as if he were some slow-moving creature to be injected with her youth and speed. He still felt the frustration, the cold anger of a man not allowed to reach some climax of emotion and concentration.

Air Vice Marshal Chatterton waited till Zweig had settled himself down, determined not to betray by ineffective hurrying the anxiety which consumed him.

"While Helen fetched you, I got onto Air Ministry."

"Well?"

"Their attitude is . . . it's our job. We're on the spot. We've got you with us. *You're* the final authority on K6! So it's up to us. . . ." He picked up an automatic pencil, wound out the lead, stared at it thoughtfully. "To settle it," he drawled softly, "with the minimum possible damage . . . the minimum loss of life."

Helen Durrant heard the words with her head down, her hands folded on the table in front of her. She knew what they meant. Hopes of rescuing the crew of 577 were fading. It remained to do what they could to ensure as few other people as possible died, too. It was like listening to news of a mining disaster when in the end trapped miners had to be abandoned, the area sealed off; the fire, the disaster confined. In one awful moment, in which her love and anxiety for John Falkner seemed to topple over all her humanity, she wished they had dropped the bomb . . . Icelandic fishing-fleet or no. The trawlers were nameless, faceless, and to her . . . loveless.

But as quickly, she was bitterly ashamed. She glanced around the table guiltily as if she had said her thoughts aloud. But no one was looking at her. The scientist was talking.

"Oh, come, Chatterton! That's not *quite* accurate . . . we have indeed advanced in the hangar. We've proved it can't be certain possibilities. We've tried a number of different combinations. . . ."

"But anything positive, Zweig?" The A.O.C. lit a cigarette. His hand, she noticed, was very still. *Too* still. He pushed the packet toward her and said, "Help yourself and pass them around."

"Positive? *Positive?* Surely, that is!"

"Not positive enough."

"You can't have a solution just like *that!*"

"That's what we *must* have."

"Impossible! We must have time—"

"You've *had* time."

"We've done a lot." Zweig shrugged his shoulders. "We can see how the fuse *could* remain live. And I've found a way to defuse this K6 by hand."

"Can't see how that helps 577. They can't get through the bulkhead to do it themselves. Nor would they know how."

"Quite."

"So we still can't help her till she lands. And she can't go through five thousand, five hundred without the damn thing going off!"

Helen Durrant watched his eyes travel to the clock. Another ten minutes had gone. The electric hand was creaking them away like the slow time of an Air Force funeral march.

"Then I can suggest nothing. Nothing *more!*" The scientist sat back. "That K6 was delivered in perfect order. Right? You accepted it in perfect order. Then something went wrong—"

"We won't go over that again," the A.O.C. said sharply. "We're faced with a *situation!* We must deal with that *situation! Quickly!*" He cleared his throat, leaned slightly over the table as if to command the special attention of all those around it, tapping with his pencil on its polished surface.

"No jettison areas sufficiently clear remain." He paused to let that sink in. "Were any still available, on three engines 577 is now below height to jettison safely."

Another pause. Nothing and no one moved within Operations. Outside, a van changed gear, an airman's disembodied voice shouted, then died away. The faint sound underlined their own detachment.

"And eventually," the A.O.C. went on, "the other three engines will seize up for that self-same lack of oil."

One by one he held each pair of eyes around the table, as if they were children and he were teaching them some elementary lesson upon which all their future understanding depended.

"Therefore within a matter of hours, 577 will lose height anyway . . . inevitably will drop to five thousand, five hundred feet and"—gently—"will explode."

The spell in which he momentarily held them was broken by Zweig. "I'm not of any use to you here. This is *policy*, not *science*. I'm more valuable in the hangar. Doing my own job." He got up. "This is *your* job."

It struck Helen Durrant that in everyday life the bomb for Dr. Zweig was no more than a successful mathematical formula, a triumph of his brain and his persistence over the apparently impossible, and that now he flinched from the equating of his work into terms of humanity.

But her reactions, she said to herself, were off-key this morning. They were *all* concerned. Everyone in this room, on this Station, in this country. Here they all were the brains, the rest of the country the body, and John Falkner was the hand that now they were preparing to slice off.

"I'd prefer you to stay here," the A.O.C. said shortly.

"Then," Group Captain Lucey said, leaning forward—it was the first time that she had seen him say anything without prefacing it with a quick automatic smile, "I take it there's little chance, sir, of making the bomb safe?"

"As far as I can see, none."

She had never guessed that she would feel nothing. These last words finally crystallized the implications of the last half-hour. She tried to say over in her mind . . . There is no hope of John Falkner landing safely. In a little while, the whole crew will be dead. But her mind refused to believe. It was all some Group exercise, that was all. Bandits have shot down a number of aircraft. Bandits have attacked London . . . all our ports are out of action. They were sitting around here, planning . . . and at noon the exercise would be over. Jolly good show chaps, bang on! . . . better than Four Group . . . drink up, my round!

"So"—Group Captain Lucey placed the tips of his fingers together and stared ahead—"all we can decide is whether they proceed"—he got up and stood against the map of the world spread out on the wall—"north of their present position." He tapped the little flag that marked 577's present orbit. "Or whether they fly *south* across the Atlantic . . . reaching if possible the deserted area *here*. Flight refueling tankers are already in position."

Softly she murmured, "Why don't you let them choose? Do you want to be exploded at the center of the bomb, or sucked into the mushroom? Give reasons and a second choice." But no one heard her. Maybe she didn't say it aloud. She could feel hysteria like spittle rising into her mouth.

There was a queer patch of whiteness around the Group Captain's nose, and his red face had taken on a bluish tinge, but apart from that he looked the same, exactly the same. He was saying, "I take it there is no alternative to the suggestions put forward by Air Ministry?"

The A.O.C. glanced around the table. "I'm open to *any* suggestions, gentlemen."

Has the prisoner anything to say before sentence is passed? In a little while, Chatterton should put on his Black Cap, and they all might stand for a two-minute silence, and at the end of it they might say . . . Jolly good bunch of boys, fine lot of fellows!

"Then we'll discuss those two." He cleared his throat. "A thermonuclear explosion in midair has twenty times the destructive capacity of one on the ground. Inevitably, if it exploded in northern waters, Russia would be affected. If we could get 577 to the South Atlantic, it would be better. . . ."

She was waking up out of some dream. She glanced from face to face of the men sitting around the table. She expected to see them altered, made monstrous. But they remained the same lined, reasonably ambitious, reasonably kindly faces that had smiled with her last night, the men who had bought her a drink, said, *Thank God the crisis is over,* and had gone on to talk of their cars, their children or their dogs.

No one was trying to save John Falkner. Though they had relied on him not to try to save his own life . . . when, not many minutes ago, he could have. Now they were merely making the orders to send to him to show where it would be politically best for him and his crew to die.

She clenched her fists. She wanted to lie on the floor and scream. Every womanly instinct, every desire to love, to protect and cherish, her feminine respect for life, waxed in wild revolt. She wanted to kneel in front of the A.O.C., to cry and sob and use every female weapon that she had.

But she dare do none of it. Her hold on this man's world was a fingernail hold. She was in the A.O.C.'s confidence, not because she was young and pretty, but because she had a cool brain and a ticker-tape memory. Now if she broke down, lost her head, they would be kind and understanding, but they would cast her out. Her thoughts gabbled through her brain. Emotion and anguish were in full tide. With grinding will power, she sought in some way to use the power of her grief.

Like a beacon to an airman, a pinpoint to discipline her eyes and then her mind upon, she stared at the small red flag on the map. She sought out an engulfing wave of her emotion, scrabbling with all her imagination and intuition, to tear truth out of untruth, to claw improbability from probability.

But like some crazy chant, 5,500 feet went on and on, till there only seemed that flag, and revolving around it the figures 5,500 feet.

Like a mountain top marked on a relief map. And . . .

She jumped to her feet, and touched the flag. Breathlessly, like waking up with a dream one must remember, must say out loud before it vanished, she cried out, "A mountain . . . a mountain! Couldn't they land on a mountain top?"

The men around the table stopped talking.

"Look," she said. "There are peaks all over . . . here, Greenland. Ten thousand feet . . . the ice cap—"

The A.O.C. was staring at her cooly and assessingly and yet with compassion. In a little while he might say, "You're tired, Helen. Go and get some rest."

"Most of them snow-capped," Group Captain Lucey said quietly. "Craggy. They couldn't get away with it."

Almost angrily, Zweig said, "K6 would inevitably detonate on impact."

The brief half-hysterical excitement drained out of her. But she still stood by the map. She had the feeling that on it there was something she must hold on to. She went on staring at its green belts, its blue seas, its brown peaks.

Surely somewhere, that benign-looking world contained one safe landing place?

The Roof of the World—the Himalayas; she touched them with her finger, trailing down through India, across the Indian Ocean. Afghanistan, Arabia. Mountains everywhere, high heights marked: 8,765, 9,214, 18,565. . . .

And then, suddenly, another spot height caught her eye. A little red triangle, and beside it the numbers 5900. Near Nairobi. *Very* near Nairobi. . . .

There couldn't be. Not at that height. They would have thought of it. And yet . . . would they? Obsessed by the one thing . . . get rid of it, jettison it, they had abandoned looking for other possibilities. Their eyes were high up there, riveted on the Arctic.

And at that fantastic altitude . . . No!

And yet, it was very close to Nairobi—that spot height. On the southwest side, too.

She put her finger on the map—so hard that the blood was forced out of the nail. All the jumbled, groped-for fragments of a puzzle seemed about to fall into place.

It *must* be. . . .

She was afraid to say it aloud, lest after all there was some flaw unknown to her. Then abruptly, stridently, she heard her voice call out, "That plateau near Nairobi—" Her lungs hurt suddenly as if she'd been running. "Isn't an airfield there? You know, sir . . . Eastleigh! *Eastleigh* . . . on the high ground at Nairobi—"

A silence swallowed up her voice. No one spoke. No one seemed stirred either to hope or scorn. The A.O.C. said, "Let's see the Route book. Check on Eastleigh's height above sea level."

She heard the airwoman's shoes crossing the Ops Room floor . . . the soft shuffling of papers . . . her return.

"It's an idea, Helen," the A.O.C. was saying, as though already he had discarded it.

The books were spread out on the table, like those circuit diagrams of last night had been. The A.O.C. turned the pages rapidly.

"Here." She saw the plan of the airfield, the runways, the radio frequencies . . . but she couldn't focus her eyes to read the height.

"Five thousand, seven hundred feet above sea level!" A silence. Then quietly, the A.O.C. said, "Dr. Zweig, is it worth trying?"

"Well, first . . . could they get there?"

The A.O.C. glanced behind him. "Depends on the oil situation, of course . . . but they might."

"It's a possibility," the scientist said.

"One obvious snag, of course." Air Vice Marshal Chatterton leaned across the table toward the scientist. "How near accurate is the setting on K6?"

"Accurate? Completely accurate! It's set to the pressure altimeter. Must be accurate."

"It was also supposed to defuse after a given procedure. But it didn't."

With the stern tone was contained enough condemnation

to make the scientist get up, stand stiffly, legs apart, mouth hard, and say, "Some unorthodox procedure was undoubtedly used—"

"Not again . . . we won't go into that again! That's not the point now! Is it *accurate? Dead* accurate?"

"Certainly!"

"If it's not, I daren't risk bringing 577 in there. They'd be lost. Nairobi'd be lost. God knows what else would go up as well!"

"It's accurate. It's *one hundred* per cent accurate!"

It struck them all that the professor had frozen on to this accuracy as a pilot in dire danger sometimes freezes on to the controls . . . this was his reputation's last stand.

"Remember we've only two hundred extra feet to play with! And some of that will get used up by difference in barometric pressure . . . by inaccuracies in contour measurement. Are you still sure?"

"Definitely sure."

The A.O.C. stared at him for a full minute. Then he straightened.

Helen wanted to say, "Shall you try, sir?" But she dare not. She held herself parade-ground straight. Her eyes moved from the A.O.C.'s face to the clock on the wall, then back to his face again.

Eventually, he cleared his throat, and said, "That makes the possibilities *three.*"

Continuing in a pleasant conversational tone, he said, "By jettisoning, or by continuing in the air until the aircraft blows up, the aircraft and crew are written off. With luck, no one else."

Luck . . . *luck!* She clenched her hands.

Group Captain Lucey said sharply. "And we'd never find out what went wrong either."

"Nor should we," the A.O.C. said, "if it blows up anywhere else." He see-sawed his hands. "One balances the other. But against the Arctic is the fact that a nuclear explosion, unwarned and unadmitted, is liable to spark off total war. Yet if we bring her into Nairobi . . . blow up half of Africa . . . what then?"

He spread his hands flat on the table, palms downward. Helen Durrant knew him well enough to recognize that this was the moment. That when he spoke, his mind would be made up, his decision unalterable. She didn't know what to do. Part of her wanted to pray. Part of her, craven and superstitious, searched for omens. Part of her wanted to will the C.O.'s thought into compliance with her own. But all she could make herself do was stand up straight, almost at attention, her pink-varnished fingernails digging into her palms, and strive for a quiet face and an unprotesting voice.

She neither looked at the A.O.C. nor tried to guess the thought processes that went through his mind. She could not have, had she tried. He knew so little of any of the solutions that to judge would have been like taking a pinch out of this mountain, another out of that, weighing them, and saying . . . this mountain is bigger. Instead, he struggled for quietness of mind, for some moment of truth, for something to stand out, clear and true. In the end, what spoke to him was the old human call of rescue crying out above the equations of science, the coldness of fact. That while any hope remained, the human spirit could not give up, nor could he abandon those under his command. They were his airmen, expendable only if it was necessary. If it was not, then to be fought for as they had fought for others.

"Of course, it's a risk," he said. "Air Ministry might not agree. The Cabinet will anyway have the final say. Kenya, of course, will have to be alerted . . . the Governor told. Though what he could do, for better or worse, except worry . . . I don't know." He paused again. "But I think it's worth trying." His eyes had a piercing unblinking quality as they turned on the scientist. "What do you say, Zweig?"

"If I could only be allowed more time—"

"Time's out of the question now."

Zweig shrugged his shoulders. "Then it seems the only thing to do."

"You could defuse by hand, if we got you there?"

"I could."

Air Vice Marshal Chatterton rose from the table, and walked over to the glass Controller's box. He was rubbing his hands. He seemed pleased, suddenly lighthearted. "Right! I'll get onto Command straightaway! And Lucey . . . rout out the Duty Crew and a serviceable Venger. Once we've got the go-ahead, we'll signal 577 . . . and get going ourselves. Me, Lucey, Zweig. . . .

He was just opening the door, when he was aware of her hand on his arm. "Yes, Helen?"

"Sir . . . I thought of it, didn't I?" Emotion was overwhelming her tautly held discipline. Tears brimmed over her eyes. Momentarily the young girl vanquished the cool W.R.A.F. officer. "You can't leave me here! Sir . . I'm coming, too!"

Night had come down over central Africa. Through the square of window high in the side of the fuselage opposite her, Helen Durrant could see a square of ink-black sky and a handful of brighter, changing-patterned stars.

She had watched that square since they had left Oakwood. It had marked for her the passing of time, the only sense that she had of movement. She had seen it change from the cloudy morning sky over England, to the drops and rivulets of wet as rain clouds blew up over the Channel; then as quickly as it had come up, the rain was whisked away again, blue sky over Europe interspersed with build-ups of distant cumulus. The navigator—no more than a broad back, and a head haloed in an angle-poise light pool till then—had turned and smiled and said, "We're over the Alps . . . if you want to have a look-see . . . fine sight with the sun on the snow. . . ."

But she hadn't bothered to get up from her jump seat, although it was hard and uncomfortable. It was as though she were badly injured and if she got up, she would fall apart.

The navigator had then gone back to his charts. The radio operator had handed her a cup of tea, and a ham sandwich, and the square of sky had become glassy with Mediterranean sunlight. When the sunlight had faded and the sky had reddened with a quickly lost evening, the whistle of the engines over the desert seemed to take on a more mournful, haunted note. Opposite her, Dr. Zweig carefully folded away the notes upon which he had been working the entire trip, and studiedly relaxed his arms and legs. Whenever her eyes had left the square of window and had rested on his trim, stocky figure, trilby hat still on, shading his face, her feelings had rocked between hatred through alarm to sympathy. But always the pivot was alarm. Untrustworthy, inaccurate . . . one mistake, bound to be another . . . the engines seemed to wail it as they went.

Now that it was dark, the lights from the lamps caricatured his figure against the fuselage. The shadow of the brim of his hat reached to the bottom of the companionway that led up to the flight deck. The shadow of his nose, witch-like, scornfully touched the Loran set.

They must be getting close now to Nairobi. The radio operator was listening in, quickly writing down a message. He folded the piece of paper, edged himself off his stool, passed her with a vague smile, and clattered up the metal steps to the flight deck. Leaning forward and following his figure upward, she could just see their shadows and the red fluorescent glow of the instrument panel. She listened for their voices but they were speaking too softly for them to carry above the whine of the engines. She envied the A.O.C. helping to fly the thing . . . having something to do . . . instead of sitting here knowing nothing of the ins and outs, imagining everything.

She scanned the radio operator's face as he returned. Maybe it was bad news. Maybe 577 had already come down, blown up. But he was still half-smiling. He went back to his set, tapped out some message, leaned over to the navigator, said something, looked down at the chart. Two fingers pointed across the pool of light. Then the radio operator sat back, and as if he had received her mental questioning, leaned back and yawned. "Estimating Nairobi in fifteen minutes." He put his hand to his mouth, shaking his head apologetically. "Good trip, eh?"

"Yes."

They were coming down. She could feel the pull of the earth through the soles of her feet. Now they were banking. The window caught the red glow of the port navigation light. Zweig had taken off his spectacles, was polishing them. Now he sat, hands clasped, staring glassily at the twin of the window above *her* head, at which she was staring.

The engine note went softer. She heard the scream of the airbrakes going down. Now she could hear the A.O.C.'s voice, hard and clear, calling out the Field Approach Check to the Captain . . . did his voice betray that he was thinking as she was . . . what will happen in the next Venger to land here, when the next Second Pilot calls out those orders?

She rubbed her forehead with her hand and stared up at the window again. Around again . . . they were lining up with the runway now; she could feel the pilot pulling back on the aircraft, holding her. The window had caught a light high up that wasn't a star. Some high building, way up on a hillside. Lower, steadily lower. Nothing but blackness now. No stars. Then the window was full of movement like a tiny cinema screen. Yellow lights, white lights speeding past, square patterns of lights flashing and gone, their places taken by new ones.

The tires squeaked softly. She could feel the brakes pulling them back. They were down.

She glanced across at Zweig with a small smile, half of encouragement, half demanding reassurance. Then she got up, adjusted her cap, put on her leather gloves, stroking the fingers smooth on and on, to keep her hands apparently steady, till she saw the small movement focused in the scientist's spectacles, and knew that it irritated him.

It seemed a long time before the aircraft halted. Before they climbed down the steps. And onto the tarmac at Nairobi.

The dome of the sky seemed higher and blacker than over England. The flarepath and the lights glowed brighter and nearer; and the air was warm—yet dry and clear. Around the yellow lamps, flies moved continuously, like a lightly whisked net curtain. And from the dark plateau beyond the airfield came the noise of what sounded like crickets and the deeper harshness of bullfrogs.

"We'll go to the Control Tower," the A.O.C. said, touching her arm. "It's just behind us. Coming, Zweig?"

They turned toward the square neon-lit building. Her eyes, getting used to the dark, saw among the grasses that edged the pathway, the glow of fireflies. And now she could pick out a horizon beyond the airfield. The stars were out, bright and clear. But to the north, high peaks blocked them in solid darkness. Mountains . . . what were they called? She was too tired to remember. She glanced at the Control Tower, wondering how many more steps it would take them. Then back to the sky again.

At first she thought that fatigue had made her dizzy. To the northwest, where the mountains had petered out, and the horizon was clear and low, she saw a tiny red pin-prick like a firefly up there instead of in the grass beside her feet. Then another. This time green. A long way away. Close together. But coming steadily . . . inevitably . . . nearer.

The nightmare had caught up with her. The moment had come.

"Thirty-five North, twenty East? Sure, Terry? Sure it's *East?*"

These orders were unexpected. East? Where was there a place in that direction where they could jettison the K6? After McQuade had assured him the longitude was correct,

Falkner still puzzled in his mind where they were going to now. That particular position was over the Mediterranean. They wouldn't be going to drop the thing there. Might, of course, be the Sahara . . .

He shrugged his shoulders, swung the Venger onto a southeasterly course. He was glad enough anyway to keep straight and level. At five hundred miles an hour, they swept down from the north.

Soon, the Faroes showed up. An old shepherd, sitting on a hillside with his sheep, saw the purposeful white triangle go directly overhead, and marveled at its height and speed. All over the world, after the crisis, things were settling down to normal. There had been no more incidents in Kanjistan. Foreigners were returning. A visit of the Shah of Persia was again announced. The British paratroops were back home, all on a forty-eight-hour pass. The headlines in the newspapers now announced the divorce of a film star. Opinion in America and the NATO countries toward Great Britain thawed. It was only in Downing Street, in the Air Ministry, and at R.A.F. Station Oakwood that activity—unaccountably for a Saturday morning—hummed under a heavy veil of Security.

Over the ether now in plain language came many anxious messages—

577 . . . *how much oil?*

577 . . . *how are your other engines?*

577 . . . *what height are you maintaining?*

577 . . . *report serviceability.*

On the W/T, Pinkney was continually sending and receiving. He wiped the sweat out of his tired eyes as he wrote the endless communications down in his log.

The sun climbed higher in the sky, pouring in through the perspex. From the flight deck, they saw other aircraft and civil airliners, well below them, crawling toward Paris or Rome. A shipload of continental travelers looked up from the deck, studied the Venger as an object more interesting than the sea. A lighthouse keeper off Dunkirk remarked on the incongruous asymmetry of two trailing vapor trails on one side of the aircraft, and only one on the other.

577 had crossed the French coast, was headed well inland, still on the same course, before over the intercom, Pinkney called out, "There's a message coming through now, Skipper! Emergency priority—"

And then he had started quickly to take down: *Cleared to Nairobi. Most direct route. Rendezvous with tanker off Benghazi. Then proceed Eastleigh. Airfield height above sea level 5700 feet . . . repeat 5700 feet.*

For a few seconds, he stared down at the words, not comprehending. Then slowly it dawned on him. He yelled through his microphone, "Skipper . . . they're going to get us down! Eastleigh . . . we're to land at Eastleigh! Above the explosion height of the bomb!"

"Eastleigh, eh? Yes . . . of course! Thank Christ for that!"

An enormous weight came off John Falkner's spirits. The unexpectedness of the news was a sudden refreshment to his dead-tired mind. Jettison . . . that was the word around which all his thoughts had revolved. He had never even considered getting down safely. He knew that the impact fuse would go off if he crash-landed on a mountain. He had never been to Kenya; and the idea of an airdrome existing at that impossible height simply had not occurred to him. Somebody down there had had a bright idea, he thought to himself. Somebody had used imagination to bring them to safety. He would not allow himself to think how close 5700 was to 5500, of the possibility that the altimeter detonator would not be accurate to within so small a margin as two hundred feet, or that the atmospheric pressure over Nairobi might be lower than average.

He had an airdrome to land at—that was enough for him. And a wide smile curled up the corners of his mouth.

They crossed over the Alps. It was cloudy over the Adriatic, but the Mediterranean was clear. A Venger came up near Benghazi to do their final refueling; and then 577 set course over the endless Libyan desert, still scored by tank tracks and marked by burned-out trucks.

"Clocking in our thirty-sixth hour in the air," Halloran announced.

"That the longest you've been up, Mick?"

"Too true! Previous record . . . twenty-five in a Liberator. And that was too damn long!"

It was hot now. Pinkney already had his overalls off. Now he removed his jacket. Sweat poured over his face. "Christ, Terry . . . what's happened to the water?"

"Been a run on it."

"My tongue's hanging out."

"You'll just have to wait till we're down."

Pinkney turned gasping to Halloran. "What's our estimate, Mick?"

"Eighteen hundred thirty. Nine local."

"Three more bloody hours!"

Gradually, in the west, the sun was sinking. Night with its bright stars was again coming up. Falkner looked up at them, saw Polaris, Vega, the vast sideways lean of the Cygnus. How often in old piston-engined aircraft he had struggled, pushing up through heavy cloud, fighting the weather to reach them! Then, getting at last on top, seeing the universe silver-bright on the tops of cloud, it had always been a victory. And now— at 41,000 feet—even on three engines, effortlessly they flew on, high above everything.

Ahead in the distance, he caught sight of the high cone of Kilimanjaro, saw on his starboard the shimmering waters of Lake Victoria.

And now suddenly over the V.H.F. came cheerfully: "577 . . . 577 . . . Eastleigh Tower calling 577."

"Roger . . . Eastleigh. This is 577."

"577 from Eastleigh. What is your position?"

"A hundred miles northwest. Estimate the field in twelve minutes at eighteen hundred forty-one G.M.T."

"Roger . . . cleared straight to the field. Weather clear. Wind light. High-intensity runway and approach lights on."

Within minutes, they could see it: a great round brooch of lights intersected by the smaller pearls of the runway lamps.

Looking down at it, Pinkney said fervently, "God . . . that's the finest sight I've seen!"

Slowly, they lost height. There was at the back of everyone's mind the idea of those two red lamps, still flaming on the bomb-aimer's panel, proclaiming that the bomb was fused and would detonate at 5,500 feet.

"Altimeter setting . . . 1010 millibars."

Slightly lower than usual. Falkner's face was frowning as he set it up on the millibar scale. Then he saw the great bonfire of light that was Nairobi over on his left-hand side. Pushing the nose down even further, he called out, "Field Approach Check!"

Beauchamp called out, "Take-off Cruise Selector Switch . . . take-off, indicator green. Tank pressurization?"

"Shut."

They were at 7000 indicated. Carefully, Falkner lined up on the runway lights, turned downwind.

"Give me the wheels, Dick!"

Beauchamp pushed down the lever with his left hand. "Down. Three green lights."

"Brakes?"

"Pressure three thousand one hundred pounds. Parking brake off."

"Fuel?"

"All pumps on. Transfer switches off."

"Air conditioning?"

"Off."

"Autopilot?"

"Off."

Very gradually, Falkner reduced speed to 165 knots.

It was warm down here. The Venger was beginning to

buck. For three quarters of a minute, 577 flew beyond the airfield, then turned crosswind.

Once more now, they could see the flarepath on the port bow.

They were at 6500 feet. On the airspeed indicator, the speed showed 160 knots.

577 was coming more and more in line with the runway. Falkner began turning. His hand was on the throttles, pulling them back.

The altimeter showed 6300 feet. Six hundred feet above the ground. Eight hundred feet above the detonating height of the K6.

Beauchamp called out, "Speed 155!"

They were lined up now. The runway, two long straight strings to safety, stretched out its arms in welcome toward them.

The altimeter crept lower . . . 6100 feet.

"Speed 152!"

"Give me high-drag airbrake!"

"Coming out!"

Falkner felt the Venger shudder as the drag of the extended airbrakes slowed them. Momentarily his eye caught the altimeter: 5800 feet. All sorts of ideas whirred through his mind. What would be the first sound if it *was* going to go up? A click? A slight jar? Or would it detonate instantaneously?

5750 feet.

They were coming up to the threshold. Ahead green threshold lights winked.

"Speed 140."

"Landing lights!"

They flared out immediately in a bright cone before him. Illuminated now was the elephant gray of the runway surface, the too-vivid green of the grass.

577 was swaying a little now. The left wing dropped. Hauling it up again, it seemed unnaturally heavy.

Sweat collected on his forehead, ran down his cheeks in rivulets. He bit his lip, feeling the blood warm and faintly comforting in his mouth. He was tired. His reactions were slow. Knowing that, he tried to steel himself into a cool detachment. He mustn't make a mess of this landing. He mustn't crash! That would be the end, not only for them—but for millions all around.

"Speed 135."

Over the hedge now. The altimeter flickering at 5725.

He pushed the nose down, firmly closed the throttles. Then, just above the runway, he flew level, waiting. . . .

Nothing happened. Then very slowly, the lights came closer. He saw them like great daubs of butter spread on the night, beyond the red and green sparkle of the wing-tip lights.

He eased back on the stick. The nose started rising. He could feel the Venger sink toward the earth.

Then softly . . . the brushing of the rubber tires on the tarmac. The speed slowed. Gradually the nose started dropping, the nosewheel slid onto the ground. He heard Beauchamp call jubilantly, "We're down!"

Falkner was conscious of the lights flashing past him like huge signs; of Beauchamp grinning beside him; then of the red boundary lights coming up ahead.

He braked gently. "Stream the tail parachute!"

Beauchmap's left hand pulled. There was an immediate and sudden jerk. All at once their speed was reduced to that of a bicycle, ambling gently between the lights, till finally at the west end taxiway, 577 was crawling along and the high screech of the hydraulic brakes had replaced the whine of jets.

The Second Pilot jettisoned the parachute. Falkner turned left off the runway, wiped the sweat from his smiling face and, opening the side window, breathed in again and again the sweet night air, as slowly he taxied the Venger toward a great green sea of neon-lighted illumination that was the ramp at Eastleigh. Silhouetted against all that brightness, he saw a man with a torch. Like any other aircraft—civil, military, private—the marshaller was waving him in.

And then, as he turned, he saw in the landing lights men in overalls, a parked jeep, airmen with walkie-talkie sets, darting between the twin beams. There were two cars parked on the grass, and figures standing beside them, their faces turned toward him, hands shading their eyes.

Momentarily, he thought it was as though the bomb had gone off, and they were frozen there in an eternal attitude of self-protection. Then they, too, moved into the beam—heads down, hurrying. No one seemed to wait for the last turn of the tires before throwing a net of activity over 577.

He eased the brake full on. The aircraft whispered to a stop. His ears seemed to thunder with the sudden silence.

They were down. Not out of danger. But down. This was solid earth beneath their tires. Above him, the stars stayed still.

He did not want to move. He wanted to stay as still as this forever. He felt no relief that he was alive. He felt no apprehension about the bomb. He felt only scoured out, aching with an empty feeling that nothing more was required of him. He'd done as he was told. He had brought 577 safely down. No nightmare temptation now to drop the K6—anywhere; no waiting for orders. No studied calm. No certainty of death. Nothing! If the bomb went off now, he was too tired to care. His mind boggled at imagining its destruction. He'd done what he was told. From now on, somebody else must take over.

Voices shouted below him on the tarmac. He thought he saw familiar figures . . . Chatterton, Zweig—

"Keep the electric circuits on!" someone shouted up. And on the intercom, dragging his voice up from miles of fatigue inside him, he called out, "I'm opening the bomb doors! They want to get cracking on it. Zweig's here—"

He turned the switch beside him, heard the familiar hydraulic whine. Then he blinked his eyes and looked outside again.

"Looks as though we've got a reception committee!" he said to Beauchamp, not turning his eyes toward his Second Pilot, because somehow he could not keep them controlled.

Or his eyes were playing tricks—he couldn't tell. A moment ago, they certainly had, shimmering all the neon lights together into a quivering zebra dazzle. Or was it his imagination playing him up? As it had tried to, coming down, till when they had dropped below 6000 he could have sworn that he'd heard something, felt a warning quiver in the aircraft, had almost shouted out. Or was it the sweat in his eyes, and the noises in his ears, and the weakness in every muscle?

No, it wasn't imagination. This time for certain behind Chatterton, he saw her, still standing away from the lights, still in shadow. How Helen Durrant had come here, he did not know. He was glad. Her presence in some strange way straightened up the world for him, put him right side up after those topsy-turvy hours.

He smiled at Beauchamp. "We made it, eh?" He clasped the younger man's arm briefly. "Thanks."

He got out of his seat, and led the way down the companionway. In the crew compartment, he looked at them: Halloran, Pinkney, McQuade. Red-rimmed eyes, red-veined eyeballs stared back at him out of pale, bearded faces. Strange faces, the faces of survivors of shipwrecks or jail-breaks. They all wore the same expression—relieved certainly, but sheepish, as if the moment called for some higher feeling they found impossible to show. He opened up the main door, gave each one a light punch on his shoulder as he passed. Only McQuade, struggling for jauntiness, in a caricatured English accent, said, "Smooth landing, Skipper. The thing won't know it's down!"

Falkner was the last onto the tarmac. He walked from unreality to unreality. The warm sweet air after the sweaty interior of the aircraft cabin made him feel lightheaded. He saw his crew standing, hats on the back of their heads, saying nothing, like men waking up from a dream. Then they were surrounded, lost among other dark shapes: alert, hurrying.

Flashlights bobbed. Feet clipped quickly past. Unfamiliar voices talked. Someone bumped into Falkner. He heard Zweig's voice from under the bomb bay shout, "Keep 'em away! *Away!* Give me room! And lights! Bring more lights!"

There was no sign of Helen. Zweig had disappeared. So had Chatterton. For Falkner now, everything was one vast light. He was in some curious limbo, where reality was shot through with sudden vivid imaginings, and he could not distinguish where the one began and the other ended. He was like someone very drunk, except that he knew his state, and walked with care.

The grass felt wonderful under his feet. He trod it slowly and carefully, smelling the night fragrance, the knowledge of being alive when he should have been dead offering itself to him in extraordinary heightened physical sensations.

Again now, suddenly he was back in reality. He was here—on the ramp in Nairobi. He saw Zweig crouched under the bomb bay, working up inside that gray-white pod. A weird blue light spilled down onto the tarmac. From here, he could hear the slight scratching of the scientist's slow and careful movements, his heavy breathing.

He was starting to defuse the bomb by hand.

Seeing the A.O.C. standing by the aircraft, Falkner went across to him.

Chatterton was smiling. "Good show, Falkner! Shouldn't take long now." And to Zweig: "Well?"

"I can see what's wrong."

"What is it?"

"The slave motor isn't working . . . seems to have failed. I'll have to disengage it by hand."

"Fused . . . really *live?*"

"Of course."

"Can you fix it?"

"Should be able to." Zweig rubbed both his hands together, blowing on them gently.

Now should have been the moment when he felt the same agonizing, melting tension of lowering the aircraft through 6,000 feet. Instead, he felt alive, alert, calm. He didn't watch Zweig now. He stood staring at the stars above him. He could hear the dry whisper of the grasses, the shrilling of some insects, the cry of an animal out on the plains.

It was then that he heard her footfall behind him. He recognized it, but he did not turn. She stood beside him, and he could smell her perfume, incongruous here. He caught her hand, holding it without looking at her.

Then he said, "Where did you hide yourself? I thought you were a mirage."

"I wanted to wait until . . ." Her voice trailed. He knew that in some way her relief and her emotion were as those of his crew had been . . . impossible to express, something to be ashamed of, to conceal.

"Where did you go?"

"Just over there. Not far. I wandered around awhile. Watching you."

He turned and looked down at her. He saw with dismay the shadows under her eyes, the paleness of her face. Gently, protectively, he said, "You shouldn't *be* here. It might still go off. You ought to be in some safe place."

But as soon as he'd said them, he knew that the words were only instinctive, without reality.

"I'd rather be here," she said, softly. "Anyway, there *isn't* any safe place."

"I suppose not." He looked away from her, keeping very still. He could just see Zweig's hand, spotlighted, luminous in the glow from the bomb bay. Now he felt his blood thundering, his mouth dry.

"Bomb defused!" Zweig said, his voice still tetchy, irritable. "Tell them to see if the red lights are still on."

"Pinkney." Was it his own voice calling or Chatterton's? "Get in and check the panel. See what it shows."

Pinkney's face appeared briefly at the perspex panel. "Lights off now, sir!"

Relief slowly sifted down. Normality returned. Everyone seemed to be talking, going backward and forward. From the far side of the airfield, twin points of headlamps appeared.

A huge bomb trolley was coming up for the K6. Beside him, Helen didn't move.

"Except with me," he said as if she had just spoken. "You have a safe place with me."

He saw her glance at the aircraft, the bomb trolley, and then stare up at him again. "Have I?"

"I reckon. If you want it."

Cars were coming up to the Venger now . . . the whole paraphernalia for a newly landed aircraft had begun. Routine and everyday life smoothed over memories so that the dangers of these last days eluded him like a bubble.

"Transport's here!" Halloran called.

"Right!" John Falkner said. Automatically, together they turned their feet toward the cars. "Coming!"

"As you have with me," she whispered.

"I know." Standing here, he could see the sweep of the hills. He'd first seen those peaks looming up on the starboard wing when they were at thirty thousand. Then he'd wondered if this trip of theirs would blow those hills out of that skyline. He could see over in the east the pulsing flash of the Nairobi beacon, a light beyond the airfield of a car traveling up from the city. "I think," he said, "that it's the only thing I *am* sure of."

He held her hand while they got into the car. He still held it as the car gained speed, the darkened aircraft faded, merged with the night.

And only the bright blind eyes of Operations confronted them.

Calories Don't Count!

News about a revolutionary reducing plan, based on a new biochemical discovery, available for the first time in a new book

UNBELIEVABLE—but true! You need to eat fat to be slim. In CALORIES DON'T COUNT, Dr. Herman Taller outlines his sensational 14-point reducing plan based on a new understanding of the body's chemistry.

With this plan you eat heartily—three full meals a day—large portions of meat, fowl, sea food —even french fries and piecrusts. You never know hunger. Yet you lose the bulges you want to lose.

"There have been no failures."

In the preface to his book, Dr. Taller writes: "The concept has been tested in medical laboratories and among large numbers of patients. There have been no failures, nor can there be any when the principle is properly applied. For it is based on a medical breakthrough so dramatic that it will probably invalidate all you know, or think you know,

Dr. Herman Taller

about the causes of obesity."

The plan is a simple one. But its rules, especially in regard to the types of fats you must eat, are specific. They are clearly outlined in Dr. Taller's best-selling book. Read it and liberate yourself, once and for all, from both starvation and overweight.

Free 30-Day Examination

Use CALORIES DON'T COUNT for THIRTY DAYS FREE. Unless it is the sanest, *best* reducing book you've ever seen, send it back and pay nothing. If, however, you keep it, remit only $3.95 (plus postage) as payment in full. Mail coupon below to: SIMON AND SCHUSTER, INC., 630 5th Ave., N. Y. 20, N. Y.

MAIL FOR 30 DAYS' FREE EXAMINATION

To your bookseller, or

SIMON AND SCHUSTER, INC.
Publishers, Dept. M4230-C
630 Fifth Ave., N.Y. 20, N.Y.

Please send me a copy of Dr. Herman Taller's exciting new book, CALORIES DON'T COUNT, for thirty days' Free Examination. If not convinced that it will help me reduce substantially and sanely, I may return the book within thirty days and pay nothing. Otherwise, I will send only $3.95 (plus a few cents postage) as payment in full.

Name...
(PLEASE PRINT)

Address...

City.............................Zone..........

State...

☐ SAVE POSTAGE! Check here if you send $3.95 WITH this coupon as payment in full. Then WE PAY POSTAGE. Same 30-day return privilege for full refund GUARANTEED.